JESSICA SIMS

BEAUTY DATES THE BEAST

Pocket Books

New York   London   Toronto   Sydney   New Delhi

Pocket Books
A Division of Simon & Schuster, Inc.
1230 Avenue of the Americas
New York, NY 10020

First Pocket Books paperback edition November 2011

POCKET STAR BOOKS and colophon are registered trademarks of Simon & Schuster, Inc.

For information about special discounts for bulk purchases, please contact Simon & Schuster Special Sales at 1-866-506-1949 or business@simonandschuster.com.

The Simon & Schuster Speakers Bureau can bring authors to your live event. For more information or to book an event contact the Simon & Schuster Speakers Bureau at 1-866-248-3049 or visit our website at www.simonspeakers.com.

Cover design by Min Choi; art by Aleta Rafton

Manufactured in the United States of America

10 9 8 7 6 5 4 3 2 1

ISBN 978-1-4391-8823-1
ISBN 978-1-4391-8825-5 (ebook)

For Holly Root—I've said it before, but I'll say it again. Thank you for showing me how great an author-agent relationship can be.

Acknowledgments

I would love to give a big, happy thank-you to the Pocket team for taking my lump of coal and making it into a diamond of a book. Thank you to my fabulous editor, Micki Nuding, who knows just what my weaknesses are in the first version so that I can fix them in the next one and make the book terrific. And a thank-you for the production team—and my copyeditor!—who always impress me with the thorough, amazing job they do.

I would also love to thank my daily email peeps—you know who you are—who make me feel connected even though we are thousands of miles apart. You guys keep me sane and make me laugh my head off. I am richer for having you in my inbox.

And for my husband, a thank-you for being endlessly patient when I whine, understanding when I'm lazy and messy, and always, always ready to lend a helping hand when I need it. I know I don't ask for help as often as I should, and this book wouldn't be nearly as cool if you hadn't given me the idea in the first place. Your genius is under-stated but never underappreciated. Love you.

Chapter One

*M*idnight Liaisons," I said as I cradled the office phone to my ear. "This is Bathsheba. How can I help you?"

"Hi," the man breathed nervously into the other end of the phone. "I'm looking for . . . company. Tonight. Maybe a redhead."

I winced. There was no way to misunderstand what he was looking for, as he'd clearly stated "redhead" in a rather obvious (and breathy) fashion. We got at least one of these kinds of calls a day, and I'd become an old hand at deflecting the creepiness of misguided callers. "Midnight Liaisons is a dating service, sir. Not an escort service." *Now please, never call again.*

There was a pause on the other end of the line. "Oh," he said. "Well, that's fine. How can I access your website to look at the dating profiles? It won't give me a password."

"The password is your Alliance ID number," I said, my voice effortlessly pleasant from years of answering questionable phone calls. "Or I can check your credentials and get you set up with a temporary log-in. If you can tell me who your pack leader is, I'd be more than happy to send through the background check—"

"My what?"

Definitely a civilian on the line. A "natural," as my boss liked to joke around the office. I decided to play dumb anyhow. "If you don't have a pack leader . . . perhaps your master?" If this guy was familiar with undead society at all, he'd catch the hint.

"Huh?"

"Coven? Fey king?" I couldn't resist. "High lord?"

"What are you talking about, lady?" The man on the other end of the line had lost his patience. Gone was the smarmy tone, replaced by your typical, run-of-the-mill angry customer. Except he definitely wasn't one of *our* customers.

"I'm sorry," I said in my most sugary voice. "But Midnight Liaisons has an exclusive clientele. Our dating service is open to referrals from current clients only. Have a nice day, sir—"

"Now just a minute," the man began, but I hung up on him anyway. The chances of him ever becoming a client were slim to none, unless he had the luck to run into a vampire looking for a new friend.

From the back of the room, Sara snickered as she typed at her desk. "You always get the weird ones."

"Of course I do," I said, turning in my chair to glance at her. Sara's gaze was glued to her screen, but she had a smile on her face. "We get weird calls because the company name sounds like an escort service. And I get them because *you're* not answering the phone."

"I'm busy," she said, but her mouth quirked.

"Part of your job is to answer the phone," I retorted, exasperated. "I'm the office manager! If anyone shouldn't have to answer the phone, it's me."

"But you're so good at it," Sara soothed me, grinning. "I'm not half as patient with the freaks as you are."

I snorted.

Sara just laughed. Seeing as how she's my baby sister, she got away with just about everything. She flipped through the slender stack of profiles on her desk. "Midnight Liaisons is a stupid name, but what else would you call a dating service that caters exclusively to the paranormal?"

"Bangs for Fangs? Flea-Collared Submissives?" I quipped, turning back to my screen to get rid of the flashing pop-up reminding me to log the call into the database. "Fresh Meat for Deadbeats?"

Sara made a small noise of dismay. "You're

too hard on them. Not everyone who has a tail is a jerk."

I winced. That was careless of me. "Sorry," I said, keeping my voice light and playful. "You know I didn't mean that. The hours are strange, the clients are even stranger, but I like it here."

It was true—my job paid well, I ran the office like it was my own, and I got to watch over my baby sister twenty-four hours a day, ensuring her safety. Life was good, if a little strange.

My job was to set up new profiles and match up clients, in addition to running the office. Sara's job was to check in with our clients to see that dates were still on, to follow up after the date to ensure everyone enjoyed themselves, and to update profiles with "exclusive" status if necessary. It was the easiest job in our small office. She usually finished it within hours and then flipped her computer over to gaming mode, spending the rest of the day playing Warcraft.

Across the room, Sara sucked in a breath. "Oh, *shit.*"

I turned to glance back at her again. "What's wrong?"

"Profile #2674, that's what's wrong," she said anxiously.

Oh, boy. I didn't even have to access the profile to know who it was. "What's Rosie done now?"

Rosie cancelled on dates regularly, was aggressive as hell, and had given more than one guy trouble—and not just the flea-and-tick variety. Some guys were into it; they expected a werewolf chick to be fiery and aggressive.

Everyone in our office hated her.

"What's she done now?" I repeated, anticipating the complaint call certain to come in.

"She's cancelled a date with a cat shifter through the website." Sara raked through her short, swingy brown bob, scattering the fine strands across her cheeks. "Don't worry, I can handle it."

I stared at Sara's stiff posture with alarm, watching her arms for any telltale sproutings of fur. When Sara panicked, she *really* panicked, and it was my job to calm her down and take care of the situation. Her life depended on it.

I made my voice soothing. "Why is that an 'oh shit' problem? Rosie always cancels on the cats."

We had a string of complaints in her file a mile long. If someone cancelled on a date, they were charged an inconvenience fee. But our boss, Giselle, always waived her fees, and Rosie abused the privilege. I suspected that Rosie and Giselle had some hidden agreement beyond the standard contract, but I wasn't about to ask.

The only reason Rosie was still allowed in the dating service was because the pool of female Alliance members was so small compared to the male membership. Especially ones as attractive and willing to date as Rosie. We couldn't afford to lose her; she was brisk business. So we put a note on her profile that she preferred canine dates in the hope of deterring some clients. It didn't deter many.

"But this isn't just *any* cat shifter," Sara said as I headed over to her desk. Her eyes flicked back and forth across the screen. "He's a new account. One of the Russells. And his account is flagged."

A flag meant that someone was powerful and dangerous, and not to piss them off or the boss would do terrible things to us. It also meant Giselle had circumvented the regular setup process and had set this account up herself. She had a vested interest in its success.

We'd learned long ago not to mess with the flagged accounts. Not if we valued our jobs.

"Oh boy," I breathed. "Do I need to call Giselle about the cancellation?"

Giselle was the siren who had started Midnight Liaisons; she was a bit of a hard-ass. She wouldn't be pleased when she found out Rosie had screwed with a flagged account.

"Hell, no," Sara said, looking at me as if I'd grown another head. She hunched over the keyboard and began to type frantically. "I can handle this. Just give me a minute."

"Sara," I warned, concerned about her reaction. "We need to be careful when it comes to the flagged accounts. Let me call Giselle and see how she wants to handle it."

"No way. I'm fixing this," she said as she typed furiously, her gaze fixed on the screen. "Give me five minutes and I can fake a database failure and wipe out all the records for the past twenty-four hours—"

"Sara! Jeezus, no!" I tried to grab her wrists, but my little sister was quicker than me. "Don't you touch the database. You're going to hose every single record that's been updated since the last backup. Don't touch *anything*. I'm calling Giselle."

I moved back to my desk and flipped through my interoffice directory. Giselle was on vacation, so I needed her cell number. I hated the thought of calling her and disturbing her while she was out, but I hated the thought of her firing me even more. And she was sure to fire someone if she figured out that we'd somehow messed up a flagged account. I dialed.

"This is Giselle," said a throaty voice.

"Gis! Hi! I—"

"I'm in Vegas right now, and you're not," the recording continued. "And I can't make it to the phone right now. I'm a bit . . . tied up." A sultry laugh. "If this is work-related, it can wait until I get back. Otherwise, leave a message."

The voice mail beeped. I hung up. I'd made

the mistake of leaving a message once and she'd chewed me out and threatened my job. I knew better than to do it again. When one of Giselle's rich boyfriends took her away for the weekend, she did *not* like to be disturbed.

Back to square one, then.

"If we lose the account, we're in deep shit, Bath," Sara said. "She's going to fire me."

I was afraid she was right. Not only did Giselle have a sensitive (read: tenuous) relationship with the Russell clan, but she also had little tolerance for humans. The only reason she staffed her business with quiet, "normal" girls like Sara and me was because we could work all hours of the day and were forbidden to date the clientele. Giselle's circle of friends was limited by things like daylight and a full moon.

Sara turned her worried gaze to me. "What are we going to do?"

I moved to the back of the office and leaned over Sara's desk, determined to take control of the situation. "Okay. Let's figure this out. Pull up Rosie's profile. See if she logged where she was heading with her Russell date tonight."

Midnight Liaisons strictly monitored the activities of clients. The date, time, and location of a date were recorded and detailed, for their protection as well as ours. You never knew when an interspecies war was going to break out because someone had dated someone else's bitch. Literally.

Sara's fingers tapped on the keyboard, and then she whistled. "She logged it, all right. Dinner at Un Peu de Goût and a couple of nights at the Worthington afterwards."

"Dinner and a private party, eh?" Rosie moved in faster circles than most girls, human or otherwise. Still, she had good taste, and the restaurant was pricey. At least she was getting this guy to treat her right.

The phone on my desk rang again. I automatically went over to pick it up. "Midnight Liaisons. How may I help you?"

"Yes," the man on the line said in a fake gruff voice. "I'd like a date tonight. A redhead."

Him again. Now was *not* the time. I rolled my eyes and hung up the phone, then went back to Sara's desk. "Pull up the Russell's account again."

The phone rang.

Now I was starting to get irritated. We rarely had so many calls so close together, and it almost never happened before dark, which was our busy period due to the vampires waking up. Since it was midafternoon, it meant the freak was probably calling back again.

Time to fix this. I marched back to my desk. "Give me a moment, Sara, and we'll figure this out." The phone rang a second and third time before I picked it up and answered in my breathiest voice. "Midnight Liaisons. If you keep calling us, you fucking pervert, I'm going to call the cops and tell them you're soliciting our business for sex."

A deep laugh rumbled through the receiver—most definitely not my last caller. Warmth flooded through my body at the liquid sound, and I felt my face flushing at the sensation.

"Do you call all your customers perverts," the man asked, "or am I just lucky?"

I bit my lip. "I'm sorry. I thought you were—never mind. How can I help you, sir?"

"I have a bit of a problem," he said in a delicious voice, pleasant and smooth. "I had a very important date tonight and she just cancelled on me."

My heart sank. "What is your profile number, sir?"

He gave it to me and I typed it into the system, though I already knew what it would show. Rosie's date.

The caller's profile pulled up. Leader of the Russell clan—oh, *hell*—and very much a VIP with our service. No picture in the database, and his history was brief, his profile number brand-new. He hadn't used our service before setting up the date with Rosie. My superseductive caller was apparently named Beau Russell. I'd bet he was absolutely gorgeous. Tall, blond, and handsome, to match his cougar genes. A sensual face to match the sinful voice. And lots of muscles.

"You got quiet over there, sweetheart." He paused, then said in a low voice, "You see my problem?"

That pulled me back to earth. I quit picturing the client's abs and tapped on my mouse, my cheeks hot. "I see Rosie Smith cancelled on your date, correct," I said. "And I'm not your sweetheart."

"Rosie agreed to spend the week with me," he said, his words easy, as if he couldn't imagine there being a problem. "It's vital that I have a companion through Sunday."

Irritation flashed through me. The gall of shifters, always talking down to humans. "Well then, sir, I would suggest next time that you examine your date's profile a little closer. If you had looked at Rosie's date history, you would have seen she has a few bad habits, like accepting dates from cat shifters and then dumping them at the last minute. A bit of simple research could have avoided this heartache." Realizing my tone was a bit unsympathetic, I tacked on a "sir."

He chuckled low in his throat at my tart lecture. "You'll have to forgive me for not being too familiar with your website." His voice thrummed low in my ear. "I'm not used to searching for women online."

No, I'd bet not. If he was half as sexy as his voice, they'd be falling all over him on a regular basis.

"Regardless," he continued, "we need to fix this. Is Giselle in? Should I talk to her?"

I ignored the last two questions. Obviously he was on good terms with my boss. Obviously this was bad news for me. "I can't force Rosie to go out with you, sir."

"Call me Beau," he said, the inflection in his voice changing to coaxing. It made my thighs quiver traitorously. "And if Rosie won't go out with me, I need you to find me another date."

I brightened. "I can do that." Piece of cake. Tucking the phone against my shoulder, I began to type, entering his number and today's date into the profile generator. "Give me just a moment and I'll go through the database. I'm sure we can find you someone on short notice."

"No vampires," he said, "or any sort of undead." Then he paused. "What's *your* name?"

I typed his search criteria into the system with a frown. The whole "no undead" thing limited my search by a lot. Female shifters were rare, and if I counted out both men and undead, we might have a problem getting someone for tonight—let alone the next week. "My name is Bathsheba Ward," I said absently, crossing my fingers as I waited for the profile results to pull up.

Just as I gave him my name, the door to the office rang and a gorgeous man walked in, a pair of sunglasses obscuring his eyes.

My jaw dropped. He was beautiful—tall, dark, tanned. His suit was expensive, and he grinned and flashed pearly white teeth at me. Even at my desk, I could smell the thick musk of his cologne. A bit heavy, but typical of the confident sorts.

Sara immediately got up and went back to the filing room, as she always did when a shifter entered the building. I smelled the powdery stink of the perfume she was dousing her pulse points with, the smell overpowering and cloying when combined with the stranger's cologne.

The man must have come in for a new profile setup. Giselle preferred that I handle those in person, and I raised a finger to my customer, indicating that I needed a moment.

He nodded and sat down directly across from my desk, eyeing me with interest.

I felt the heat rise in my cheeks and hit the Enter key a few more times, just to distract myself. *Look busy, look busy.*

"Bathsheba?" The man on the phone sounded amused, and I had to drag my attention back to the phone call. "That's a mouthful for a modern girl. Are you a vamp?"

Intensely uncomfortable, I flipped through

some files on my desk, avoiding the scrutiny of the man across from me. "If I were a vampire," I said lightly, "I'd be burnt toast right now since it's midday." Sunlight poured in from the window behind my desk, and the entire front of the strip-mall office was windows. "I'm human. Sorry to disappoint."

"Oh, I'm not disappointed," he said in a low voice that made my toes curl.

Between the phone call and the man across from me—who looked altogether too interested in my conversation—I was going to die of embarrassment.

My search results finally came in and the computer pinged at me. Thank God.

One lone, lousy profile popped up on my screen. "It looks like we've found you a good match, Beau," I said, turning on the sales pitch. "Lorraina Murphy happens to be free tonight, and she's very interested in dating all kinds of shifters, according to her profile."

He made a rumbling sound of assent. "And what is she?"

"A shifter," I said evasively.

"What kind?" he pressed.

"Avian."

An uncomfortable pause. "You're going to have to be more specific than that."

I held back a sigh, knowing where this was headed. "Harpy."

The man across from me smiled.

There was a pause on the phone, as there always was when the harpy's profile came up. Then, very softly, he said, "I'm not going to go out with a harpy, Bathsheba."

I couldn't blame the man. Harpies had a bit of a reputation. They gave psycho-girlfriend new meaning. They tended to get unhinged over small stuff, and then things got really ugly. Shit hit the wall, no joke. "We have a doppelganger on file," I said desperately. "Jean can pose as a man or a woman, depending on your needs."

The phone grew very quiet.

Then, "Bathsheba, are you married?" God, his voice sounded sexier than ever.

Say yes. Lie and say you are married. "No," I breathed. "I'm not." I didn't dare look up at the man across from me; too bad I couldn't hide under my desk.

"Seeing someone?"

"No." My personal life was way too complicated to even think about throwing a boyfriend into the mix. Worried, I glanced at the doorway to the filing room, but I didn't see Sara. I hoped she was all right.

"Then it sounds like you're my date, doesn't it?"

"What?" I sputtered, then immediately threw the standard rejection at him. "The Paranormal

Alliance doesn't permit human/supe dating unless allowed by a special visa."

"I've got lawyers. Leave the details to me."

"Mr. Russell," I said, desperate, "I don't date clients."

The man across from me sat up and leaned forward, as if his interest had sparked. He murmured, "That's a real shame."

My face couldn't possibly get any redder. Not. Humanly. Possible.

"Make an exception—or let me talk to Giselle." The man on the phone wasn't going to take no for an answer, and I turned all my concentration back to him. I was starting to get a little irritated at his high-handed demands.

"Giselle's not available."

"Then it looks like we have only one option."

Shit. Giselle was going to flay me alive if I went out with a client. It was forbidden. I'd lose my job. Then again . . . I stared at the star on his profile. I was going to lose my job either way, wasn't I? Maybe if I went out with Mr. Russell, I could convince him to keep it a secret. Giselle would never have to know we'd botched his account, and I'd have a few drinks with the man and then let him down easy. He seemed nice enough.

I sighed. "I think you are making a mistake, Mr. Russell."

"Beau."

"Still a mistake."

"Why is that? You have a lovely name, a sexy voice, and you're free tonight," he said, his tone cajoling. "You're at least an auxiliary member of the Alliance if you're working for Giselle, so there won't be anything awkward to explain, like why I grow a tail sometimes. And you already think I'm a pervert, remember? So there won't be any surprises."

Was that a joke? My protest came out as a dry squeak. This was such a bad idea.

"I have to say, I'm looking forward to our date," Beau continued. "I'll get the chance to put a face to that sweet tongue of yours."

I blushed again. Dammit.

Thinking hard, I glanced over at the file room and saw Sara pacing, rubbing her arms. That was a bad sign. Right now she had a lot to stress over: the messed-up account, Giselle's wrath, and the shifter in the room. A panicked knot formed in my throat as Sara slammed the file room door shut. Very bad sign. Since it was my job to keep Sara from getting agitated, that meant getting rid of the shifter who sat across from me.

And to do that, I had to get the *other* shifter off the phone.

I turned away from my desk, trying to get a

semblance of privacy. "Just dinner," I breathed into the receiver, caving despite my misgivings. I couldn't look at the man across the desk from me as I gave in to Beau's demand. Everything in me shouted *big mistake*, but I had to do something. Sara was seconds away from losing it. "Not the whole week. And I won't go back to the hotel with you."

"Unless you want to," he added.

I rolled my eyes at his cockiness. "I won't want to. Trust me."

"We'll see," he said, supremely confident. "I'll meet you at the restaurant at seven thirty. See you then, sweet Bathsheba." He hung up.

I set the phone down with relief. One problem down, one to go.

The man across from me smiled. "Hi, I'm Jason," he said, extending his hand.

"Was that him?" Sara called, her voice muffled through the door. "Am I totally fired now?"

I cleared my throat and gave the man across from me an apologetic look. "Could you excuse me for a moment?"

"Of course," he said with a nod.

I dashed into the file room and closed the door behind me. Immediately, I put a hand to my mouth, gagging at the thick, cloying perfume. My eyes watered. "Jesus, Sara. If you spray any more of that stuff, he's going to think we have a rose garden back here."

"He's a shifter," she hissed and sprayed another squirt into the air. "I'm just being careful. So, am I totally fired?"

"Not quite," I said, fanning the air. The goofy, nervous feeling wouldn't leave me, no matter how hard I tried to calm down. "I've fixed things."

Sara looked confused. "What do you mean, you 'fixed' things?"

"I'm going out with Beau Russell tonight. Taking Rosie's place."

Sara's jaw dropped. "*What*? We're not allowed to date clients. You're a *normal*, not paranormal. You don't have the appropriate paperwork." She shook her head, glancing at the closed door behind me to make sure our guest wasn't going to enter. "That's really sweet of you, sis, but Giselle will have a cow if she finds out."

"I won't tell if you won't," I said. "By the time she gets back from vacation, it'll be taken care of."

She shook her head, her short, fine hair flying about her shoulders. "Don't be crazy, Bath. I can fix this—"

I grabbed her arm and pinched it, like I used to when we were kids. "If you erase one file out of that database, I swear I'm going to pour water onto your motherboard at home. Understand me?" At her glare, I continued, "I'm the office manager. Let me manage this."

She stuck her tongue out at me in response, and I knew I'd won.

"Are you going to be okay?" I asked abruptly, changing the subject. "Do you need to leave?"

"I'm fine," she said as she rubbed her arms again. "Everything's under control."

"Bullshit." I wanted to reach for her again, but I knew from experience that would just aggravate things. "I'll take care of this guy. You stay in here and I'll cover for you until you feel better, all right?"

Her lips pinched into a tight line, and she nodded.

"Knock something over so you have an excuse to stay here and clean up. Just not the perfume bottle. My lunch won't stay down if you spray it again."

Again, Sara gave a tight nod.

I gave her a thumbs-up and slipped out of the room.

Jason smiled at me as I returned to my desk. "Everything all right?"

"Just fine," I agreed with my best smile. "Now if I could just see your Alliance ID, I can get your profile set up."

It took forty-five minutes to set up Jason's account. I usually got them set up faster while still being polite and chatty, but Jason was a talker and a flirt to boot. I worked steadily, sneaking glances at the closed file room door. There wasn't a single sound, which concerned me a little, but I couldn't show it.

Jason was determined to hit on me. I declined his advances and kept things strictly business, sending his request for a date to a pretty little were-fox that I thought might suit him. Once Jason had his profile paperwork printed out and his latest flirtatious comment rebuffed, there was nothing else for him to do but leave. I kept working for a few minutes after he left, just in case he decided to come back, but he didn't. Then, I bolted up from my desk and ran to the file room and opened the door.

A sleek gray wolf lay on the floor, her head between her paws. Sara's clothes were discarded on the floor, mixed with some fallen files.

"Oh, Sara," I chided her.

The wolf whined.

I picked up her torn shirt, examining it to see if it was mendable. It wasn't. With a roll of my eyes, I went back to my desk and opened my bottom drawer, then lifted a big, manila envelope to reveal a stack of emergency shirts. I picked out a pink one and shut the drawer again.

Living with a werewolf meant a lot of torn

clothing. In the six years since Sara had been transformed, I'd learned to adapt to her needs.

But it didn't mean I couldn't give her crap
about it. I went back to the file room and dangled
the pink shirt in front of her. "Last one in a normal color," I teased. "Change one more time, and
you're reduced to those SpongeBob T-shirts we
found on the clearance rack."

She growled at me, her canine lips curling back
in a snarl.

I grinned and tossed the shirt down at her. "Just
a little added incentive."

I warred all day with what to wear to my date.
Part of me wanted to wear something that was
about as sexy as a funeral. Since Mr. Beau Russell was planning on getting laid, I wanted him
to understand as soon as he looked at me that he
was not scoring tonight. I needed something that
screamed off-limits, puritanical, and possibly
Amish.

But the feminine part of me rebelled at not
looking my best. Beau was probably handsome
and confident. I, meanwhile, hadn't been on a date
in six years.

It was the first thing to have changed in my life
after Sara had turned, and I'd willingly given it up.

Protecting Sara had become my life, and everything I did revolved around her.

And yet . . . here I was, about to go out on a date. Just me and some guy looking to meet a pretty girl, charm her, and hopefully score. I swallowed. No pressure. To make matters worse, we were going to a fancy restaurant. I needed to look like I belonged there, to be glamorous and confident.

After all, I had to be on my guard around Mr. Russell. I needed to be supremely self-assured, and poised as hell. Balls-to-the-wall, take no prisoners, not-interested-in-you strong female who was human and normal, and didn't happen to have a werewolf sister.

After work, I spent an hour picking through my closet. Most of my clothes were practical, and nothing seemed quite right for a date. I ended up settling on a sleeveless, swingy A-line dress in black, edged with aqua satin. It was pretty and feminine. The skirt was shorter than I remembered and the neckline deep enough to show generous cleavage, which was probably why it had sat in my closet unworn for so long, the tags still attached. It really wasn't all that seductive, but for someone like me, there was never an occasion to wear it.

I put on a couple of bracelets and hoop earrings, and pulled my long, straight, superfine blond hair into a bun high atop my head. I didn't have time to blow-dry it into fluffiness.

After all, I wasn't really trying to impress Mr. Russell, was I?

And just because I wasn't trying to impress him, I added a second coat of lip gloss.

Before heading out the door, I gave my clothes a squirt of Febreze and tumbled them in the dryer with a floral-scented dryer sheet just in case Sara's distinctive werewolf scent lingered on me. I couldn't smell it because I was human, but just about every shifter had a nose ten times keener than mine, and we'd had several close calls. My black strappy sandals had been airing on the porch for the same reason.

Un Peu de Goût was in the heart of Sundance Square in downtown Fort Worth, where it catered to a business clientele and tourists looking to spend money on dinner. The last restaurant I'd been to was Burger King, so I was nervous.

My sister was at home sleeping off her most recent change. It always took a toll on her, so I left the car with her and took a cab to the restaurant. I stared out the window as we drove, trying not to get too anxious, my purse clutched close to my chest like a football carried into enemy territory.

As I walked into the restaurant, my heels clicked

loudly on the marble tile, drawing the attention of the maître d'. This was a big fat mistake. I should have worn something with a longer hemline, or a less plunging neckline. Or just turned the date down. If Giselle found out I was dating one of the clients, even at his request, I'd be out of a job, no matter how important the account.

Humans were a dime a dozen, even the ones who wouldn't freak out over the weird proclivities of the boss or strange client requests. The Alliance community was an exclusive one, and all of the clients were rich and powerful. Some had tons of money, thanks to long life spans, and some simply had a natural charisma that drew humans to them.

A couple of sorry humans like Sara and me— well, maybe just me—were outclassed. If she had to choose between loyal human employees and clients, Giselle would always pick clients.

"Yes, mademoiselle?"

I smiled at the maître d', hoping he couldn't sense my nervousness. "I'm here to meet Mr. Beau Russell," I said breathlessly. "We have a dinner reservation."

The maître d' didn't even look down at his list. He gave me a tight, knowing smile. "Mr. Russell will be here shortly, mademoiselle. You may wait at the bar."

"Oh," I said, a bit surprised that my date wasn't here yet. "Certainly." I let him lead me in.

When I approached the bar, I started to feel a little irritated at the absent Mr. Russell, who couldn't bother to show up on time. If this was some sort of passive-aggressive move to put the little human in her place, I wasn't amused. With a small frown, I ordered a mojito and sat down on my barstool to wait.

The mojito was expensive but tasty and did wonderful things to relax my frazzled nerves. I'd sucked down half of my drink before I forced myself to slow down. I didn't want to be plastered by the time the man got to the restaurant.

Ten minutes passed, and I played with the lime on the edge of my glass. Where was he? Maybe he wouldn't show up. Maybe he'd called the agency back and told Sara that he wasn't going to meet me. I knew what the Alliance went for in a woman, especially the shifters. All their dating profiles read the same—muscular, lean, aggressive. Gorgeous. Enthusiastic. Morally ambiguous. Most shifter women pursued the men as hotly as they were pursued back. Even the vampire women were elegant, delicate creatures.

Me? I was a desk jockey for the glamorous. A mousy blonde encased in power panty hose that were going to cut off her circulation. He'd take a look at me, laugh, and ask to meet the harpy after all. Twitchy at the thought, I took a bite out of my lime and sucked on it. After ten more minutes, this guy could consider himself out of a date. I wasn't going to wait here all night like some pathetic loser. I put my lime rind on a napkin and tossed back the rest of my drink.

By the time seven more minutes passed, I'd had it. Enough was enough. Mr. Russell wasn't coming to our impromptu date. Part of me breathed a sigh of relief. At least Giselle wouldn't have anything to be upset over, and I'd fulfilled all my obligations. I left a couple of dollars for the bartender, tucked my bag under my arm, then stepped away from the bar—and saw him.

He lounged nearby, leaning against the bar as if he owned the place. He was turned toward me, a half-full beer on the bar beside him. It was obvious he'd been there some time, and just as obvious that he'd been watching me without bothering to introduce himself. The jerk.

A slow smile curved his lips, and my heart stuttered. I'd seen beautiful men, and I'd seen sexy men. But I'd never seen a man who was as powerfully masculine as this one.

I was finding it hard to breathe.

It wasn't the sleepy, sexy eyes with the dark lashes. It wasn't the piercing gray irises that assessed me as if they could see me naked. It wasn't the impressive spread of his shoulders or the narrow waist, or the thick fall of tousled brown hair over his tanned forehead. None of that caused my breath to evaporate quite like the confidence that poured from him. It was there from the easy way he carried his big frame to the crooked smile that tugged at his lips and emphasized his amazing cheekbones.

This man was going to be trouble.

The room grew fuzzy at the edges, and black stars flashed in front of my eyes as he crossed the floor to meet me. Everything about him was effortless, graceful motion, like a predator stalking its prey.

He leaned in close to me, and I could smell his musky clean scent. "You need to breathe, Bathsheba."

Breathe. Right. I sucked in a breath and my vision cleared.

He smiled at me again, that soft, lazy smile. "That's better."

I fought the urge to wipe it off his face, annoyed that he'd made me wait while he'd been here all along.

He gestured at the sea of white-linen-covered tables. "Shall we sit?"

That depended on his answer. "How long have you been here watching me?"

The smile widened into a grin. "You caught me," he admitted. "I wanted to watch you for a few minutes. Is that so wrong?"

"It was very uncomfortable for me," I said coolly. "I believed I was being stood up."

He took my hand in his and lifted it to his mouth for a kiss. His lips brushed against my skin, sending a shiver through me. "I apologize," he said, looking serious. "That was thoughtless of me."

I tried pulling my hand out of his.

He didn't budge.

I raised an eyebrow. "Mr. Russell, you know that humans aren't allowed to date in the Alliance. On behalf of my company, I didn't want to leave you stranded tonight—but I could lose my job over this. So *if* I stay, Giselle must never know about it."

His thumb rubbed against the back of my hand. "Of course not. The last thing I want is for you to get in trouble at my expense. Please stay—I ordered the tasting menu," he coaxed.

I'd never been to a tasting dinner, with its multiple courses of fancy tidbits, all designed to show off the chef's culinary skills and imagination. It would be fun—and he seemed sincere. I pulled my hand away and nodded. "Fine. I'll stay."

"Thank you." At the table, he pulled my chair out as the waiter hovered nearby, then he sat down across from me and flicked his napkin into his lap with a flourish.

The waiter opened a bottle of expensive wine and, as we each took a sip, I said, "I feel that I should point out my first rule of dating, Mr. Russell. Just because you wine and dine me doesn't mean I'm obligated to have sex with you. So going to the Worthington after dinner is not happening."

He smiled, clearly not offended in the slightest. "I wouldn't dream of it, Miss Bathsheba. If I pay for dinner, the only pleasure I expect is your company."

I stared at the six and a half feet of masculinity on the other side of the table. He looked amused, as if he liked a challenge. This could end up being very, very dangerous in a way I hadn't expected.

I changed topics, trying to put a wall up between us. "So why did you want to watch me at the bar, Mr. Russell? Just in case I had warts and a hunched back, so you could make a hasty escape?"

"I wanted to see if the voice and name matched the body."

"And? Do I look like a Bathsheba to you?"

"You do," he said. "Soft. Delicious. Warm. Curvy." His eyes glinted as he leaned across the table. "I bet you'd taste the same."

Oh. My. An instant flush crossed my cheeks. "That's a first," I said, recovering swiftly. "Usually I'm told that the name Bathsheba reminds them of an old lady clutching her knitting."

"They'd be wrong."

Red alert. Red alert. All hormones on deck. "Mr. Russell—"

"Beau," he said, interrupting me. "Short for Beauregard." He gave me a sheepish look. "Old Southern family."

I finally smiled. "I'm not about to give you a hard time about your name. You're speaking to a woman named after one of the greatest adulteresses in the Bible. My sister's lucky she wasn't named Whore of Babylon."

He laughed, his silvery eyes warm and crinkling at the corners. He lifted his wineglass and raised it to me. "Two very unusual names for two very normal people. We're a match made in heaven, Bathsheba Ward."

I wasn't sure how normal he was, but I clinked my glass against his anyhow. I wasn't used to hearing my full name all the time, so when we set our glasses down, I said, "My friends call me Bath."

He clasped my hand between his warm ones. "But I don't want to be your friend."

His skin against mine was incredibly distracting. I felt the calluses on his palms, felt the strong grip of his warm, large hands, his nails lightly scratching at the back of my hand in an absent, comforting gesture.

Oh, dear. I liked that far, far too much for my own good. Licking my lips nervously, I asked. "So what's on the tasting menu tonight?"

He grinned. "I have no idea. I just asked the maître d' what was good and that's what he recommended."

The waiter arrived and we pulled apart, though Beau's hand seemed to linger on mine.

"An amuse-bouche for the monsieur and the mademoiselle," the waiter said, a hint of a Texas drawl coloring his French. He set down two tiny plates. "A patisserie with caviar and crème fraiche," he said, then left.

Beau popped the amuse-bouche into his mouth. After a moment his expression changed and his chewing slowed.

I eyed the concoction on my plate. "How is it?"

He chewed for a moment more, then swallowed hard. "Interesting."

Well, *that* was a ringing endorsement. I eyed mine, and nodded that I was done when the waiter arrived to take the plates away. He returned a moment later with two bowls of bright orangey-yellow soup.

My eyes widened at the brown thing floating in my soup.

"Butternut bisque," the waiter announced, "with quail egg in nest."

Oh, dear. The waiter left and I looked at my bowl, then at Beau. He was staring at his food with an odd expression on his face.

"Is that a real bird's nest?" I asked him. "Are we supposed to eat it?"

"I don't know," he admitted, then tapped his spoon against the egg. "I know I'm a were-cat, but this is ridiculous."

I giggled and took a large swallow of wine, no more eager to eat mine than he was. "Maybe I'm not as adventurous as I should be when it comes to eating," I admitted. "What's next on the menu?"

"Cheese," he said, looking down at the piece of paper.

"Why the face? That doesn't sound so bad."

"A savory mixture of goat and . . . yak cheeses," he said, continuing to read.

"Er . . . oh." I took another swig of my wine. "The wine is very good, at least."

Beau looked chagrined. "I'm sorry you're not enjoying the meal."

"We haven't even started the meal," I quipped. "The entree will probably be some unfortunate exotic animal served on a bed of seaweed. French seaweed."

He laughed, then glanced at me. "There's a sports bar next door. Want to go grab a burger?"

"And leave my bird's nest behind?" I pretended to protect my plate, resisting the urge to break into laughter. At his grin, I put down my wineglass and stood. "Let's go."

He threw a wad of bills on the table.

In the sports bar, we grabbed a comfortable booth and ordered. As we waited for our burgers, an uncomfortable silence fell. Sitting across from him in a cozy booth in a dark corner felt far more intimate than sitting stiffly across from him at a fancy French restaurant had.

I clasped my hands together, trying to think of something to break the silence, but nothing came to mind. Crap. I hadn't dated in so long that I didn't know what to talk about. Football? I didn't know if he was a big sports fan. The weather? No, that was just stupid—

"Do I make you uncomfortable?" he asked, misinterpreting my awkwardness.

"I'm just not very good at small talk. Or dating. I don't date."

He looked fascinated. "I can't imagine why not. Tell me about yourself then."

I froze. Talking about me meant talking about

Sara, and I couldn't talk about Sara. "There's not much to tell," I said in a stiff voice. Was this a probe for information? Was he going to sell it to the wolf packs? "I'm a very boring girl."

He shook his head, that beautiful smile flashing across his face. "I sincerely doubt that anyone with a name like yours could be boring."

I remained quiet.

"You really *aren't* good with small talk," he teased.

Shoot, what could I talk about that wouldn't alert him to our secret? "I . . . like to read."

He smiled at me over the plate of cheese fries the waiter set down in front of us. "Who doesn't?"

Well, how could you not like a man who said that? "That's about it, really. Now, your turn. Tell me something you like."

I caught a flash of white teeth. "I like women. Soft, curvy women."

I rolled my eyes. "That doesn't count."

"Why not?"

"Because it's a given—like if I said I liked men with large packages." I reached over for a cheese fry. "That's like saying that you like breathing, or eating."

"Sounds like we're a match made in heaven," he said lazily. "I like to eat, love to breathe"—he leaned over the table—"and I have a very large package."

I choked on my cheese fry. "Not nice," I coughed, trying to catch my breath. "You play dirty, sir."

He picked up a fry and gestured at me with it before popping it into his mouth. "Your turn."

"There's really nothing else to tell."

He cocked an eyebrow at me. "Nobody's life is that dull. I get the impression that you've got something to hide, Miss Bathsheba."

Why, yes, Beau. When I was nineteen, my younger sister started dating a werewolf. He bit her and turned her, and I had to drop out of college to take care of her as she adjusted to growing fur and a tail. And since the werewolf pack wants her back, we keep a low profile in case we have to leave town again. Oh, and I like frat boy comedy movies. You?

I finished chewing my fry, pretending to think it over. I needed something bland and nondescript, to angle the conversation back toward safer ground. Aha! "I like bookkeeping."

It was the one phrase guaranteed to scare a man off. Most women would say that they liked to date, or dance, or curl up at home with a movie. I liked general ledgers and balancing someone's books.

He did a catlike tilt of his head that was a bit unnerving, reminding me that he was slightly more than human, for all his sexiness. "Bookkeeping? Like accounting?"

I waited for his eyes to glaze over with disinterest. "I find it enjoyable."

He reached for another cheese fry. "Do you like math, then? The challenge of it?"

That wasn't the bored look I was used to—or worse, the derisive sneer. It startled me, and I gave him a genuine smile. "I like the control aspect, being the one in charge. At first I hated it, but then it became like a puzzle to me, to figure out how to balance the books and find the right numbers that make everything click." I enjoyed managing Giselle's office. It made me think I could own my own business someday, so I considered it good practice.

"You ever think about starting your own business?"

"Maybe someday," I said, uncomfortable again. I didn't want to talk about my personal hopes and dreams with him.

"You could start up your own accounting business. I'd hire you to do my company's books."

"I'll pass, thanks."

He grinned back at me and my heart flip-flopped. "The offer stands. You're welcome to get your hands on my books anytime."

It was amazing that he could make something

as benign as accounting sound like a turn-on. I turned to my drink—a fresh mojito—and took a gulp, feeling a sudden need for liquid courage.

He smiled and leaned back, studying me like he might a delicious roast that he was about to devour. But then the smile faded and his shoulders formed a tense line.

Someone slid into the booth next to me. "Well, hello," said a man in a low, growling voice.

I looked over in surprise, scooting farther back reflexively. Beau's jaw had clenched into a hard line.

"What do we have here?" The man gave me a roguish grin, displaying big, crooked teeth. He had wild, thick hair that stuck up in tufts from his head, and a wrinkled polo shirt hung from his enormous frame. There was something wild about him that I couldn't quite put my finger on, but I recognized the way his nostrils flared, sniffing the air to catch my scent.

Shifter.

My pulse pounded in my ears and I stiffened, thinking of Sara. Fuck. Fuck. Fuck. This man could be a wolf, and therefore dangerous.

The man tilted his head, the crazy grin never leaving his face, his eyes on Beau. "Who's your friend? She from out of town?"

I waited, afraid to breathe, for him to pick up Sara's scent on me. To expose my secret.

Beau's eyes narrowed into a distinctly unfriendly look, though the pleasant smile remained on his face. "Go away, Tony. This is my personal business, not the pack's."

Tony leaned even closer toward me. I shoved him away, not caring in the slightest that it was rude. "Get away from me."

Undeterred, Tony grabbed my hand. He sniffed me and his eyes widened. He looked back to Beau with a knowing grin. "She's not a were at all, is she?"

I took another gulp of my mojito, relief warring with anxiety. Sara was safe . . . but now I had a whole new set of problems.

Beau was supposed to have been dating a supe through the agency, but I was a normal. This was sure to get back to my boss. Shit.

As I drank, Tony reached out to touch my ear. I jerked hard, spilling my drink all over the table.

Beau reached over and plucked Tony's hand off me. "If you touch her again, I'll break your fingers," he said in a bored voice, but his eyes were flinty with dislike. "Understand?"

"Tsk tsk," said Tony in a mock-playful voice. "It's silly to get upset over human trash, Beauregard."

Beau's eyes narrowed into slits and I could feel the rage radiating off of him.

One wrong move and these two would fight. Beau looked ready to destroy the man, and Tony didn't seem to have a lick of sense in his body. He just continued grinning and looking at me, his gaze flicking over my neck and pulled-up hair as if he wanted to touch me. "She's cute for a normal, Beau. Not what I'd call your type, though." He looked me up and down once more, his eyes a little too interested, then turned to Beau. "So where's Arabella?"

I got a sinking feeling in my stomach. Oh, God. Was Beau involved with someone? Or even married?

"I don't know," Beau said, his words a careless drawl. "I'm not her keeper."

I checked his finger—no sign of a ring-sized tan line. Good. Not that I cared, of course.

"I can see I'm not wanted here," Tony stood and grinned. "You know you're not supposed to date humans. I believe that rule was set down by your very own little Alliance. Funny how you're the one to break the rules."

Beau looked right at me and answered Tony, "It's none of your business who I date. When I need permission from someone, I'll ask."

"Suit yourself." The shifter smirked in my direction. "The others are going to find this really interesting, though." Tony winked at me. "Later, chicken."

Silence fell as he turned and left. Beau clenched

his hands, glaring at Tony as if he'd like to jump up and rip the man's throat out. The other man didn't look back, as he took his sweet time circling back to the far side of the restaurant and disappearing from sight. The waiter stopped by to mop the table and left me a new drink. Beau said nothing.

I was the first to break the silence. There were a hundred things I wanted to ask about. "Chicken?"

Beau's response was grudging. "Chicken is Tony's term for non-supes. He likes to say that they taste like chicken."

"That's fairly disturbing."

"He's trying to be tough. His pack is full of ass-holes who like to push around as many people as they can. They refuse to join the Alliance."

Well, that explained why they'd been going at it like cats and dogs. It also made me want to throw up. To think that he'd sat next to me . . . tried to touch me . . . to think that he could have smelled Sara if I hadn't been careful. I took a hasty sip of my mojito, my hands shaking. And then I choked, my throat too tight to swallow properly.

"You all right?" Beau said, the growl receding from his voice. "I'm sorry if he scared you."

I shook my head. "No, I'm fine. My drink just went down the wrong way. So who's Arabella?"

He sighed. "My ex," he admitted. "I haven't seen her in months."

"Word must travel slow."

"Yeah. We don't talk to the wolf pack much." He didn't seem to want to expand on the subject.

Thank God for that. "What kind of supe is Arabella? Were-skunk?" I asked, my tone sweet.

His lips twitched with mirth. "No, just a were-cougar that hung around far too long. Haven't you ever dated someone like that?"

I gave him a look. "I can't say that my little black book is full of were-cougars."

He laughed. "Then I am delighted to be your first."

My entire body tensed. But that was silly. Beau couldn't possibly know that I was a virgin.

"Before I forget," Beau said, pulling out his wallet. He flipped through it, then handed me a small salmon-colored card. "Sign this."

I took it from him and turned it over, reading. Lots of very small print crept across it on both sides. "What is it?"

"Your visa." At my startled look, he flashed a grin. "It says you are legally approved to date in the Paranormal Alliance."

From what I'd heard, this sort of permission took forever. "So why did you let Tony think that I don't have one?"

He picked up his drink. "Maybe I want you all to myself."

Chapter Two

Several drinks and a delicious, normal meal later, we wandered out of the restaurant, smiling. He had my hand clasped in the crook of his elbow, and I had enough drinks in me—and good conversation—to let him.

I found myself liking Beau quite a bit more than I should have. It was a mistake, through and through, but when he smiled down at me, I got a little weak in the knees and even weaker in resolve.

He was supernatural, I kept reminding myself. That meant bad news for Sara, bad news for me. He was everything I was supposed to avoid. Dating Beau meant Alliance politics I couldn't even begin to understand, mortal enemies (every supe had them), and all kinds of complications. As a human on the fringes, I knew my fair share about how their secret society operated, but there were levels that I'd never be privy to. For all I knew, the guy turned into a ravening, man-eating cougar at the full moon.

Suspicious, I glanced up at the sky. No full moon.

Everything about the setup of our date told me to run away, and run away fast. But he was charming, and funny, and incredibly sexy. He listened to everything I said with an interested look on his face. I could talk about the bizarre goings-on at Giselle's office and knew that he'd understand because he was part of the Alliance. It was seductively freeing, even more so when he chuckled at my anecdotes.

I also learned a bit about him. Beau was the eldest child of his family and had three younger brothers. His dad had died when he was eighteen, and his mother lived in California with her second husband—a were-lion. He loved his clan. He was the head of the Paranormal Alliance and owned a large security firm staffed by shifters.

He was . . . nice. I liked him. I *couldn't* like him, though. Sara was in danger if I allowed my feelings for someone—especially a supe—to come between us. I was her shield to the world.

Lost in thought, I was quiet as we walked out of the restaurant. Neither of us spoke, but he still had my arm in his, possessive. A taxi stand was just down the street.

He started to steer me away from the taxi line and toward the restaurant's private parking lot, and my happy, almost-bubbling mood dissipated. I stopped. "I think it's time for me to head home."

"Want to go have a nightcap somewhere?" His hand slid over my shoulder.

I slid it right back off again. His hand was very warm and felt great on my bare skin, but I wouldn't let that sway me. "I'm not going to the hotel with you."

His lips quirked. "I won't lie—I would love to get you into my bed. But I was thinking more along the lines of a drink. Or coffee, if you'd rather."

Sure, and I was just whistling Dixie. "I'll pass, thanks." I pulled away and turned toward the cab stand.

When a cab pulled up, Beau opened the door.

Before I could get into it, however, he shut the door. Irritated, I slapped his arm lightly. "What are you—"

"Shhh," he said, turning back toward me. His eyes were slitted like a cat's, gleaming yellow-green and reflecting light.

I stared at him, openmouthed in surprise. His nostrils flared slightly as he sniffed the air, searching for something. I wanted to ask him what was wrong, but I remembered his request for quiet and obeyed.

He blinked and the unnatural shine faded from his eyes, his pupils a regular size once more. Then he looked down at me. "Don't take the cab."

"Why?" I glanced over at the waiting taxi, unnerved.

He pulled me closer to him in a protective grasp and led me back down the sidewalk. "The cab driver smelled like . . . like alcohol."

Something about his statement rang false. I remembered the way his eyes had gleamed, as if he'd been hunting prey. "Uh-huh."

"I'll take you home. How far are we from your place?"

"About twenty minutes," I said.

"Got a roommate?"

"My sister," I said, wariness returning. "Why?"

"Good." He handed me his cell phone. "Call her and tell her you will be home in twenty-five minutes, and to call the police if not."

That seemed trustworthy enough. I took the phone from him and dialed my home number. Sara answered on the second ring, and I could hear her computer game blasting in the background. "Hello?"

"It's me," I said, my eyes on Beau. He watched me calmly, his hands in his pockets. He didn't seem like he was setting me up, at least. "I'm still out with Mr. Russell. He's driving me home, so I'll be there in twenty-five minutes."

"All right," she said slowly, and I couldn't tell if she had picked up on my anxiety. I needed to tell her about the other wolves we'd seen tonight, the veiled references he'd made. Maybe we needed to move again.

"Tell her that if we're not there on time, to call the police," he said, misunderstanding my awkward silence.

I parroted it back into the phone, feeling a bit like an overly paranoid freak. He was being so calm and easy about this.

"I guess I don't need to tell you that Giselle just called and gave you a late assignment?" Sara said, reciting the excuse we'd agreed upon in case the date went badly and I had to exit fast. She dropped her voice into a whisper. "He must be cute."

Oh, jeez. Had my were-cougar date heard that? I glanced over at my date and saw his mouth curl into a faint smile.

"Very cute," he agreed.

I nearly died of embarrassment. "Look, twenty-five minutes, okay? Will you keep track?"

"Sure," she said, yawning. "I'll start an egg timer or something. You two kids have fun."

I hung up and handed him the phone back, disgruntled. Sara wasn't taking this seriously, and Beau had just heard the entire conversation, thanks to supernatural hearing. "We have twenty-five minutes," I announced.

"I know," he said. "We'll be there in fifteen."

"You're very confident in yourself."

"I am," he agreed. "I know what I want, and I get what I want." He gave me a pointed look.

I ignored it. "All right then. I'll get in the car as long as you tell me what you smelled back there."

He hesitated. "A shifter. I know you don't want to be seen with me, so I thought it might be best if we took my car."

That made sense, and I felt relieved that he'd been so quick to catch that. "Thank you."

He simply grinned at me.

Beau's car was a Viper. I nearly melted at the sight of it. The valet at the parking lot had the same expression I did—he looked loath to hand the keys over to Beau.

I ran my hand along the hard top as he opened my door to let me in. The inside was cramped, but posh—just what I expected for this kind of car. It was amazing that a tall man like Beau could fit in the car. I eyed the size of the seats. Pretty much in the clear, here. This was a date-rape-safe car—there just wasn't room for that sort of thing.

He slid into the car next to me and paused, his eyes flashing that odd color again for a moment.

"What is it?" I asked.

He shook his head. "Nothing. Just me being paranoid."

The drive home was a brief one. I'd considered not giving him my home address, but Sara knew he was taking me home, and we had his information on file at work. If there was one thing that the Alliance didn't cater to, it was killers and lawbreakers. They were extremely careful to keep up appearances, and someone who couldn't follow the basic rules of normal society was usually "disposed of" pretty readily.

Kind of like the mafia, but a little hairier and with less garlic.

About fifteen minutes later we pulled into the driveway of the small suburban house Sara and I rented. I saw her part the drapes and look out the window. She saw the car and I raised a hand to let her know it was me.

She nodded and pulled the curtains shut again, giving Beau and me privacy.

I wanted to stay in his company for a few minutes more, but part of me was on edge. My mind was stewing with Tony's appearance tonight, my thoughts full of wolves and Sara's safety . . . and I couldn't stop thinking about Beau's smile and when his fingers had brushed my palm earlier.

But I'd accepted my role as my sister's protector a long time ago, and it didn't leave room for a man in my life, especially one with a tail.

Beau put an arm behind my shoulders and I stiffened, but he only toyed with a lock of hair that had escaped my bun, his fingers brushing against my neck in a small motion that sent shivers down my spine.

"I had a nice time tonight," he said.

Lord, he was gorgeous. His dark brown hair looked inky black in the darkness, his eyes pale. "Listen, Beau—"

He laid a finger over my mouth, silencing me before I could shoot him down.

"Shh," he said, not perturbed in the slightest at my reluctance. "The week is young, Bathsheba. There's plenty of time. I have until Saturday before things get desperate."

"I don't follow you."

He tilted his head, eyes gleaming in the moonlight. "How so?"

"You call the agency and demand a date—any date. And when you decide you don't want to date a harpy, a vampire, a doppelganger, or anything else I can pull up on file, you ask for a stand-in. Me." I threw my hands up in the air. "And now you're saying it's okay, because we have time until Saturday. What does Saturday have to do with *anything*?"

He stared at me, and then he laughed.

I crossed my arms over my chest, feeling

wounded and embarrassed. "What's so darn funny?"

"I thought you knew. I figured someone in your line of work would guess . . ." He smiled. "I have to say that this puts a new spin on things."

"What are you *talking* about?"

He leaned in close, setting my pulse to thrumming hard, and I instinctively leaned back.

"I'm going into heat," he said.

Chapter Three

I shied back at his declaration. "You're what?"

He reached for the lock of hair again, playing with it. "In heat. So to speak."

"I . . . I . . ." I blinked, trying to gather my thoughts. "I thought only females went into heat." Didn't men have the wrong equipment for that? Trying to be nonchalant, I flicked a glance at his package. Well, now. Either he truly was in heat, or he was as well built as he claimed.

"We all use the term, and you're right, only females go into heat." His mouth twisted. "One of the female cougars in my clan is about to go into heat in a few days. Her need affects all the males, so there's fighting among the unmated guys to claim her, and clan politics get really messy right about now. Normally she would just leave town if she didn't have a mate, but . . . she can't this time." His face grew tight.

"Oh," I breathed, thinking hard. My gaze darted rapidly to the sensual curve of his mouth, the hint of tongue that touched his lips. Oh, my. "So why don't you and the female hook up?"

"It's complicated," he said, and slid a little closer to me. "And I want you."

"Oh," I repeated, retreating. The back of my head smacked against the fogging window of the Viper. Maybe it was taboo for him to date her? I didn't know much about Alliance politics—or cougars in general—but they had their own special hierarchy. "Is that why . . . Rosie . . . ?"

He nodded and whisked his hand to my hair, pulling out the clip that kept my tight bun in place and releasing the blond strands to spill over my shoulders. "I've been wanting to do that all night," he said, running his fingers through it and then kneading them against my neck, like a cat kneading its paws. His voice was a low growl. "Your hair is sexy as hell. How long is it?"

"To my waist," I breathed, my breath quickening to match his, my eyes locked on his face. "So you were using the dating service to find someone because you were in heat?"

He lifted a handful of my hair and let it slide between his fingers like silk. Definitely a hint of purring in the back of his throat. "I don't give a shit about Rosie. Your dating service was the only option available for a last-minute date that wouldn't mind what I am, so I paid the ridiculous fee and set up a profile in the same hopes."

I jerked my hair back out of his hand. "Our business is not ridiculous. We cater to a very specific need."

"It's a dangerous business, and Giselle knows it. What's worse is that she doesn't care." His gray eyes searched mine. "She's a fool for hiring humans to do a delicate job. You're going to cross some line you won't even know about, and then you'll all end up in trouble."

"Oh?" I shoved my hair back over my shoulders. His eyes followed the move, and my body tingled with awareness. "Like the way you crossed a line by dating a human?"

"Something like that," he growled, leaning in.

I planted my hand on his face and shoved. "You picked the wrong girl for your heat."

His smile curved against my fingers. "What makes you say that?"

"I'm a virgin." No one had gotten into my panties for twenty-five years, and this cocky guy wasn't going to be the first.

"I suspected as much," he said.

I opened my mouth to ask why when something caught the corner of my eye. A shadow passed behind the upstairs window, blocking out the light.

"Someone's in my bedroom." I leaned forward, staring out over the dashboard.

Sara never went into my room. She was too afraid of her scent contaminating my clothing.

His eyes were intense on me. "Are you trying to distract me?"

But then Sara peeked out of the downstairs window—in the living room—and the shadow passed behind my bedroom window again. My heart pounded, and out of the corner of my eye I saw Beau tense.

"Hold this," Beau said, handing me his keys and his cell phone and leaping out of the car.

"Wait," I called after him, throwing my door open. "Where are you going?"

"I'll get her out of there," he said. "Stay in the car." He disappeared to the far side of the car and out of my sight.

I stared at my bedroom window, wanting the shape to reappear so I would know I wasn't mad, and dreading it at the same time. Sitting in the car was pointless. I jumped out of the Viper and dialed the home phone, my hands shaking so hard it was difficult to dial. I had to try twice before the call went through.

"Hello," Sara said, confused.

"Sara, are you there with Beau? Is he in there with you?" I was babbling so fast that I sounded incoherent.

"Beau? I thought he was with you. Why are you calling from the driveway?"

"Never mind. Just get out of the house, right now. Come meet me on the front lawn."

"I'm not dressed—"

"Just *do* it, Sara!" I ended the call and scrutinized every window. Where was the intruder? Where was Beau? He was nowhere to be seen.

And neither was my sister. Damn. If she wasn't coming out, I was going in after her.

I tossed Beau's keys on the hood as I ran forward . . . and stumbled over a man's shoe. Confused, I looked down. There was the match to it, along with a pair of slacks and an expensive shirt matching the one Beau had worn to our date.

It didn't register in my mind at first.

The sound of breaking glass made me look up, and I saw an enormous tawny shadow disappear through the downstairs window.

Had . . . had Beau shifted to go after Sara? I heard the roar of the cat inside—and Sara's scream.

Shit.

I ran forward, the urge to protect Sara overwhelming, nearly blinding me with fear. My sister needed me—

As my hand touched the doorknob, the bushes on the side of the house rustled. I turned, drawn in that direction despite myself. My purse wasn't heavy, but I'd use it as a weapon anyhow if I needed to. I took a few steps toward the bushes. "Beau? Is that you?"

A low, unearthly growl met my ears.

Was it Beau . . . in his cat form? I took another step toward the bushes, then stopped. Would he recognize me if he was in his cat form? Was this quite possibly the dumbest move ever?

I took a step backward and decided to try another tactic. "Sara," I yelled at the top of my lungs. "Beau!"

"Over here," Sara said, her voice distant and odd.

I turned and saw the most beautiful sight in the world—Sara's tiny frame was cradled in Beau's arms. They stood on the far side of the Viper, having emerged from our small backyard on the far side of the house. I bolted toward them. "Sara! Thank God!"

My sister was in a pair of pajamas, her body stiff with fear, shoulders hunched in a way that I recognized—trying to make her body smaller in the hopes that she might curl it tight enough to mask her scent. As I ran toward them, I realized Beau was buck naked. With the massive breadth to his shoulders and the light sprinkling of hair on his chest—much lighter than I'd imagined for a werecougar—and the narrow hips and . . .

Oh, boy.

"Hi," I blurted, my voice cracking, but fear for Sara quickly overrode my awkwardness at Beau's nudity. "What happened? Is she okay?"

"She's fine," Beau said, still holding her against him. "When I came in through the back of the house in cougar form, I scared her and she fainted."

Of course she had. She had probably thought he'd been coming for her, or she'd been on the verge of doing another shift. Sara gave me a tiny smile of embarrassment and rubbed her arms, as if warding off another involuntary shift.

I could understand that. I felt a little faint myself. "Who was in our house?"

His gaze darkened. "No one that I could find. When I went upstairs to check, the place was empty. It was like no one had been there, except there was a smell . . ." He frowned to himself.

"What sort of smell?"

"Like rotten meat," Sara added. "I didn't know what was going on, just that the house stank. I was changing the garbage when you called."

I gestured at the bushes on the opposite side of the house from where they'd come. "I thought I heard something over there, but I didn't smell anything."

"I'll check it out." Beau immediately set Sara down and crossed the yard.

I watched his buttocks flex in the moonlight as he walked toward the bushes. It was hard to force myself away from the sight, but concern for my sister drew me back to her, and I turned, touching her arm and examining her with my gaze. "Are you all right?"

"Just trying to hold it together," she said in a shaky voice. "He caught me by surprise. I . . . I hope he didn't smell me."

"I'm sure it'll be fine," I said, lying to comfort her. To be safe, I surreptitiously hid my hand behind my back and wiped it on my dress to try and remove her smell.

She looked over my shoulder, and choked a little. "He's coming back."

I turned. Blood roared in my ears as I stared at the man striding across the lawn, all tawny skin and rippling muscles and completely, utterly naked. And judging by his casual, graceful stance, he didn't care that he was naked.

"Oh, I am in so much trouble," I breathed, watching him move. Then I picked up Beau's pants, holding them out to him with my eyes closed so I wouldn't see anything else and be tempted.

"I'm fine, really," Sara protested from beside me in the Viper. The wind was high and icy outside, so I sat in the driver's seat while we waited for Beau. "You're making too big of a fuss."

"I always fuss over you. Besides, you fainted." I ran a hand over her bare arm, feeling for telltale fur. "How are you now? Are you good?"

"I'm fine," she said, shoving my hands off of her like she would an overprotective mother. "It just startled me. Tell me about your date." A shadow crossed her face. "He didn't ask about me, did he?"

"Dinner was very nice. The restaurant was lovely. You would have liked it." *If you ignored the car thing, the drop-in from the werewolf, and my date telling me he was going into heat.*

"Your face is red," she said. "You like him, don't you?"

I focused on the front yard, avoiding her gaze. "Don't be silly. I'm just going out with him this one time. It's not going to go anywhere. You know it can't."

"You like him," she restated slowly. "And you don't like anyone. Huh."

I ignored her, scanning the house for Beau again. He had insisted on checking out the place one more time in cougar form. When that yielded nothing, he shifted back and made a few phone calls while Sara and I waited in his car.

All of my suggestions to go into the house were met with a small growl.

"Should we call the police?" I rolled down the window and asked.

He shook his head at me. "I don't think what was in your house was human. We can't notify the police—that would compromise the Alliance members in the immediate vicinity."

I didn't give a crap about the Alliance. I wanted to get back inside my house and see what was missing or touched or disturbed.

Beau circled back toward the car, pulling his pants on and buckling his belt. "I smelled a mixture of things. Like werewolf and something else."

Sara stiffened next to me, and fear clenched my heart. "We can't smell anything," I told him. "You're the one with the shifter nose."

He gave me a sheepish look. "Right. I keep forgetting."

"Isn't it safe to go back in?" I asked again. "You've gone over the property three times."

He shook his head and reached for his shirt. "One of the tigers in the Merino clan knows forensics. He'll be over shortly to dust the house and look for evidence." His hand stretched toward me. "House keys, please?"

I held my purse tightly. "Why?"

"So Mike can check out the house while I take you two to a hotel."

No way. Not with Sara's scent all over the place.

Beau continued, "Mike insisted that we leave the crime scene intact, and that's what we're going to do. I can go inside and get you some clothes once he gives the okay."

Sara's hand clutched mine anxiously, and I knew what she was thinking. If Beau went inside and dug through her things he'd find wolf scent all over her clothing—or worse, he'd find the clothes that she had last used when she changed: a torn T-shirt and a wrinkled pair of shorts that reeked of the change.

"We're fine," I blurted. "We don't need clothes. Let's just go."

Beau's eyebrows went up and he glanced over at Sara in her pajamas. "All right," he said slowly. "I'll buy you girls some clothes and we can check things out in the morning. Sound good?"

I still didn't like the thought of a stranger poking around in our house, especially one with a shifter's nose. "We sometimes take care of the neighbor's dog for her," I lied, to explain the canine scent sure to be in the house. "Tell Mike that if a woman with a dog comes to the doorstep in the morning to call me."

A smile tugged at the corner of Beau's mouth. "I'll tell him."

Without another reason to stall, I handed him the keys.

He walked away to greet the car that pulled up.

Mike turned out to be an enormous man with short, close-cropped black curls and a cheerful expression, despite it being nearly midnight and freezing outside. He and Beau talked for a couple of minutes, then Beau showed Mike to the front door and they went inside. I clasped my hands tightly to stop myself from dashing inside and dousing the house with some scent-masking sprays—or better yet, chasing the men out of the house.

"I'm sure it's fine," Sara told me, trying to ease my worry. "You know I'm careful. And if Beau didn't notice anything before . . ."

At least I had the clothes on my back. Poor Sara had only her pajamas.

Beau returned a few moments later and I got out to meet him. He moved to my side as if he belonged there and began to rub my shoulders. "Mike's going to be several hours, so he's going to drop your keys off to me in the morning."

"All right. Sara and I will stay at the office," I said.

"You can't sleep at the office," Beau argued, putting his warm arm around me. He gestured at Sara, still huddled in the car, her legs tucked under her. "She looks a little freaked out. Wouldn't you rather stay in a nice, comfortable hotel room?"

I glanced over at my sister. She was a dainty, fragile sort, so unlike me with my tall, sturdy frame. Tonight she seemed even smaller, staring at the house with worried eyes, waiting for Mike to discover her secret and ruin her life. She was shivering, too.

I sighed. "She could use a good night's sleep. Thank you. We'll stay at the hotel."

He nodded and pulled me against him, tucking me under his chin and cradling my body to his.

I stiffened a little, but he only ran his hands gently up and down my back. It felt lovely and soothing, and I finally relaxed a little.

Unfortunately, snuggling with a man was not the way to get rid of him.

At the hotel, Beau got us the room adjoining his. The hotel room was lovely, the blankets turned down, and fluffy robes hanging on the back of the bathroom door. I felt sleepy just looking at the big, plush bed.

"I'll be on the other side if you need me," Beau said, standing in the doorway that connected the two rooms. "Sleep tight, ladies."

With a wink at me, he closed the door.

As soon as he was gone, I slumped on the edge of the bed and sighed. "God, I wish he wasn't so hot. That would make this all so much easier."

Sara tapped her ear, indicating that his shifter hearing could hear our conversation.

Oh, well. It wasn't like I'd done a good job hiding it anyhow.

She moved to the closet and opened it, scanning the contents. Then she turned to me and mouthed, "Are there extra blankets?"

"Why?" I mouthed back.

She gestured at herself. "I still smell like whatever was in the house," she mouthed, her voice barely audible. "I need to shower and get the stink off of me. But if I do . . ."

She'd smell like herself again. And if I slept next to her all night, I'd smell like her, too, because I didn't have any other clothes to sleep in.

Should I go downstairs and get a third room? Beau was sure to be curious if I did, and we would have to be more cautious than ever.

Unless . . . he'd already figured out that Sara was a werewolf? I discarded the thought. He'd have questioned me about it immediately if he had, or demanded to speak to Sara. Our secret was still safe.

Sara trembled slightly as she stared down at the bed, knowing she couldn't get into it and relax.

Knowing that our being here wasn't a full reprieve, that in the next room was a man who could give away everything we had worked so hard to conceal. As I watched, she rubbed her arms. They were covered in goose pimples, a sure sign that she was about to shift due to stress.

I waved a hand to get her attention, then gestured at the connecting door. "I'm going to go sleep with Beau," I mouthed. "You take this bed."

Her eyes went wide with shock and she forgot to whisper. "Bath, what—"

I cut her off with a quick wave of my hand, then mouthed, "Not like *that!*" I moved closer to her to explain my plan. "I'll just tell him that you snore and I won't be able to sleep. It's perfect, because if I sleep in the same bed as him we'll have the same scent, and he won't suspect a thing."

It *was* a perfect plan, but it wasn't why I wanted to sleep next to him. I wanted to sleep next to him because the very thought made me shiver with excitement.

"Bath, *no*." Sara mouthed the protest. "What if he's a creep?"

I shook my head. "He's not a creep," I whispered back. "He's nice. He won't do anything." I decided not to mention the whole "in heat" thing.

She didn't look convinced, but I saw her gaze sneak back to the bed, and she sighed. "I can sleep on the floor," she began, but my eye roll cut her off.

She sat down on the foot of the bed, then gave me a weak thumbs-up that I returned. When she was freshly showered and wrapped in the bathrobe, I flicked the lights off, then closed the door behind me, stepping back out into the hall.

A loud, fake snore began to rise from the room, so I took a deep breath and knocked on Beau's door.

He opened it a few moments later, his hair tousled, chest bare. My gaze went immediately to the low-slung plaid sleep pants around his waist, noticing the dark trail of hair that crept down his abdomen.

"Hi, again," he said.

I jerked my head up, caught staring. "Oh. Hi."

"Something wrong?"

Not in the slightest, I thought as warmth spread through my body. I gestured at our room. "I hate to ask, but my sister snores and I thought I might sleep with you."

He raised an eyebrow.

"Sleep in the same room as you," I amended quickly. "We could put pillows between us or something. And it'll give us a chance to . . . talk."

"I can get another room," he began.

"I'd rather stay with you," I said. "It's not a

come-on. I just feel safer with you in the room, if that's all right."

He stepped aside to let me in. "Of course."

Ever the gentleman, Beau immediately offered me a spare set of pajamas, and I took a quick shower and brushed my teeth with the complimentary toothbrush. When I emerged the room was empty, with a note that Beau had gone to get extra pillows from the front desk.

He returned a short time later. The click of the lock on the door was the only thing that let me know that he'd come back; other than that, he moved as silently as a cat. Hah.

I had already prepared the bed for his return. Pillows were stacked in the middle and I'd wrapped myself in one of the extra blankets, leaving him the sheet and the duvet. His lips twitched at the sight, but he said nothing. He simply put the extra pillows down and clicked the light off.

"I thought we were going to talk," I reminded him.

The other side of the mattress dipped with Beau's weight as he chuckled. "My mouth works just fine in the dark, Bathsheba. I imagine yours does, too."

Now *that* was a blatant double entendre. My heart pounded with nervous excitement. Oddly enough, I was a little breathless at his pursuit.

Would he shove the pillows aside and take me into his arms? Kiss me senseless?

I squirmed a little at the thought and forced myself not to think such things. I had told him this would be innocent, and he had agreed. Why was I fantasizing about him ravishing me? I rolled over on my side, facing away from Beau, and tried to relax. It was a near-impossible task—my body was utterly conscious of the man who lay so close to me.

I tried to think of something to say. After all, the premise of my being here was that I wanted to talk to him, right? So I needed to talk.

One arm snaked out and grabbed me by the waist, pulling me across the bed. Instead of the wall of pillows I expected to meet, I slid across the sheets and bumped into his chest. "Shhh," he said softly in my ear, his breath warm. Hot snakes of desire coiled through me.

"So tell me," he whispered quietly in my ear. "Who would want to kill Sara?" His thumb began to stroke my arm in a rather distracting, shivery pattern.

I stilled in his arms, shocked by the rush that crept over my skin. It took me a moment to re-cover, and then I realized what he was asking. Lots and lots of people probably wanted to kill Sara, but I couldn't tell him that. I feigned ignorance. "What do you mean?"

"Whoever was in the house." He pulled me closer until my backside was spooned against his front. The breath stole out of my lungs at the warmth that flooded through me. His arms enveloped me, and huddled next to him, I felt like the smallest, daintiest woman in the world rather than my five-foot-ten self. It was pretty close to heaven.

"The intruder?" I asked. "No one who knows Sara wants to kill her."

It was all those wolves that *didn't* know her that were the problem.

I could feel his warm breath against my ear and neck. "Any ex-boyfriends or angry lovers?"

I was silent. The only ex-boyfriend she had was a dead one.

I knew he was dead because I'd shot him.

"No angry lovers," I said. "Sara's not seeing anyone. Do you think she was the target?"

I could feel his chest moving with every breath. His hand slid off my arm and down my waist, then across the cradle of my hips in a very intimate embrace. "Would someone be after you, then?"

He was making it damn hard to concentrate. I struggled to gather my thoughts and shook my head. "Not unless I've pissed off the bookkeeping mafia. We're dangerous people, you know."

"Shhh. Keep your voice down," he said, then bit my earlobe gently.

That playful caress made my entire body flare, and I flexed my hips back against his instinctively. A small whimper rose in my throat.

I heard his groan in my ear, and his spread hand flexed across my belly. "Did you like that?" he murmured, and repeated the action. His teeth scored against the edge of my earlobe, and I felt his tongue flick against my earring. "Shall I tell you how sexy you look wearing nothing but my pajamas?" Nip, nip.

Dear God, this was the best thing I'd ever felt. Why in the world was I still a virgin? My hand covered his, my fingers pulsing in time with his, kneading the flesh of my stomach as well. I felt his cock against my backside, hard and obvious, and began to entertain some very naughty thoughts.

But I couldn't. I removed his hand from my belly and could have wept. "I'm not going to sleep with you, Beau."

He chuckled as I tried to move my head. He was lying on my still-damp hair. "Who says we have to sleep?"

I jerked on my hair and he moved, leaning over me instead of next to me. His breath fanned across my neck. Though I was free now, I made no attempt to move, excited and quivering. What would he do?

To my surprise, Beau leaned over me and bit

my collarbone. Too low to be a vampire bite at the carotid, but I felt the definite scrape of teeth at the base of my neck, and then the sensual slide of his tongue over my flesh.

It felt so good that I wasn't able to contain my moan of pleasure, and when his tongue stroked over the sensitive spot again, my hand twined in his hair to hold him in place, encouraging him to do it again. With every stroke of his tongue, a whimper of enjoyment slid from my throat.

"Shhh," he whispered against my ear before nibbling at it again. "You're going to wake up the neighbors."

Through the wall, I could hear Sara fake-snore loudly.

I froze.

What was I *doing*? I wanted to thank Sara for the obvious reminder, and smack her on the head for interrupting. As smoking-hot as Beau was, he was a shifter, and off-limits in more ways than he could imagine. He also just wanted someone to slake his needs while he was in heat.

My sister was probably scarred for life, listening to me make out with Beau. My hand went to his face and I pushed him away. I felt Beau's snort of amusement against my fingers, but he took the hint and backed off, returning to his side of the bed.

There, he grabbed my hand, then pressed a kiss to my palm. "We'll talk in the morning, Bathsheba. Get some sleep."

"Good night," I whispered back. I lay there, awake and breathing hard for long minutes. My body still thrummed and my legs felt curiously liquid. Just from a nip or two at the neck and ear.

I fell asleep picturing myself and Beau in some naughty situations, hoping I wouldn't say his name in my sleep.

Chapter Four

*W*hen I awoke and squinted at the sunlight streaming in through the window, Beau's side of the bed was cold and he was gone. A note sat on a nearby stack of clothing, along with my keys.

I sat up and grabbed the note—not that I was eager to hear from him. Nope. I squelched the shadow of disappointment that I felt at not seeing Beau this morning. Like I cared how he looked in the morning. Or if he had a five-o-clock shadow. Or if he had those cute, tousled cowlicks in his hair when he woke up. Or if his eyes had that sleepy look that made my legs jelly. Nope. Didn't care.

His handwriting was scrawly and loose, but somehow intimate, and just looking at it gave me the warm fuzzies.

Bathsheba,

Mike didn't find anything unusual in the house. I'm going to go and check things out for myself. I'll be watching the house to make sure nothing—or no one—returns. If you can, please stay away for a few more hours, until I know it's safe. I went down to the gift shop and got you both some clothes—I guessed at your sizes. Hope that's okay. There's some money in the pocket for a cab, and use my credit card if you need it. You have my cell number. Call me later today and we can make plans. I'm not letting you get away easily.

I sighed.

In true masculine form, Beau had incorrectly guessed at both our sizes. The Dallas Cowboys sweatpants and T-shirt he'd gotten for Sara were about two sizes too big. Her slim form swam in the sporty clothing, but she gushed about how thoughtful Beau was.

My clothes—me being taller and bustier than Sara—were too tight. The shirt was indecent and the jogging pants were so short they could have been capris. I put them on anyhow and wore my minidress over them as a tunic.

"Good thing Giselle is never in the office," Sara said, rolling up her sleeves. "She'd have a heart attack if she saw us dressed like this to come to work."

Luck was not on our side. We'd no more than arrived at the small Liaisons office and told the nighttime girls (Ryder and Marie) about our harrowing break-in before Giselle breezed in, a vision in a red minidress. Her dark, wavy hair cascaded over her shoulders.

I swallowed hard at the sight of my boss. "Giselle," I said weakly. "You're back early." Well, shit. That just complicated things.

"Bathsheba," she called in a clipped accent. "I want to see you in my office. Now." She didn't bother to look at the four of us gathered at Sara's desk.

All my senses on alert, I straightened my clothes. Giselle must have somehow heard about my date with Beau and had come into the office to put the smack down on me. Shit.

Sara gave me a wide-eyed look as I passed, but she didn't scurry for the file room. The other girls in the office weren't shifters, and Giselle was a siren. Sirens had a lot going for them, but the preternatural sense of smell wasn't one of them. It was why we'd been able to work here for so long.

Giselle was not the most understanding boss, however. She kept odd hours, expected her employees to be held to higher standards than her own, and had a bunch of weird quirks that I'd written off as supernaturally based, but she wasn't a fool. She might chide us for dressing down for one day, but it wouldn't affect how we answered the phones or handled clients. Her anger had to be because of my date.

I'd let myself get carried away with Beau's attractive face and my own raging hormones. Stupid, stupid, stupid.

As soon as I entered Giselle's posh corner office, she shut the door behind me. I picked an empty chair and sat down. Her office was furnished far better than the rest of the building—the chairs were plush and thick, and fine art hung on the walls.

We had one lousy motivational poster in the outer office.

She took her time crossing over to the far side of the room and sat down at her desk, a coy look on her face. "Why don't you tell me what's going on, Bathsheba?" Her voice was singsongy and deliberately sweet.

Not a good sign.

I plucked at the hem of my dress and hoped she hadn't noticed that the pants underneath had a sports logo on the hip. "I only met Mr. Russell to tell him that I wouldn't be going out with him. I tried calling, but you were unavailable."

Giselle pulled out her cell phone, flicked the screen a few times with her thumb, then offered the phone to me.

I looked at the picture she'd pulled up. Beau and me, sitting at the restaurant table. My eyes were closed, the look on my face rapturous as Beau fed me something.

Whoops.

She leaned over and snatched the phone out of my hand. "Isn't the first rule of working here that you cannot date the clients? Haven't I explained to you that humans and Alliance do not mix? Ever?"

I swallowed hard. "I know." Oh, God, I was going to lose my job.

"And yet you disobeyed my rules." She pointed at me. "His mark is all over your neck. Do you know how I heard about this?"

"No." I touched my neck and blushed. The spot where he'd bit me didn't have a visible mark, though it felt hot to me. Did sirens have X-ray vision?

She crossed her arms. "I had no less than four— four!—calls last night. The werewolf community is quite upset and they're threatening to boycott my service if I fix up more humans. They've made calls to several other important leaders, and I've already had one VIP pull his account. Not only is the entire Alliance upset, but they're furious that *I*"— she stabbed her finger at her chest—"have given an authorized visa to a *human*. Even worse, I have not extended the same offer to other leaders as I have to the leader of the Russell clan."

I put my hands to my forehead and slowly went over everything she'd spouted at me. "Could you repeat that?"

"If one clan of weres can date a human, *all* can date a human, or so I'm being told. As you can see, I have a problem." Giselle gave me a look of disgust. "A big problem that you have created. My best clients with the biggest accounts want to know why the were-cougars are so special that they get exclusive treatment over my regular clients. Exclusive access to a papered, pedigreed human virgin—"

"Wait," I interrupted. She made me sound like a dog. "Pedigreed human virgin?"

She gave me a look that said I should be quiet, then continued. "Rights to a human woman who has been cleared and declared fit for the Alliance. What am I supposed to tell these very important men?" Her eyes narrowed into slits.

I wrung my hands in my lap and hoped she didn't notice. "I only met him because . . ."

"Because?"

Could I tell her the truth? That Sara had been freaking out and I'd been distracted by another customer and the answer had blurted out of my mouth before I'd thought about it? Finally, I admitted the truth.

"I tried calling you, but I got your voice mail and knew you didn't want to be disturbed, so I had to make a decision. He asked me to go out with him, and I thought maybe one teeny date wouldn't hurt."

Giselle's mouth formed a hard line. "You thought wrong. I should toss you out on the street, along with your sister."

My heart sank. Giselle paid us both very well. If we were fired, it'd be hellish trying to find jobs that paid as much as working here. And here we were safe, because we knew where the packs were and what they were up to. We knew that the werecougars lived up in Little Paradise on the edge of Fort Worth. We knew that the wolf packs lived on the far side of the Metroplex. We had tabs on every single shifter in the area who used the service, which made Sara safer, knowing who and where to avoid.

If we were fired we'd have to leave the city and start all over again. We had some money, but not enough for a move cross-country into blind territory. What if we moved to Portland or San Diego and the weres were thicker there than here?

"Please don't fire me or Sara," I begged. "We need this job."

Her eyes were hard as they focused on me. "Are you loyal to me and my company?"

"Yes." Anything to keep my job.

"Will you do whatever it takes to get back in my good graces?"

A few unpaid overtime shifts would be well worth it. "Whatever you want. My schedule is open."

Giselle leaned back in her chair. "Good. I should almost thank that were-cougar for marking you," she said absently, staring at my neck. The patch of skin burned under her scrutiny. "His mark makes you infinitely more desirable to others, now that you've been staked out as someone else's property."

That wasn't the answer I'd been expecting. "Beg pardon?"

Her perfect mouth curved in a smile. "You, my succulent little human virgin, are going to go on another date. Several of them, actually."

Beau must have called and made arrangements early. That made my stomach give a happy flip, but I quelled it. I had to think of Sara, not my hormones. "Mr. Russell is charming, but—"

"You're not going out with Mr. Russell," she snapped. "You are done with the Russell clan unless they go through the service and pay the fees."

My brow wrinkled. "I'm not following—"

"This is a *dating* service. And you know as well as I do that desired females are very much in demand."

Giselle stood up, towering over me. "As I said, since last night, I have gotten calls from four very important account holders. They were not aware that we had sanctioned human women available, much less a virgin." Her lips curved into a smile. "I told them that it was a new offering, of course. And since you have the blessing of a clan leader, not only are you papered and authorized but you are also very desirable." She strolled around her desk and approached the chair that I huddled in. "You, my dumpling, are going to go out on dates with these men. Or mermen. Or werewolves. Or naga. Or whatever I decide. They are going to pay an extra charge to go out with our sweet human virgin with the pretty blond hair." Her pitiless mouth curved. "And you are going to keep them interested in my dating service, or you are out on your sweet, virginal ass. Understand?"

Each date meant Sara was in more danger—but I couldn't afford to lose my job, either. "What exactly do these dates entail?"

"No sex," she said bluntly. "Most of your appeal is that you are virginal. That's rare in a full-grown human these days. You play sweet and coy and you blush, and you keep them interested. And then you get to keep your job. You and that little Sara bitch."

I stood up, liking that when I stood, I was half a foot taller than her. "Don't call my sister a bitch, Giselle."

"But isn't that what she *is*, Bathsheba? A little bitch."

I stared at Giselle, my mouth dry. Was she hinting at what I thought she was?

"You and your sister think you are so smart. So smug that you're keeping a secret from your supe boss." Her eyes were ice cold. "Nothing goes on in this business that I do not know about. Understand? All it takes is one phone call to the wolf pack and she's done for. Do you understand?"

She knew. I didn't know how she knew, but she knew. My legs felt weak. Everything we'd worked so hard at, and Giselle knew exactly what Sara was.

"I understand," I said numbly.

"Good. Now go and talk to your sister, if you like." Giselle made a shooing motion in my direction. "See if she wants you to go out on these dates, or if she wants to explore that wild side she's been suppressing." Her expression was all sweetness and light. "I've heard that the wolf pack is *very* friendly to females."

I'd seen—and had—firsthand experience of how friendly. Most of the women who dated a werewolf didn't date one a second time. They were cliquish, irritable, possessive, and liked to fight. In short, they acted like the wolves they were.

She flicked her hand at me. "We're done now. Go. Let me know when you've made up your mind."

"Made up my mind?" I laughed bitterly. "We both know what my answer is, Giselle. I'm not going to let anyone touch my sister, including you."

Her eyes gleamed with avarice. "So . . . ?"

"If I do this, you can't tell anyone about Sara's . . . problem. If you do, all bets are off."

Giselle's smile was wide. "My dear, it's far more profitable for me to keep her secret. It's safe with me as long as you play by my rules."

"I have one additional rule," I said, thinking fast. "Wolves are a deal breaker," I said in a hard voice. They'd pick up Sara's scent immediately and know an unfamiliar werewolf was out there somewhere. Then it wouldn't take them long to realize it was Sara.

She shrugged. "I don't see why I'm bargaining with you, but I'll allow this. We don't do much business with wolves anyhow."

I left her office, shutting the door behind me, a sick feeling clenching my stomach. Giselle knew *everything*. Someone must have told her; she couldn't have sniffed it out on her own. That meant someone else knew about Sara's secret and was keeping quiet.

Who else was going to show up and attempt to blackmail us? I felt nauseated at the thought.

Sara waited by my desk, her face white and anxious. Immediately, my resolve strengthened. I'd date whatever bird, cat, or rat shifter Giselle dug up, and do it with a smile. And once I had enough money in the bank account, we'd leave in the middle of the night and start over again.

I couldn't tell Sara what Giselle knew, though. She'd be paralyzed with fear and completely unable to work. So I gave her a cheerful smile that hid the fact that I felt like crying. "Giselle was mad about Beau, but since it's set a precedent, she wants me to go out on a few more dates. It's nothing big."

"Really? Are you sure?" Her expression was clearly surprised. Then a slow smile spread across her face. "Is it because of Beau? You really liked him. Do you get to go out with him again?"

I waved my hand in a carefree manner. "Maybe so, maybe not. You know just as well as I that it can't go anywhere."

She hesitated, clearly confused by my reaction,

then swallowed. "What about . . . you know." She brushed a finger under her nose, indicating scent.

"We'll be very, very careful," I said firmly. "Like we always are."

The phone rang, interrupting us. "I bet that's Mr. Russell," she said. "He called twice while you were in Giselle's office."

Of course he had. He wanted to make sure we were on for the rest of the week. Being in heat, he wanted to hedge his bets. I remembered how nice it was to be curled up against him in bed last night, then overlaid that brief, tantalizing thought with Giselle's cold face and Sara's pinched, worried one.

It would never work.

I picked up my phone and put on my business voice. "Midnight Liaisons. How can I help you?"

"I've been thinking about your ears all morning," he said, then his voice dropped a little. "Thinking about the sweet curve of your earlobes, and how I'd love to nibble on them again tonight."

Warmth unfurled in the pit of my stomach. God, he knew just what to say to make me tremble. "I can't. Working."

"You've been at work since seven a.m. Don't tell me you'll be working at, say, eight tonight?"

"I'm pulling a double shift," I said immediately.

"What time does your shift end?"

Giselle's red dress flashed in the corner of my eye as she cut across the office. I froze. "If you want to see me again," I blurted, "you'll have to schedule it through the dating service."

"What—"

I hung the phone up before he could finish and buried my face in my hands.

Sara's safety came before my heart, and if chasing Beau off was what I had to do to keep her safe, I'd do it.

I repeated that to myself over and over again, hoping it would make the ache in my chest go away.

Beau wasn't the type to give up easily. He showed up at the office a few hours later, an enormous bouquet of flowers in his hand.

I stood up at the sight of him, clenching my hands so I wouldn't do something girly like straighten my hair. "You shouldn't be here. I can't see you unless you go through the service."

"The service," Beau drawled, "is exactly why I'm here. Where's Giselle?"

I frowned and gestured at her office. "Back there."

Beau nodded and knocked on her door. A moment later, he disappeared inside. I turned, looking for Sara; her supernatural hearing would come in handy for spying on their conversation. But in true fashion, she'd disappeared as soon as she'd seen Beau.

Beau stayed inside Giselle's office for an hour and a half. Not that I was timing it. Or listening at the door—not that I could hear anything. Quiet, conversational chatter continued the whole time he was in there, muffled by the occasional throaty peal of laughter from Giselle. The sound of Beau's rumbling bass laugh made my knees weak.

Gee, I was glad they were having *such* a good time together.

Beau emerged from Giselle's office without flowers and gave me the lazy, confident smile I was already getting used to. "Hello again," he said, heading toward my desk, where I tried to look busy. He stood across from me, directly in my line of view.

I got up and grabbed a big stack of filing. "I'm really busy, Beau."

"Aren't you even the slightest bit curious as to what I talked to Giselle about?"

I opened the file cabinet and dropped a stack of Qs into a *J* folder. Who cared? I'd fish it out later. "All right, then. What did you talk about?"

"You and me seeing each other. Giselle is fine with it; you're not in any trouble. In fact, we're going out tonight."

I plopped another set of files randomly into the drawer. If only he knew the truth: I wasn't in trouble because of the simple fact that I was being blackmailed. "Great," I said, trying to force enthusiasm into my voice. "I can't wait."

Actually, the small, selfish part of me was very excited about going out with him again. The practical, thinking-of-my-sister's-safety side was worried. And all of me was concerned about Giselle. "What about the rest of the week? Until your heat?"

"Taken care of, If you're willing to put up with me," he said with a smile.

I didn't have a choice. "I'm sure I'll manage," I said in a voice that I tried to make light and teasing. "You're pretty hard on the eyes, but I'll try and suffer through for a good cause."

A slow, wicked grin spread across his face. The warm feeling fluttered in my stomach at the thought of seeing Beau again so soon. It grew when he moved closer to me and put his hand on my arm. He smelled terrific, sun-warmed. I wanted to lick him and taste it.

I blushed at the thought.

"Tonight at eight," he said, reaching out to touch the soft end of my long ponytail. "Dinner. Wear your hair down, please. For me."

Giselle emerged from her office, a hint of a

frown crossing her lovely face at the sight of the two of us standing so close together. I skittered backward and rammed into the file cabinet. Ow.

Beau glanced over at Giselle, then took my hand and pressed a light kiss to the back of it. "I'll pick you up here," he said, and left the office with a quick nod and smile to Giselle.

Uck. Giselle. I froze against the file cabinet and didn't move until Beau disappeared from sight and the bell on the front door clanged against the glass. Then Giselle slithered forward like a snake with prey in its sights. "You're going out with him at eight."

The tension in my shoulders eased. "I know." I took the information sheet from her with cautious fingers.

"To be on time, you'll need to be dressed and ready to leave by two."

Where were we going to dinner? Timbuktu? "Two?"

Her smile was brilliant. "You have a date with one client at two thirty. Another client at five. Then you see Beau at eight to placate him."

She was going to stack my dates one after another, for maximum use of her new toy—me. I immediately felt dirty but shoved the feeling aside. I'd agreed to do this, even if it made me feel used. "Okay," I said, taking a deep breath. Then I asked, "Clothes?"

She handed me a pink business card from her dress pocket (where did she have pockets in that thing?). "You're going to see my friend Francesca over at Saks in the Galleria. She'll get you set up with some decent clothing." Giselle studied my appearance. "See if she can't do something with your hair and makeup, too. We want innocent but seductive."

"Right." I said, taking the card from her. In the corner of my eye, I saw Sara exit the filing room, and just as quickly go back in at the sight of Giselle.

"So who am I dating?" I forced a smile to my face.

"Do you remember Mr. Jason Cartland? He was in yesterday."

I drew a blank for a moment, then gasped. "The hot guy? Were-cougar?" We seemed to be brimming with horny were-cougars lately.

"It would seem so," she said smugly. "He's your two thirty."

Well, this might not be so terribly awful. Jason was a beautiful man, and he seemed nice. Comfortable, despite his too beaming white smile. "Who's the five?"

"His name is Garth," she said with a look of delight, as if she'd just seen dollar signs flash in front of her eyes. "He's very rich. Middle-aged, never been married. Country music song writer. He likes baseball and trucks. He'll be quite a catch."

Blech. "Sounds lovely," I said. "And he is . . ." Tall? Short? Fat? Desperate? Deaf? Mute? Lord, I hoped he was mute.

"Naga."

I blanched. "Snake?" I hated snakes.

"Snake," she agreed. "And you're going to tell him that you love snakes. Understand?"

"I love snakes," I parroted back in a gushing, idiotic voice. "Snakes and baseball and country music. They're my favorites."

"Good girl," Giselle said, patting me on my cheek like I was a dog.

Chapter Five

A couple of hours later, I looked utterly delicious and felt completely miserable. Francesca had picked out a few outfits for me, not one of them practical in the slightest. I was currently trussed in a black lace cocktail dress with terribly cute but impossibly high heels. My feet hurt after just five minutes, but I had to admit that the effect was impressive.

So was the bill for everything.

Francesca had sent me to a beauty salon after she'd picked out my clothing. My long straight hair had been fluffed and teased and blown-out within an inch of its life, and the resulting white-blond mess atop my head was gorgeous, artfully tousled, and crunchy with hairspray. It looked great as long as you didn't touch it. The makeup artist had lined my eyes with a delicate gray liner that made them seem bigger, and had pinked my complexion with some artful blush. The resulting effect was dewy, and I looked very much like a nubile ingénue.

Jason seemed to think so, too, and the looks he was giving me were going to cause a permanent blush.

He was every inch as dazzling as I'd remembered. He had a heavy build, all muscle and tanned flesh, whereas Beau ran toward lean (but with very broad shoulders). He wore a charcoal wool jacket with an open-neck pale blue silk shirt. He looked every inch the rich playboy—except for one thing. For all his gorgeous looks and his money, Jason was very heavily into cheap cologne. Very. Heavily. Either BRUT or Old Spice.

Still, the character of a man wasn't determined by the quality or quantity of his cologne, and I resolved to look past it. I gave Jason a faint smile over my water glass.

"Is that all you're going to eat?" he said, indicating my small salad. "Please order anything you'd like."

I gave a small shrug. "I'm really not that hungry." Actually, I was ravenous, but Giselle had two more meals scheduled for me, so I was holding back. Plus, everything I put in my mouth seemed to taste like Old Spice. So I drank my water and pretended interest as Jason talked.

And tried not to think about Beau. He'd smelled

really nice. Last night when I'd been cuddled up against him, a faint, spicy scent had clung to his skin that I hadn't been able to figure out. Deodorant or body wash, maybe. Very subtle, and clean.

My nose itched. I decided that I liked subtle and clean.

"—friends with Beau Russell?"

I focused back in on my date, who was beaming a megawatt white smile at me. "I'm sorry?"

"I was asking about Beau. He's a friend of yours?"

Blank, I stared at him. He'd heard my phone conversation and wanted to call us "friends"? "I guess you could call it that." Is that what Giselle was calling it? Best to play along.

"I hear he's an important man in his clan."

Talking about him made me unhappy, so I said, "I wouldn't know."

To my relief he took the hint and switched the topic to other things. Jason was a wonderful date— he was witty, charming, laughed at my attempts at humor, and made me feel pretty. Women slowed as they walked past our table, checking him out. He touched my hand repeatedly, devoured me with his eyes, and made it obvious that he wanted to eat me up like candy.

So why was my brain entirely focused on the man I'd been out with last night? Both men were

were-cougars. Both men were handsome. Jason was the epitome of niceness, while Beau's playful smile drove me crazy with desire.

Torn between two cougars. Strangely enough, not a problem I'd ever thought I'd have.

My next date wasn't much better.

It was another restaurant (the default setting, of course) and it started out well. At least for the first five minutes. After that we steered directly into uncomfortable territory.

"So," Garth the naga said, "what do you do?" His eyes watched me with entirely too much interest, his gaze focused on my cleavage. At least Jason had had the decency to look me in the eye.

I toyed with a bit of chicken parmigiana. Was I supposed to admit that I worked at the agency, or should I lie about it? As I hesitated, Garth's tongue flicked over his lips. Good God, was that thing forked?

Distracted momentarily, I had to regroup. "I'm a professional bookkeeper."

The forked tongue was seriously giving me the creeps.

"That's fascinating," he said in a tone of voice that meant it was less interesting than Styrofoam. "So how did you get into Giselle's agency? It's very exclusive." As in, how did a lowly human manage to become worthy of notice?

"Oh, the usual way." I didn't know what the usual way was, but I was willing to bet he didn't, either. Something slithered against my shoe and I recoiled. What the fuck? Was that his tail?

He gave me a look that I assumed was supposed to be seductive. "Sanctioned humans are rare," he said, his eyes glued to my neck like I was wearing some sort of flashing beacon around it. Could he see Beau's mark as well? "Especially virgins."

"Giselle told you I was a virgin?" I tried to ask it in a casual tone of voice, as if I hadn't been screaming inside. As one might ask if their date was a Republican or a Democrat. Or a naga.

Garth looked surprised at my question and took another drink of his wine, his tongue flicking at the edge of the glass. Yep, definitely forked. I suppressed a shudder.

"Indeed. A virgin is highly desired," he said. "You have been claimed as worthy of notice, you are disease-free, and you are considered a fair mate for any member of the Alliance."

I was glad I wasn't eating—if I had been, I was pretty sure I would have thrown up. "A mate?" I said. "How nice." Lucky me. I picked up my glass of wine and swirled it around, hoping I looked like

I knew what I was doing. I had no idea why people sloshed their wine around in their glass.

Garth leaned forward. "Is your heart claimed by another?" His whatever-it-was slithered against my shoe again.

Ugh. If Giselle thought she could blackmail me into marrying one of her clients—after she'd squeezed them for every dollar she could, of course—she was sorely mistaken. I was *not* about to mate this guy. In fact, I was starting to dread the rest of the dates that she had lined up for me, except for Beau. Garth was staring at my neck again, as if he'd like to cover Beau's mark with one of his own. My hand slid to my collarbone and I hid the mark. "Oh, my, look at the time," I said, feigning surprise. As if I'd been so charmed by our date that I'd completely lost track of the hour. I put my napkin down on the table. "I really should be going soon."

He reached for my hand, an ardent look on his face. "I've never met anyone like you," he declared, his moist palms gripping my hand between them. "You're beautiful and sophisticated and . . . virginal."

Obviously Garth didn't get out much if he thought I was sophisticated. And it was a little creepy that he kept tossing in the "virginal" thing. I tried to extract my hand from his. "How sweet of you."

"We need to go out again," he said, refusing to let me do said extraction. "I could be falling in love." His eyes flicked again to the wonder spot on my neck that everyone seemed able to see but me.

Would he be half so smitten if I hadn't already been staked out as private property? I doubted it. "Excuse me, I need to go powder my nose."

He lifted my trapped hand to his mouth and kissed the back of it, his tongue flicking against my skin. I barely managed to hide the shudder that rocked through me. "Bathroom," I yelped and jerked my hand away hard, then grabbed my purse and raced to the ladies' room. There was an attendant in there, and I offered her a twenty. "Can you tell me if there's a back way out of here?"

She gave me a knowing look. "That your date out there in the bolo tie and the yellow vest?"

"None other. You've got to help me," I said and leaned in. "I think he's wearing spurs."

She shuddered. "There's a door through the kitchen. I'll take you back there."

Chapter Six

*A*fter penning a note on a napkin, I asked the attendant to give it to my date. It was a brief explanation, one that I hoped seemed innocent and coy (to please Giselle's sensibilities). I cited "female troubles" and apologized for leaving him so abruptly. I had a hunch that girly issues wouldn't scare him off, though. There was a reason men like him were single, after all. It was because they were clueless.

All coherent thoughts fled from my mind as soon as I entered the office and saw Beau standing there in a casual gray jacket, hands tucked into his pockets. He turned and gave me that slow sensual smile, and my brain nearly fried at the sight of him.

Gorgeous. I'd never get tired of looking at the man.

His smile dimmed as I approached and his nostrils flared. "Perfume?" Then his eyes scanned my hair. "You look . . . nice."

There was a ringing endorsement for a girl. Here I was with my hair and makeup done professionally, and he was looking at me as if I'd been an alien. I simply smiled and shifted on my painful but cute heels. "It's good to see you again," I said, then immediately felt like an idiot. It had only been half a day since I'd last seen him.

"Shall we go?" He gave me another polite smile, but it didn't have that sexy curve that I remembered. Was something wrong? He treated me as if I'd been a stranger. I might have been okay with it once, but after daydreaming of cuddling up next to him in bed again (breathless, hot daydreams that made my legs weak), it bothered me to see him look at me like that.

He glanced over at me. "Are you hungry? We can go for drinks if you'd rather."

But he'd gone to the trouble of making a reservation, and I didn't want to give him any more opportunity to be irritated at me. So I gave him a bright smile in return. "Dinner is fine. I love Italian." Too bad I'd just eaten it. Twice.

What followed was easily the most awkward date I'd ever had—which was saying something. I tried to eat like I was enjoying myself, but my stomach was already full from the previous meal and what was in my stomach was churning.

Beau was silent as he methodically ate. He had good manners, at least. Used a knife, made use of his napkin, and was polite to the waiter. It was me he ignored.

I ate a few more bites, then I couldn't stand it any longer—the food or the silence. "What is it?"

A flare of emotion crossed his face and was just as quickly hidden. He put down his fork. "It depends. Do you not want to be here with me?"

"I'm just tired," I admitted. "I had a long day at work." The previous two dates had *definitely* felt like work. I'd had to smile and be friendly and act interested, to be "on" the entire time. I picked up my wineglass. "How was your day?"

"It was hell."

I choked on my chardonnay. "I'm . . . sorry. Is something wrong?"

He ran a hand down his face. "Everything. Nothing. I'm sorry. I'm just . . . let's not do this tonight, all right?" Beau folded his napkin and placed it on the table.

"Oh," I said, feeling stupid at the hurt that bubbled up inside. "Of course."

So much for having the grand problem of whether I should date him. It didn't seem to be a problem after all. I should have been thrilled, relieved. Something *good*. But all I felt was really, really disappointed.

"Let's get out of here," Beau said, dumping a wad of cash on the table as he stood. He moved to pull out my chair and I could feel the frustrated emotion vibrating off of him.

What was wrong with him tonight?

Relief and sadness warred on the walk back to the office. A tiny part of me was glad that I wouldn't have to go through another exhausting date, one less problem on my plate full of troubles. But not seeing Beau again bothered me more than I cared to admit. We'd clicked on some deeper level, and I realized suddenly that I wanted to see more of him. Maybe we could have drinks at a smoky bar to cover Sara's scent. Something.

He needed a woman before Saturday, and if we called things off that meant he'd have to find someone else—because the heat wouldn't take no for an answer.

We reached the dark strip mall that housed Midnight Liasons, and Beau stopped in front of the door. I knew that if he walked away now, he would walk out of my life. And this was feeling like a good-bye.

He gave me a faint smile, his eyes gleaming cat-like in the moonlight. "I'm sorry, Bathsheba."

I reached out and grabbed his lapel, stopping him before he could turn away.

He looked at me in surprise. "What is it?"

"I wanted to give you this," I said in a breathless rush, and kissed him.

Beau's mouth was unyielding for a split second, but then his arms went around my back, crushing me against him as his lips parted under my own, his tongue sweeping into my mouth. I had started the kiss, but it was obvious that Beau was used to being the aggressor.

And oooh, just the feeling of his tongue sweeping against mine made my toes curl in my shoes. Warmth pulsed through my body, matching the strokes of his tongue against my own, and my fingers curled deeper in his lapel as if I could pull his body closer to mine.

The kiss was dark and possessive; with each stroke of his tongue, I felt like he was claiming me for his own . . . and I very much wanted to be claimed. His hand twined in my hair and—

It felt like every strand was being ripped out of the back of my head. I pulled away with a screech, my hands flying to the knotted mess of sprayed curls that he'd tried to remove with his fingers. "Ow! What are you doing?"

"I was trying to touch your hair," he said. "What the hell did you do to it? It's all glued together. Your hair is gorgeous when it's not done up like a poodle."

A *what*? "Oh no, you did *not* just call me a poodle."

He tugged on a crunchy lock. "I'm sorry, Bathsheba," he said, the husky way he said my name like a caress. "Last night your hair was lovely. Tonight it looks like a nest and smells even worse. It's as if you conspired with Giselle on how to make yourself unappealing."

"Jeez. That's the last time I try to kiss you." Hurt, I took a step backward. He was right that I didn't look like myself—I suspected that was part of Giselle's master plan—but it stung to hear him say that.

His arm snaked around my waist again and he pulled me close, so close that our mouths were practically touching again. In my high heels, I was eye level to him and our gazes met. He grinned. "No, it's not."

I liked the way his arm lingered at my waist, his hand resting at the dip of my lower back. For a wild moment, I wished he'd rest it a bit lower.

Some virgin I was.

"I'm sorry about tonight," he said in a low voice, and my gaze flicked to his sensual mouth, inches away from mine. "Today was . . . not good."

"You can say that again," I muttered. "What's bothering you?"

Beau seemed to struggle for a moment, then

he gave in. "It's shifter politics. I'm not sure that you're interested."

I gave his lapel a little shake. "I'm interested in everything about you," I told him, and realized it was true.

Well, shit. That was going to make things tricky.

I was rewarded with the faint curve of his sexy mouth in a half-smile, but it quickly disappeared. "It's Savannah, the were-cougar who's going into heat. She's in danger."

"What kind of danger?"

Again, the hesitation. Then he leaned forward and put his forehead against my own, our noses bumping.

"The wolves have her. They've kidnapped her and are going to hold her hostage until I produce another female werewolf. They're convinced I'm hiding one from them."

Chapter Seven

*A*ll the air left my lungs. I stared at him. "Female . . ." I choked around the word. "Werewolf?"

"They're insane," he agreed, looking stressed. He ran a hand down his face and seemed suddenly very tired. "As if we'd hide a female werewolf from them."

Oh, God, this just got worse and worse. I forced a sympathetic look to my face, though I wanted to scream in terror. "Can you talk about it?"

Please, please talk about it. Tell me everything you know.

Beau gestured at the park bench on the far side of the sidewalk, across from the parking lot. On sunny days, Sara and I ate lunch and chatted there. Tonight, I stared at that bench as if it had been my enemy.

As I sank down on one end of it, Beau sat on the

other side of me. His hand reached for mine and I let him take it, too numb to do anything but stare blankly at him. He seemed to need to touch me, his fingers playing with mine, stroking along the inside of my palm.

"The wolves have more females than the Alliance does," he said. "It's one reason why the wolves rarely using the dating service, I imagine. Between the pack hierarchy rules and the fact that they have more females than the other shifter clans, there isn't as much of a need. But what they don't tolerate is a runaway."

I swallowed hard. "Are . . . are they looking for a runaway?"

"If they are, I don't know of any." His fingers played with mine, his gaze not meeting my eyes. "The wolf packs don't like it when someone leaves the pack. They expect the pack to rule everyone's lives—even the ones who don't want to be ruled. They're judge, jury, and executioner. And since I haven't helped them in their search, they now think we're harboring a fugitive female." His mouth grew hard. "They took Savannah yesterday. Left a note with her abandoned car and said that if we didn't have the other female back to them by this time next week, they were going to kill her."

And Savannah was going to go into heat on Saturday. This just got better and better.

"What are you going to do?" I asked softly.

Beau's mouth gave a wry twist. "I haven't decided yet. I'm not keen on the thought of handing over some young girl to the wolves, especially since I know what they're like."

I knew what they were like, too. My hand trembled in his.

He mistook it for cold and pulled me against him, tucking me under his arm. "But I don't know what to do about Savannah, either. Ramsey's out looking for her trail, but it's cold by now. So we're waiting . . . and we'll see what happens."

I pulled away from him. "Beau," I began. It was time to break it off, as much as I liked him and wanted to kiss him again. "I don't think this is a good time for us to see each other—"

His eyes gleamed in the darkness, his face showing a flash of haggard emotion. "Bathsheba, don't say that. I need you. Please."

I could tell he wasn't used to asking for things, and I hesitated—then stood up. "I'm sorry, Beau. But I can't."

Sara was busy with a project, her headphones on, when I went inside. She looked up as I passed. "Hi. How were your dates?"

I waved her off, not wanting to talk about it,

especially in front of the others. Marie and Ryder sat at their desks, chatting and waiting for the phones to ring. They glanced over at me but didn't approach, as if sensing I needed space. Giselle wasn't in, at least.

That was good. I didn't want to see her gloating face right now. I needed to process.

I sat down and stared at my computer. My inbox was overflowing, my voice-mail light was flashing, and my monitor was littered with sticky notes . . . but it could all wait until tomorrow.

I didn't know what to do.

The wolf pack was looking for Sara. Beau's clanswoman had been kidnapped and was being held for ransom. I'd just broken up with a smart, funny, gorgeous man who I liked far more than I had any business liking. And my boss was going to make me date a naga.

If ever there was a time to run, now was the time.

I grabbed my shawl and took off my shoes. "Sara, let's go home." We could have a nice, calm conversation. I would explain to her what Beau had just told me, then we could pack our things and quietly leave town and never, ever come back. We'd start over again. Someplace where there was no wolf pack, if such a place existed.

Maybe Greenland. They needed office managers in Greenland, didn't they?

Then I thought of Beau, and my shoulders slumped with exhaustion.

I couldn't think about that. I couldn't.

Sara pulled off her headphones. "You bet. I'm done anyhow." Her wariness was apparent; she scented my fear.

"Great," I said, forcing a lighter note to my voice. "I want to check out the house. Ten bucks says that Mike went through my panty drawer."

She laughed, some of the tension easing from her shoulders, and I felt a little less tense at her returning smile.

Since the car was still at the house, Ryder gave us a lift. As we drove home, my thoughts were torn.

Sara was in danger.

I couldn't stop thinking about Beau.

Sara and I needed to run . . . but I really wanted to call Beau and explain. But what if he told the wolves that Sara was the one they were looking for?

Exhausted from the mental ping-pong, I gave Ryder a halfhearted wave good-bye as I slid out of her car and headed to the porch. The lights to the house were off, and I dug around in my purse for the extra house key. My hands were shaking so badly that my purse tipped the wrong way and the contents slid across the porch, scattering in every direction.

I swore a blue streak.

"You're edgy tonight. Date must not have gone well," Sara said and brushed past me to shove her key in the lock. "Let me open the door."

I started picking up the spill of junk and throwing it back in my purse. "Sorry," I said. "My head is just not functioning tonight."

"I know how you feel," she said, twisting the key in the lock. Sara grabbed the doorknob and shoved against the door, only to bounce backward in surprise. "That's weird."

I scooped up the last of my junk and zipped my purse. "What's weird?"

Her delicate brown brows furrowed together as she stared at the door, then back at me. "I think . . . I think I just locked it." She turned the key again and the deadbolt clicked. "Wow, that's really weird."

Unease swept over me. I touched her arm before she could step inside. "Do you smell anything?"

She grimaced. "Just my perfume. We had a were-lynx in tonight and I dosed up just before you got there."

I dug out my cell phone, clutching it tight. As I stared at my sister, the thought kept echoing in my mind that the wolves were looking for a runaway. "I'm going inside," I said in a whisper. "You stay out here!"

"No way!" She shook her head. "What do you think it is?"

I couldn't tell her yet, so I pushed the door open, putting a finger to my lips to shush her. Swallowing hard, I forced myself to step inside our small foyer. The interior was completely dark, filling me with fear. We always left a light on. Either Mike had turned the light off, or someone else had. "Wait here," I whispered, knowing she probably wouldn't.

Moving down the hall, I fumbled for the light switch. The hall light flicked on and I squinted, noticing that Sara had followed me in. Her nose worked as she scented the air.

I stared around the hallway, then took a few steps in. I could feel something was off, and unease spread through me.

"I smell . . . something," Sara whispered.

"What is it?" My blood went cold.

"Almost like the garbage turned . . . like last night."

Forcing myself to step forward, I headed for the kitchen. We had a baseball bat in the pantry for safety against intruders.

Upstairs, something shuffled and the floorboards groaned.

"What's that?" Sara asked, though we both could guess.

I turned and shoved her toward the front door. "Go. Run."

She shook her head at me. "No! I'm not leaving you."

Damn it! My fingers gripped her arm and I dragged her toward the kitchen. "Come on," I hissed.

The boards overhead creaked again, and whatever it was upstairs was heading in my direction. *Our* direction. In a few moments, it would turn the corner and come down the stairs.

Sara's light frame made it easy for me to drag her along beside me.

"What are you doing—"

"Shhh!" I opened the pantry and shoved her in. "Don't come out until I say it's safe."

"But—" Her eyes were wide, frightened.

"Just stay. Good dog!" I told her and shut the door.

The ceiling creaked overhead, loud, and I heard a heavy foot land on the top of the steps, then another.

I bolted around the small island and scrambled for the cutlery. Our big carving knife stuck out of the wooden knife-block, and I grabbed it, twisting the handle in my hands nervously.

The heavy feet continued to slowly stomp down the stairs, and I heard the scratch of claws as they landed on the hardwood floor at the base of the stairwell.

It wasn't human.

The urge to scream in fear was overwhelming, and I forced myself to concentrate. If it wasn't human, it was probably fast. That meant I had to be ready.

A thick, rancid smell filled the air, and the knife suddenly didn't feel like enough. Whatever it was, it smelled . . . horrible. Like three-day-old, rotting-in-the-sun roadkill. And through it all, that horrible, slick clicking of claws.

A low growl sounded through the house.

I crossed the room. I wouldn't be able to outrun or outmuscle it, but I could at least lead it away from Sara.

Emerging from the kitchen, I saw a dark shape turn to face me from the other end of the hallway.

It wasn't a wolf, which surprised me. It was like no shapeshifter I'd ever seen before. It was some sort of cat . . . thing. Thick, bulging muscles distorted its body under the taut, dirty fur. The teeth were distended in a contorted snarl, and the eyes were red. At the shoulder it was twice as high as any normal lion, nearly to my chin.

Shit, I was going to need a bigger knife.

As the creature started toward me, I backed into the kitchen and slammed the door shut. It crashed into the door, which shook on its hinges. Gasping for breath, I darted to the island and yanked out my emergency drawer.

I pulled out a sharpened wooden stake and tossed it aside. Not a vampire. A cross, holy water, a mirror—all no good . . .

The doorframe rattled again, and I heard the sound of the wood splintering.

Hurry, hurry! My fingers closed around the plastic baggy where I kept the wolfsbane—it was empty. *Shit.* I frantically reached to the back of the drawer . . . and found it: colloidal silver—liquid silver mixed with water. The perfect anti-shapeshifter potion.

The beast on the other side of the door snarled, then the entire doorframe shattered. The red eyes stared at me, and the creature opened its long-fanged mouth and let loose an unearthly scream.

I slammed the top of the long bottle against the counter and the neck shattered. The creature took two steps toward me, and I flung the contents of the bottle on it.

A thick splash struck the creature across the face. It screamed in pain, skidding to a halt and writhing on the floor. One of the big, clawed paws tore at its face, and the yellow teeth bared in a hideous grimace. Then the undulating muscles rippled, and when the creature stood to face me again, my mouth went dry. Maybe colloidal silver didn't stop this creature? . . .

It roared and burst out of the kitchen.

I grabbed my knife and followed it, skidding on the wet, dirty floor. A shard of glass bit into my foot, but I didn't stop.

Glass crashed and the creature burst through the window in the living room, giving one more eerie, catlike scream as it disappeared into the night.

My breath escaped me in a whoosh.

Another window broke, this one in the foyer. My hand tightened on my knife again and I raised the blade, my eyes wild as another cat shifter burst into the living room. I threw the weapon at the creature. It dodged at the last moment, and my knife skidded across the carpet.

I took a panicked step backward, my eyes on the newcomer. Adrenaline blacked my vision, spots swimming at the edges of my sight. As I took another step backward something clicked, and I realized that the creature in front of me was a cougar, rapidly shifting back to human form. One of the Russells, maybe? Still watching over our house?

The cavalry had arrived. All the adrenaline rushed out of my body. Safe.

"Bathsheba!" Sara cried. I turned to her, scanning her to make sure she was okay. Her eyes were glittering, her face wrinkling in the telltale sign that it was about to sprout a muzzle, and her arms were covered in thick, dark gray hair. Her feet were perilously close to the silver water, which would incapacitate her. "Sara! Get back! Don't let them see you."

"Forget about me," she argued back, her words turning into a snarl as her teeth elongated and sharpened into canines. "Just don't kill Beau!"

Beau? That threw even more panic into me, and I shoved Sara back into the pantry, ignoring her wolflike yelp. "Don't come out until I've cleaned all this up," I hissed, then bolted for the living room. I slipped on the wet silver spilled all over the kitchen and grasped the broken doorframe to keep my balance, then pushed into the foyer.

"Damn it, Bathsheba," Beau snarled, eyes narrow as he looked me over. "Who were you going to stab with that knife?"

He was naked. Really naked. His wide shoulders were every bit as mouthwatering as I remembered, muscles clearly defining his lean frame. He had a fine six-pack and the most amazing hard ridge of flesh along his hip bones. . . .

"I ran out of silver," I said blankly, still staring at his chest. It was remarkably perfect, without a hint of softness.

"Silver?"

"I . . . oh, yes," I said, shaking myself free of the mesmerizing hold his abs had on me. "Don't go in the kitchen. There's silver water everywhere."

He grabbed my wrist. To my surprise, he pushed me back against the wall, his hands grabbing my shoulders and running over my body in a fast check. "Are you all right? Are you hurt? Answer me."

Bewildered, I stared at him and tried to shove his hands away. "I'm fine—"

A low growl escaped his throat and he kissed me.

It was like being swallowed into the eye of a storm. All rational thought went out the window. His lips crushed mine, frantic and possessive. His tongue stroked against the seam of my mouth, demanding entrance and demanding my submission. It was glorious. I wanted more. I opened my mouth, my tongue seeking his. They touched briefly, then tangled. His tongue stroked along mine, lighting a series of flickering sensations along the rest of my body. Gasping noises emerged from my throat, followed by a possessive growl of his own. I needed this—oh, I needed this. His tongue was conquering, thrusting, dominating. God, his mouth tasted so sweet and . . .

I broke away from the kiss. Had I totally lost my head? Sara was here and turning into a wolf, and Beau was going to scent her at any moment. I grasped at his arms, torn between the urge to leap into them again and the urge to fling him away from me. "Beau, how . . . what are you doing here?"

"Making sure that you're safe," he said, releasing my shoulders. Then he jerked me close to him again, his hands roaming over my body in a motion that I wasn't sure was protective or possessive— but I liked it. His gaze met mine as he brushed his fingers against my cheek. "It's a damn good thing, too. What were you thinking, confronting that creature?"

"What was I supposed to do?" I frowned at him.

"You and Sara should have run—"

I shook my head. "It would have chased us. This way I kept her safe."

"While risking your own—"

I shoved at his shoulders, baring my teeth in fear and anger. "*My* sister, *my* responsibility. Not yours."

"You could have been hurt," he said in a softer voice. His eyes were smoky with desire, his body moving closer to my own. The look on his face could have melted butter. The press of his body against me told me Beau was really turned on by my protectiveness.

Flustered, I tried to change the subject. "Whatever that thing was, it smelled putrid. Like it was dead."

"It was a shifter of some sort," Beau murmured, stroking my crunchy hair. "But not like any I've ever seen."

"What do you mean?"

He was silent. What, was he afraid to divulge top-secret shifter stuff? Like I gave a crap. I punched his arm. "Tell me."

"Ow. Careful. You have silver on your hands." He pulled his shoulder away slightly, but his hands didn't leave my body.

"Sorry," I said, pulling my hands away.

"You can keep them on me," he said against my mouth, and then grinned. "Just keep them above the waist."

Distracted at the thought, I tried to concentrate. "The shifter . . . what was it?"

"I don't know," he said, then released me. "I need to make a few calls."

Just like that? I swallowed my disappointment when he went into my living room and picked up the landline. My life had no room for a sexy, protective were-cougar, as much as I might have wanted otherwise.

When he greeted the person on the other end of the line, I tiptoed through the silver water toward the pantry, where I'd last left Sara. It was silent.

I opened the door, caught a hint of tail and shredded clothing. "Stay in there," I whispered to her. "I'll clean up the water and get rid of Beau."

She gave a small whine of response as I closed the door. I mopped up the water and poured it down the sink, then disposed of the broken glass that littered the room. Once that was done, I left the kitchen to pull Beau away from Sara's hiding spot while she was vulnerable.

He stood in the middle of the hallway, still buck naked, and oh boy, his ass was nice. I'd already seen it once, but it was equally mesmerizing on the second viewing. I admired his body as he talked on my phone, mentally caressing the breadth of his shoulders and the slim V of his hips as he talked. Just a hint of hair dusting his chest, and none on his back. That was nice. His buttocks were fascinating. Small, firm, and taut. I badly wanted to feel the smoothness of that muscled backside and clasped my hands, not trusting them to not reach for that wonderful bronzed flesh.

He finished the call and began another. "Ramsey? It's me. I need you to come meet me."

As Beau gave Ramsey my address, I realized what had been bothering me about his appearance and rescue. He'd sure gotten here fast. I glanced back in the kitchen, thinking of Sara and frowning. Something wasn't adding up.

On a hunch, I tiptoed toward the broken window and peeked outside. No sign of the Viper in my driveway, but his clothes were strewn across my front yard. Wherever he'd come from, he'd walked. And considering how fast he'd gotten here, he must have been very close nearby.

I turned away from the window, managing to stay remarkably calm. "How did you get to my house so fast?"

He put the phone back into the cradle. His gray eyes bored into mine, challenging. "I was outside."

"Why were you outside? I broke up with you."

"And I came here to talk to you about that," Beau said. "Because I know the timing is all wrong, and I don't care. I wanted to see you again, so I decided to come talk to you, and then I smelled that thing. The same thing that I smelled in the cab, Bathsheba. I didn't tell you then, because I didn't want to worry you, but something unnatural is stalking you. Something that's stronger than any supe I've run across and that likes the taste of blood."

"I see," I said in a soft voice, trembling. "You saved us. Thank you."

"You looked like you were handling things just fine." He crossed his arms over his chest, which really emphasized his nakedness. "So are you going to tell me what's going on?"

"If I knew what it was, don't you think I'd have taken care of it? Something is hunting you. Or Sara. Maybe both of you."

I gave a tremulous laugh. "Maybe we should be asking if *you* have enemies."

His expression remained grave, which made me shiver. The werewolves had Savannah because they wanted Sara. Maybe they wanted me as well? I knew that they couldn't turn me into a wolf, but they didn't know that.

A warm arm wrapped around my shoulder. I suddenly found my nose smooshed against Beau's chest and he pulled me tight against him. "Come sit on the couch," he said in a low, hypnotic voice. "I'll go get Sara."

My arms clamped around his waist and I pulled him against me. "She's fine. She just needs a little time to recover and won't appreciate us bothering her." At his skeptical look, I laid my head on his shoulder. "Stay with me. Please."

I was not above emotional manipulation to keep him away from my very wolfy sister.

"Don't worry," he said, keeping me pressed to his side as he steered us toward the couch. "Everything is going to be fine. Whatever it was is gone. I've called my clan in and they're going to come help us."

Us. Not "you." As if we were joined at the

hip already. It wouldn't hurt to let him think we could still be together, and I huddled next to his naked body on the couch. My mind kept running through the events over and over, the growls, the horrible smell, fear for Sara, who must have been terrified, yet I couldn't get to her as long as Beau was here and she was still a wolf. . . .

We sat on the couch for a long while. Beau stroked my hair and whispered small things to me, and I . . . liked it. There was something soothing about letting someone hold me and pet me as I fretted. Though I couldn't tell Beau my problems, he knew I was upset and sought to make it better.

That was a new concept. Usually I was so busy holding the pieces together for Sara and me that I never got a chance to relax or let someone else shoulder the burden, even for a second.

It was an intoxicating feeling. It made me want things that I couldn't have. I must have trembled again, for Beau pressed his lips to my tangled hair, hugging me closer. "I'm here, Bathsheba. You're safe. I'll take care of things."

Strangely enough, that made me feel better. He couldn't possibly help me, but knowing that he was willing to try somehow made all the difference in the world.

A few men soon showed up and let themselves into the house. I jerked upright at the sight of them, but Beau wasn't tense next to me, so he knew them. After getting a good look at the strangers, I understood. They all looked much like Beau—tall, lean, dark-haired, and built. Same light-colored eyes, same bone structure. Obviously more members of the Russell clan.

Standing before them naked, Beau didn't look the slightest bit awkward as they all began to talk as if I hadn't been there.

"Humans, Beau?" One of the strangers gave me an incredulous look. Another sniffed his surroundings, nostrils flaring, as if this all disagreed with him.

"Miss Ward is my girlfriend."

No, she's not. She can't be. Not if she's smart.

Another spoke up. "Are you serious?"

The entire house grew deathly quiet, as if a massive insult had just been spoken. One of the men jabbed the other in the shoulder. "Boss," he began, and I could practically smell the apology forthcoming.

Jeez. Supes *really* didn't care for humans.

But Beau only gave them a lazy grin that made my heart stutter. "Serious," was all he said, and pulled me behind him in a possessive gesture. "Now, where's Ramsey?"

One of the clones gestured outside. "Getting his kit from the back of the truck."

Beau grunted acknowledgment. "You bring your weapons?"

Wait. Huh? "Weapons?" I interrupted. "What are you guys doing?"

Beau said, "We're setting up a sting. If that thing returns to this house, it won't live for long."

Well, shit. I did *not* need a bunch of cat shifters crawling around in the house. I needed them all to leave now, before they scented Sara. I cast an angry look at Beau. "You can't do that. I don't want weapons in my house. In fact, I don't want a bunch of strangers in my house."

Beau pulled me toward the far corner of the living room. The others averted their eyes, talking in low whispers.

"Let me take care of this, Bathsheba," he said quietly. "I'm not going to allow some creature to stalk you, break into your house, and threaten your life. You are going to be safe. I've marked you with my claim, and you are going to accept that I'm looking out for you." His words were low and even.

I opened my mouth to protest.

"The others won't touch you. They'll give you more respect than a normal human would get because I've claimed you." When I started to protest again, he continued, "You are mine. I've already decided it. And if I have to mark you all over that delicious body of yours to prove it, I will."

A blast of desire raced through me at that mental image and I swallowed hard, resisting the urge to fan myself.

The crooked smile curved his mouth again and he ran his thumb over my lower lip as if to remind me of his kisses. Then he walked toward his men. "We need to set up a defense. Bring the silver and the wolfsbane, and be careful with it. I want you to start upstairs."

They left me there in the living room, stunned, my lips still feeling the electric heat from his touch. I wandered back to the kitchen, peeking in. The pantry door was wide open and there was no Sara anywhere. That was a good sign. Maybe she'd changed back and gone to the back bathroom to disguise her scent.

A hand touched my elbow.

I jerked away, stumbling back a few steps in fright.

A big, blond man stood there with a grave look on his face. He was enormous—at least a foot taller than Beau and broader. His hair was shaggy, his features large. One hand held a toolbox, and the other colossal mitt held up a bottle of water. "Drink this."

I stared up at the giant in alarm. "Who . . . who are you?"

Irritation crossed the hard features, as if he was annoyed that he had to answer me. "Ramsey."

"Okay." Beau had mentioned Ramsey a few times. His best friend and fellow Alliance member. "No, thank you. I'm not thirsty."

He reached out, grabbed my hand, and forced the water bottle into it. "Drink."

Not exactly the most friendly man. I glared at him.

He glared back.

I drank.

Next, he handed me a silver bubble pack of pills. "Take these."

I pushed them away. "I'm fine."

Ignoring my protests, he nudged the pills at me again.

I took the pills from him and scowled when he continued to watch me, waiting for me to swallow them. "Your Mr. Russell is a bit high-handed."

Ramsey grunted. Obviously not a man of many words.

I eyed the pills—clearly something to relax my nerves. God knows I could use it. Sara and I needed to get out of Fort Worth. Away from the shifters, away from *everyone*. We could pack the necessities tonight and be out of the city by morning, but not with all these shifters hanging around my house, trying to be helpful.

"Take. The. Pills." Ramsey loomed over me, his face hard and unsmiling. His arms crossed over his chest, and he stared pointedly at me.

I returned his glare. "I'm going to complain to your boss that you're trying to drug me."

Ramsey's hard eyes glittered down into mine. "Who do you think told me to give them to you?"

Oh. Well, then. This was what I got for pretending to have a nervous breakdown to distract Beau. I could pack while medicated, I supposed. Even if I didn't want to take the pills, I had no doubt that Ramsey would force me to take them, one way or another. Ignoring the hulking giant that hovered over me, I reluctantly swigged the pills down with water.

They tasted terrible, leaving a coating in my mouth. "Does everyone always do what Beau wants?" I asked, gesturing at the men who crawled all over my house. I could still hear Beau barking orders upstairs.

"Yes," said Ramsey.

I snorted and began to clean up the glass from the two broken windows. I needed to check on my sister, but not with this overgrown behemoth looming over my shoulder. But soon I grew sleepy, sluggish. Things started to feel disconnected, and my head felt like it was spinning.

Beau suddenly appeared at my side and angled my face up, studying my expression. "How is she?"

I wanted to protest that he could ask me directly, but there was a fog settling on my brain. Ramsey showed up out of the corner of my eye, Sara standing behind him, her clothes changed and her hair wet—a quick shower?

"She took the pills," Ramsey said in that low, gruff voice. "I'd give it a few hours."

"For what?" I asked, finding it difficult to keep my eyes open.

"More than enough time," Beau said, and then I was lifted into the air. The world spun dizzily, the thick scent of Beau was everywhere, and I realized I was cradled against his naked chest. He was so warm and delicious that I snuggled in and sighed with bliss. I could go to sleep right here. "Time enough for what?"

He pressed his lips to my forehead, and the world bobbed a little as he began to walk. "Time to get you home, Bathsheba. To my place."

"We can't," I protested, trying to focus my eyes on my sister. Sara's face was ashen with stress, her arms crossed over her chest. "We're leaving."

"Yes, we are," Beau agreed.

We were talking about two different things— but I could no longer stay awake. My eyes sealed shut as I burrowed deeper in Beau's arms and let the heavy sleep take over me.

Chapter Eight

When I woke up, the foul taste in my mouth had blossomed into a whole new kind of foul, and my head throbbed. I sat up, realizing that I was on someone's couch. That explained the crick in my neck and the drool tracks down the side of my face. I wiped them away and frowned at my surroundings.

It looked like I was in some sort of rustic lodge. The couch was an ugly country plaid, and the walls were some sort of log planks.

The room itself was huge, the windows large, filling the room with sunlight. A braided rug decorated the floor, and I caught a glimpse of a spacious kitchen across the living room. This wasn't just a log cabin—this was a log cabin on steroids.

Beau's house? I vaguely remembered him saying he would take me home.

But where was Sara? Where was my sister?

The world came rushing back and I bolted

through the rooms, looking for her. She was no-where to be found. I opened a dozen doors, but I was the only one in the house. It hit me like a ton of bricks then.

I'd been drugged. That bastard Ramsey had given me something to knock me out. Stupid fool that I was, I'd thought it was something to make me relax. Nope. It was something to make me *unconscious*.

I ran my hands down my dress. My panty hose were intact and my hair was still a disgusting mess. I felt a little better.

Beau. *"Time to get you home, Bathsheba. To my place."* Alarm returned as full memory did.

A monster had been in my house. Sara had pan-icked and changed, and a bunch of were-cougars had arrived to save the day. I put a hand to my forehead. Where was Beau? Why had I been left here alone?

Fear set in. Had he gone to exchange my sister with the wolves? Is that why I was here by myself? Worried, I went back through the house again, this time thoroughly searching each room.

The ceilings were arched and spacious, and there was a second floor with a master bedroom. A massive bed dominated the room, a fact not lost on me. There was also a jet tub in the bathroom, a lovely deck surrounding the house, and miles and miles of trees.

I stared at the gorgeous scenery in dismay. We

were obviously no longer in Fort Worth. East Texas? Oklahoma? And where the heck was the driveway? I circled the deck twice to make sure I hadn't missed anything, but there was no driveway leading from the cabin; just more woods and a footpath.

So how on earth was I supposed to escape? Being a city girl, I didn't trust myself alone in the woods. I didn't even know which direction to run to. I scanned the skies, where a wall of gray clouds brought a chill, icy breeze with them.

Still frowning, I went back inside. There was a TV in the big den and a library of DVDs nestled on a nearby shelf. The movie shelf was full of current releases, and the bookshelves were lined with both classic and popular books. Tolstoy sat next to Stephen King, Dean Koontz, and Dan Brown. Most of the books were action-adventure, with the occasional classic tossed in. I pulled out a pristine copy of *The Great Gatsby* and then put it back when I noticed a well-worn paperback next to it— *An American Werewolf in London*.

The irony was not lost on me.

On the far side of the house, a door slammed. All my senses went on alert again, and I raced across the house to confront my kidnapper.

I heard the sound of easy whistling as I turned the corner and saw Beau's broad back in the kitchen. A large box was on the island counter, and as he whistled, he pulled food supplies out of it.

"You're awake," he said, turning to look at me. "How are you feeling?"

"Where's my sister?"

"Sara's fine." A faint frown crossed his face as he studied my wild expression. "Calm down. You're safe, and so is she. You're under my protection."

"Your protection?" I sputtered. "You think you're protecting me by slipping me a mickey and carrying me off into the wilderness Lodge of Love?"

There was a dark look on his face, and his eyebrows drew down over his eyes. "You're right," he said slowly. "I should have just tucked you into your bed and let whatever it was come back and kill you and your sister both."

"I had a plan," I muttered. I couldn't tell him that I'd been *planning* on disappearing from town before sunrise. "So why here? Why not a hotel? And why isn't my sister here?"

"This is my home when I don't have business in town. I like it here. It's private." His explanation was simple, but I sensed an underlying pride.

"And where are we, Mr. Privacy?"

He shook his head and returned to pulling things out of the box. A loaf of bread. A jar of peanut butter. A can of ham. "I can't tell you that."

I moved around the island to get in his line of vision again. "Why can't you tell me that?"

He shrugged. "We don't know what we're dealing with." His motions as he unpacked the groceries were calm, fluid. Everything he did, he did with effortless grace, and I calmed a bit just by watching him. "I don't know how this thing knew which house was yours, or which taxi you were getting into the other night. Maybe it can read minds. If it can, I don't want it knowing how to find you. So it's better that you don't know." He picked up a package of Oreos. "Hungry?"

Unfortunately, this was starting to make sense. "No," I said, and resisted the urge to wring my hands in frustration. "Did you have to drug me?"

He gave me a slow, melting smile. "I didn't think you'd let me carry you through the woods quietly—not with the scare you'd just had."

I blinked at that. "Did you carry me?"

He grinned and took a step toward me. I warily circled the other side of the island, keeping the counter between us. Beau chuckled. "I did. Carried you several miles."

"Several miles—is that how far we are from town?"

He smiled and didn't answer.

"You suck." I crossed my arms over my chest. "So where is my sister?"

"Safe," he said. "Don't worry about anything else."

Not worry? How could I not worry? They didn't even know what I was worrying *about*. "Where is she?"

"With Ramsey," he said, then repeated, "safe."

That made me feel a little better. Ramsey was terrifying—if anyone could keep her safe, it was him. My arms, tight across my chest, eased a little. "And Savannah? Any luck finding her?"

Tension flashed briefly across his face. He pulled out a can of coffee and set it aside. "No word on her yet. We'll find her."

No Savannah meant that Beau still needed me for his heat. I wasn't sure if that internal tremor I felt was worry or excitement. "How do I know this isn't all an elaborate ploy to get me to sleep with you in the next few days?"

Beau leaned over the counter, and I couldn't help but notice how broad his shoulders were. "Sweet Bathsheba," he said, his voice low and playful, "no one said that I wasn't going to try and seduce you."

As Beau unpacked the small box of food—the rest would be coming tomorrow with Ramsey—I felt nervous and uncomfortable. So when he handed me a bottle of scented shampoo, I grabbed it and headed upstairs. Rooting around in Beau's closets uncovered a few things—first, he was truly a bachelor. I found no extra linens besides two tow-els. Second, he clearly lived here—winter clothing hung in the closet along with summertime wear. I took a T-shirt and a pair of sweatpants, and hoped that when Ramsey came with Sara tomorrow they'd bring me some clothing.

The shower was a little slice of heaven. I hadn't realized how sticky and unclean I felt until I peeled my clothing off and kicked it into the corner. I sham-pooed my hair twice and lingered in the shower, enjoying the hot water. Once out, I dressed in his borrowed clothing and bundled my dress, under-garments, and hose into a small stack. It reeked of blood and restaurants and a faint hint of Old Spice, and I suddenly wanted to just throw it away.

When my long, wet hair was combed out, I went downstairs looking for Beau.

He was sitting with a book on the couch. The thriller was open on his chest and his eyes were closed, his breathing even. He was asleep.

I felt a surge of grudging tenderness. While I'd been sleeping the drugs off—not at my choice, mind you—he'd been up all night, bringing me out here to the boonies to keep me safe and dragging in his people to keep an eye on my place. I still didn't forgive him, but I felt grateful that he'd gone to so much effort on my behalf.

Well, only a *little* grateful. I sat next to him on

the couch and poked his arm. "Wake up, Beau. I need to know where Sara is."

His arm shot out, grabbing hold of my wrist. Before I could utter the squeal building in my chest, he dragged me toward him. The book went flying and I flew across the couch as he pulled me onto his lap, my bottom resting on his thighs.

"You smell good enough to eat," he said, and leaned in to nibble on my neck.

Delicious tingles shot through my body and I squirmed in his arms, trying to get away. "You're trying to distract me into kissing you, aren't you?"

"Is it working?"

"It is not," I said. "Tell me about my sister."

"She's safe," he said. "Don't you trust me?"

I didn't trust anyone. I stared at him for a long moment, then sighed. "All right, fine. I trust you. Now tell me about my sister."

He chuckled and pulled me against him until my chest smacked against his. His chin nudged against my neck and then he bit my earlobe, and all thought about having a serious conversation flew right out of my head. My breath shivered and my hands touched his neck, his shoulders, trying to find a good spot to land. I could feel that wonderful heat radiating through his clothing.

His teeth tugged at my earlobe, sending my blood rushing through my body and shivers down my spine. My hands curled in his hair. Something low rumbled in his chest—almost like purring, and he brushed my wet hair aside to nip at my neck again. "My tasty little Bathsheba," he murmured against my skin. "I've been wanting to do this for a while now."

It was hard to think when he did that to me. His hand wrapped in my wet, heavy hair, exposing more of my neck, and my nipples tightened in response, my pulse growing heavy. My hand threaded through his hair as he nuzzled the tender skin of my neck, the scrape of one day's growth of his beard stubble on my skin harsh yet exciting. His other hand slid down my side, cupping my bottom through the sweatpants.

He was very, very good at distracting me, I thought as I curled my fingers in his hair. Almost too good. I jerked on his hair, pulling his face away from my neck. "Not so fast there, Casanova. I want an answer."

He chuckled. "Can't help myself. You just look so delicious sitting there in my clothing."

Well, I certainly wasn't averse to compliments—or to having him nibble on me—so I returned his smile. "You're trying to distract me with kisses."

"And here you said you weren't susceptible," he said, all teasing.

"Oh, I'm susceptible all right," I said. "If you

kiss me again, I won't be able to think of anything else for the rest of the day."

A pleased smile crossed his face. Perhaps I shouldn't have told him that he scrambled my brains with his touch. Sara would shake her head at my awful flirting skills—

"Sara," I blurted, knotting my fingers in Beau's short hair again. "Where is my sister?"

"It's taken care of," he said in that now annoyingly confident voice. "Ramsey is my second-in-command. He'll handle it while you're here."

"Sara is not an 'it,' she is a person and I need her. We have someplace we have to be." Like a couple hundred miles from here.

"At work? I told Giselle you had a family emergency."

I gave a moan of dismay and sank down on the arm of the couch. God, I hadn't even thought about work. "You *didn't* talk to Giselle."

"I did. She said to tell you that she'd take care of everything."

I moaned even louder. Knowing Giselle, that was a bad sign. Given that I'd ditched Garth last night, and now I wasn't there to hit the new string of dates she'd set up for me, she'd take care of things, all right. She'd start by telling everyone that Sara was a wolf, and we wouldn't be able to get away before the wolf pack caught on.

I looked over at Beau, an idea sparking. "Will Ramsey do anything you want?"

He stiffened, as if I'd wounded his masculine pride. "Of course he will."

"Good," I said, thinking fast. "Tell him to kidnap Sara, too. She's in danger. Those monsters might be after her."

He paused, clearly thinking. "You're asking me to organize her abduction."

I threw one of the couch pillows at him. "You abducted me, you moron! What's one more?"

He grinned. "Yours isn't an abduction but a seduction. It'll never hold up in a court of law."

"Bullshit," I said. "Don't change the topic. Now, are you going to call that mammoth that you call Ramsey?"

"You're ferocious when it comes to your sister, you know that?"

"Sara's the only person I care about."

His eyes darkened. "The only person?" Before I could comment on his reaction, he said, "All right. I'll do it in exchange for a favor from you."

I gave him a wary look. "What sort of favor?" *Spread your legs and act interested?*

The smug grin returned. "You need to kiss me again."

"Kiss you?" I sputtered. "Remember the part where I broke up with you? Not seeing each other means there's no kissing." My heart pounded in my chest. He did have the sexiest damn mouth. Even as I stared at it, his lips curved into a smile that I wanted to lick right off his face.

Beau closed his eyes. "I don't think your motivations were solid. Kiss me and we'll save Sara. Those are the rules."

"This isn't a game," I snapped. "This is Sara's life."

"Then I guess you'd better get started." He didn't move a muscle.

I waited a moment longer, exasperated by his stupid game. He remained motionless, his arms at his sides. I still smelled a trap.

I slid forward an inch or two on the couch.

A pleased rumble emitted from his chest and his mouth curved into a smile, his eyes still closed. "That's it. Come closer."

I slapped his chest lightly in irritation. "Don't you mean, 'Come into my web, said the spider to the fly'?"

"That would imply that I'm going to eat you," he said, his words soft. "It's your lips that are going to be moving."

A tingle shot through me. I moved a little closer until I was near enough to kiss him. He was sprawled out and I couldn't find a good angle to lean in, so I straddled his leg and slid forward a bit more.

He groaned and shifted slightly, his thigh pressing against the V of my legs. "I liked that."

I poked him in the chest. "Hush. I'm concentrating."

"Sorry," he said in a tone of voice that was anything but.

I inched closer, moving a little bit further down his thigh, feeling surprisingly vulnerable. But he didn't move a muscle, so I leaned in. My breasts grazed his chest and I pulled back at the sensation.

He groaned, the confident smile fading. "Tease."

I had to admit, I liked that reaction. So I leaned in again, making sure to brush up against his chest once more, and I kissed him.

At first, it was just a light press of my mouth to his. I expected him to take control, but to my surprise he remained still. Then the challenge hit me and I suddenly wanted to see him lose control. If this was a contest, I was determined to win.

I excelled at tug-of-war.

So I kissed his full and sensual lower lip first, giving it a light bite and then soothing it with the tip of my tongue. His breath rasped at that, sweet and hot against my mouth, and it made me bolder. I traced both lips with my own, then repeated the motion with my tongue, every so often dipping mine into the faint crease of his mouth. He still didn't move, but his breath quickened against my own.

I slid my tongue into his mouth, searching for his. Beau tasted terrific—warm, musky, delicious. A soft noise of pleasure escaped my throat.

That sent him over the edge. Suddenly one hand was at the base of my skull, the other one grabbing my ass, and he pulled me against him, his tongue fiercely meeting my own. It was a dance, a flirtation of tongues. Taste, tangle, retreat. It went on for long moments, lips meeting with each tongue thrust, until I gasped for air and broke away.

He gave me a hot-eyed look, breathing hard. "You don't kiss like a virgin."

Irritated, I tried to shove him away. "That's right," I said sarcastically. "You've figured me out. I moonlight as a professional call girl."

"That explains your weird hair yesterday," he said, and winced when I slapped his shoulder.

"Very funny." The hand in my hair had slid down my back, holding me against his chest. "Now please call Ramsey about Sara. I'm really worried about her."

He leaned in and kissed the tip of my nose. "She's already been moved."

"*What?*"

He grinned, pleased as could be. "Ramsey took care of it last night while you were out. Sara is hiding out at a safe location, much like you and me.

We decided to separate the two of you to determine which is the target."

I knew who was chasing her, and why. She'd never be safe as long as I kept that a secret . . . but how could I tell Beau that the reason I knew the wolf pack was after Sara was that she was the runaway female they were demanding in exchange for Savannah?

I couldn't. And I needed to hear her voice to know she was okay.

"Beau," I said in a warning voice.

He shifted under me, prying something out of his back jeans pocket. "Here," he said, handing me the phone. "Call Ramsey if you'd like."

I flipped open the phone and paged through the address book—noting with irritation that a good many names were female, and Arabella's name was still in his list—and hit dial when I saw Ramsey's name.

"Yes?" he said, answering on the first ring. If I thought Beau's voice was deep, Ramsey's voice was the abyss. It definitely matched his Godzilla-sized body.

"This is Bathsheba. I need to talk to Sara."

A moment later, Sara's voice chirped into my ear, "Hello?"

"It's me, Bath. Are you all right? Where are you?"

She paused for a moment. "Ramsey says it's not

safe for me to say. How are you? Are you okay?"

It was really starting to irritate me that Beau and his cronies could waltz into our lives, turn them upside down, and we were suddenly dancing to their tunes. I glanced at Beau, who was obviously listening in on the conversation, and I was positive Ramsey was doing the same. I couldn't tell her that the wolves were after us. "I'm fine. And you? You're . . . fine? You're being careful?"

Sara sounded almost shy. "I'm good. No problems on this end. I'm being careful."

I exhaled in relief, knowing what she was saying. "That's good. That's very good."

"It's okay, Bath. I'm going to stay here with Ramsey and the rest of the Russell clan for a few days. It's going to be fine."

"Okay," I said, as if our lives hadn't all been torn to shit at the moment.

But her voice was even and steady, and didn't have the vibrato of fear that I'd become so attuned to. Whatever was going on, she felt safe, and that made me relax.

"I have to go," she said after a few minutes. "We're picking teams for Xbox and I don't want to be stuck with Jeremiah again. He sucks at Call of Duty—all thumbs. I'll talk to you tomorrow. Love you."

"Love you," I said slowly, but she had already

hung up. I felt a little stung. Wasn't she even worried about any of this?

"She knows you're safe with me," Beau offered, almost as if he could read my mind. "And that she's safe with Ramsey. He'd die before he'd let anything happen to her."

"I know," I said softly. "I just worry about her."

His mouth quirked into a half smile. "You mother Sara, don't you? For all that she's maybe a year younger than you—"

"Two years," I offered.

"—you still treat her like she's a kid. You like being needed, and you like being the one to get her out of a scrape. But it's all taken care of now, so you don't know what to do with yourself."

I rolled my eyes at his psychoanalysis. "That's not true. I'm happy that she's fine, but I'm still worried about her even if she's not."

"She's as safe as can be with Ramsey. Don't you worry about her one bit."

Easier said than done.

He touched the underside of my chin. "You do know what this means, right?"

"What's that?" I said warily.

"It means you and I can relax here and do whatever we want . . . which means you can make me pancakes."

"Nice try."

He didn't seem deterred. Beau grinned and flipped over my hand, then began to press kisses at the soft flesh of my wrist, moving up my arm with each subsequent one. "You forget that I have the heat to worry about, Miss Bathsheba. I need my strength."

"Well, I hope your hand is ready."

He winked at me, slow and sultry. "I hope yours is, too."

"That's not what I meant. I *can* resist you, you know." Though it was going to be difficult as hell if it was just me and him in a romantic cabin away from the world.

He chuckled. "But can I resist you? For two whole days? When you sit here on my lap and look good enough to eat?"

I shoved away from him. "Flatterer."

He let me go, but I felt his eyes on me as I stood and paced across the room. "My sweet Bathsheba, didn't anyone ever tell you that the more that the prey runs, the more the hunter desires it? A cat loves nothing more than a good chase."

"So what am I supposed to do? Fall at your feet with my legs wide open? Would that make you run away?"

His eyes sparked with interest. "We could try it."

I threw a couch cushion at his head.

Chapter Nine

Even though Beau was good company, I was unable to relax. Beau didn't realize that Ramsey was the enemy, too, but because I knew it, I remained on edge. Beau puttered around the house whistling as he checked the windows and doors and did a few other things that I questioned. For one, he sprinkled each windowsill with holy water.

I offered to help him, but as soon as I tried to do anything, he'd growl for me to sit down and relax.

And then he'd disappear, off to take a shower.

Confused at his actions, bored with having nothing to do, I used his cell phone since the battery on mine was low and I didn't have the charger. I called the office to check up on things and put out a few small "fires" that had arisen between badly scheduled dates and an audit.

Naturally, the girls in the office were curious

about what was going on, and I didn't have a whole lot to tell them.

One guessed, of course. "There's a man, isn't there?" Ryder said over the phone, a speculative hint in her sweet, perky voice.

"There's no man," I said, but my voice squeaked.

She laughed with delight. "Girl, it's about time. I had money in the pool that you were heading for a nunnery."

"Pool?" I echoed, not following her line of thought.

"Betting on when you'd get laid."

My jaw dropped a little. "You guys have an office pool? On me?"

"We did." She sounded disgruntled. "Sara just won it. She had you pegged for thirty."

I couldn't believe they were taking bets on when I'd have sex. What was even more incredible was that the closest bet was five years off . . . and from my own sister. Irritated, I made up some quick excuse and got off the phone, Ryder's cheerful laugh ringing in my ears.

Beau strolled by just then, his mouth curved in a smile. He'd probably heard every word of the conversation. I scowled at him and flounced up from the couch, causing his book to fall onto the floor.

I bent to pick up the book, and when I turned around he had disappeared again. A minute later, I heard the shower start once more. I frowned, puzzled by his abrupt disappearance. That was odd.

Something like . . . me? And the heat due tomorrow?

I blushed, thinking of how I'd bent over and how that had sent him running. I'd have to be more careful. With that in mind, I settled in on one end of the couch and flipped through Beau's novel. A few minutes later, I froze when I heard a door open across the house. Careful not to make a sound, I shut the book and stood. From the other end of the house I could still hear the shower going.

Nervous, I edged to the kitchen, my first thought to head for the knives.

The intruder, however, was already in the kitchen.

It was a small brunette—petite and curvy, with short, curly hair and a huge rack. Freckles dotted her nose and she had the greenest eyes I'd ever seen. She was gorgeous, dressed in a low-cut top, tight jeans, and sandals. A heavy perfume wafted around her.

She looked at me with a hint of disgust, her nostrils flaring in a way that I'd learned to associate with shifters. Her lip curled. "Who are you?"

I stiffened at her rude tone. "Who the hell are you?"

She took a step toward me and her perfume became overpowering. I wanted to hold my nostrils shut. "I'm Arabella, and I live here." She held out her hand, displaying her keys. "That's why I have these."

She lived here? All my bravado died as I stared at the keys.

But if she lived here . . . then . . . something wasn't adding up.

Either she was lying to me, or Beau was. I didn't like the ugly look on her face and decided to stick with the devil I knew. "That's funny, because I could have sworn that I was living here with your boyfriend, not you."

Arabella's lip curled. "Men are cheating whores. I'm not surprised that he decided to get himself another piece of tail, though I am surprised he decided to slum it with a human."

Nice. I crossed my arms over my chest. "Lovely to meet you, too."

She ignored me and shoved past, stalking into the living room. I followed behind her, determined to keep up a cheerful demeanor, even if I had to resist the urge to punch something. She glanced at my clothing—Beau's clothing—and her lip curled a little more. "I want you out of my house."

"Much as I would love to humor you," I said, moving to the far side of the couch to put space between us, "I'm afraid I can't."

For one, I didn't even know where we were. For two, I wasn't budging until I knew where my sister was.

That answer didn't suit her. She snarled and stalked back to me, grabbing me by the arm. Her claws cut into my upper arm.

I jerked away as she dug into my flesh. "Hey! Back off!"

To my surprise, she did. A confused look crossed her face and she retracted her claws, then sniffed her fingertips, staring at me.

She must not like human stink. Too damn bad.

"Bathsheba is not going anywhere," Beau said and I turned to see him standing in the doorway dripping with water, a towel low on his hips. The look on his face was utterly furious. "What are you doing here, Bella?"

She had a cute nickname? My dislike of her increased.

Arabella put her hands on her hips. "I live here, remember?"

"No," Beau said calmly, pushing his wet hair back. "You lived here six months ago. Then you disappeared and left me a note telling me that we were through. I haven't seen you since."

If that was true, I felt a little better. I tried to hide the smile cracking my face.

Arabella sent me an arch look. "Well, I figured it was our weekend. With Savannah's heat and all." She shrugged. "People in town told me that you were forced to shack up with a human. I thought I'd come over and save you from the indignity."

Well, wasn't she just all sweetness and light.

"No indignity at all," Beau said with a smile and moved to my side. "I like Bathsheba, human or not."

They made it sound like I was diseased. Human cooties. "Gee, thanks," I said and tried to slip away.

Beau's arm went around my waist and he pulled me in front of him, anchoring me in his embrace. He pressed a kiss to my hair and I felt him inhale its scent. His thumb grazed underneath my borrowed T-shirt, brushing against my skin in an almost ticklish motion that made me want to shiver.

Arabella noticed all of this, her pretty face growing ugly with dislike. "You and I had an understanding, Beau—"

"No," he said, interrupting her. "We had a relationship. Once. Now I have one with Bathsheba."

Her hateful gaze fixed on me. "So you're picking this lump of a human over me?"

I put my hands on my hips, ready to give her hell.

Beau's arms tightened around me and he pressed a kiss against my neck, declaring his choice and silencing any protest I might have made.

Arabella was furious at that small gesture. She flung the keys against the wall. It sounded like a gunshot had gone off, and a massive chunk of log fell from the wall, a hole punched from the impact. Good God, she was strong.

"I want my things back," she shouted.

"I gave them away to Savannah," he said. "Six months ago, when you ran off with another man."

Arabella's eyes narrowed and her gaze refocused on me. "You can have him, you stupid human bitch," she said. "He isn't worth my time." A slow smile curved her mouth and she gave Beau a triumphant look. "I hope you're satisfied with your choice. She won't make you as happy as I could." Then she turned and stomped off. I stood there, frozen by her hatred, until the door slammed shut, reverberating through the house.

"That's funny. I don't remember being happy in that relationship," he said idly.

I tried to slide out of his arms, but he didn't let me. "So what's all that about 'nasty little humans'?"

He kissed my neck, his lips moving against my skin as he responded. "The Alliance views humans as weak and diseased."

And he was the leader of the Alliance. "Oh, really?"

"You have to admit that the weaker part is true."

Weak? Diseased! I shoved his head away from me and pushed at his arms. "Let me go!"

It was like fighting with an iron cage. Beau wasn't about to release me, and that got under my skin. "Let me explain," he said, his voice patient.

I turned away. "I'm not interested—"

"You're going to listen," he said, and then I was off the ground. Damn, he lifted me like I was nothing. I looked at the gigantic hole in the wall that Arabella had created with her angry key throw and shivered. These shifters were *strong*.

He was right about humans being weaker, but it still made me furious.

Beau carried me across the room and deposited me on the couch. When I tried to get up he lay on top of me, grinning. His heavy weight was a peculiarly pleasant feeling.

"You ready to listen?" he asked.

"You're smothering me." My hands shoved against his chest.

His hair was still wet from the shower, and a warm drop slid onto my face. I could feel the heat of his hard, naked body pressed against mine, sending traitorous trickles of pleasure through me.

"Bathsheba," he began, leaning in. A rumbling began low in his throat.

Was he . . . purring? Why did I find that so charming?

He grinned at my silence. "Do you know that when you get angry, your little chin gets pointed?"

"I'm sure it's one of those icky human things," I began, but I lost all concentration when he swooped in and pressed a kiss on my chin. First one, and then another, making me all distracted. He pressed another kiss along my jawline, nibbling up to my ear.

And oh, that felt nice. His teeth played with my earlobe, gently, teasing the soft flesh in a way that I imagined he'd tease the rest of my body. Tickling, tasting, exploring. He bit at my earlobe and my breath exploded from my throat.

"Arabella and I have been through for six months. She left me for another man. I haven't seen her since then, so I couldn't get back the key." He began to work his way down my throat again, kissing and nipping each inch of flesh, then licking at the sensitive spots. "I'd never pick her over you."

I shoved at him again. "Great. You picked the cootie-riddled human over the batshit-crazy shifter. You're a prince among men."

He chuckled, and his tongue licked along my collarbone. "I think you're delicious."

"Not disease-riddled?"

"Not in the slightest," he murmured against my neck, breath warm and ticklish against my skin.

I grew very aware of his body covering mine. Hard, hot, and still slightly damp from his shower. *Very* naked. His chest pressed against mine, heavy but not crushing. My breasts were pressed against his chest, and I fought the urge to rub myself against him like a cat.

I was angry, I reminded myself.

When he nipped at my collarbone, though, a soft sound of pleasure escaped my throat and all my anger melted.

"That's it, sweet Bathsheba," he whispered against my skin. "Let me taste you."

"No," I protested, but it came out so breathy and soft that I didn't believe it myself.

"No?" He leaned in, his nose brushing against mine in a playful motion, his mouth so close I could taste his breath.

The desire to kiss him shot through me, and I closed the gap between us and sealed the kiss. His mouth immediately plundered mine in return, hot, demanding, delicious. His tongue swept into my mouth, met by my own, and the kiss grew so deep and hot that my brain started to lose focus. I heard a soft sound of pleasure and realized that it had come from me.

He responded with a growl that was sexy as hell, and I forgot about everything but the intense kiss.

His hand slid down my side as our lips parted and the kiss ended, but Beau didn't stop. He began to nip down my jawline again, the stubble on his face rasping against my skin slightly. It hurt, but it was a fascinating kind of hurt, and I squirmed with pleasure when he lapped at my neck again.

His hand slid all the way down my sweats-covered thigh in a caress, and my leg followed the pleasing motion. I didn't even realize what I was doing until my legs parted and Beau's heavy body slid into the cradle it created. And then entirely new sensations blew my mind. Our bodies fit together like magic, and his hand coaxed my thigh up, and then I was wrapping my clothed legs around his naked waist.

It felt so good, and from the heavy purr in his throat, he liked it, too. I could feel the hot, heavy heat of his erection at the junction of my legs, and when he rocked against me, I gasped. The meaning there was obvious.

Beau stilled against me, and his gray eyes searched for mine. "Are you all right, Bathsheba?" He pressed small, light kisses to my mouth, as if trying to soothe me. His hips rocked against mine in another blatant move, and liquid fire poured through me, my entire body tingling.

That felt *very* nice. Even terribly exciting. I kissed him again in response.

"Sweet thing," he breathed against my mouth, punctuating his words with tiny nips and licks. "I want to kiss your breasts."

I moaned at the visual, my hips rocking against his at the thought. He growled low in his throat and rocked back, pressing that hardness against the apex of my thighs, my sweatpants suddenly seeming too thin.

Beau slid down my body, his hands sliding down my sides, pressing his face against my collarbone and sliding lower, nuzzling me through the fabric. Inch by slow inch, he moved down until his chin rested between my breasts, and my breath came in short, rapid gasps as I watched him, waiting anxiously.

He looked up at me, and as he did so, his mouth slid over a fraction, and then lightly bit at one nipple through the fabric.

My breath exploded in my throat all over again. A thousand bursts of pleasure electrified in that one spot.

He continued to look at me, his gray eyes hot, his hands stroking and gentling me on my sides. "Are you all right?"

I nodded, not trusting my voice. Then I blurted, "Please . . . don't stop." I needed to feel that sensation again, and he was moving way too slowly.

He bent down over my breast once more, his eyes on mine, and as I watched, he bit at the fabric-covered peak once more. I moaned in pleasure. "Oh, yes . . . please. Beau, please."

Beau didn't need any more encouragement. As I watched him, his tongue emerged and he lapped at my nipple through the thin fabric of the shirt, toying with it. His mouth closed over the sensitive peak and he sucked, teasing the wet fabric against the tip. I rocked my hips against his again, a gasping sob emerging from my throat, and my eyes drifted closed. "Oh, please, Beau."

Beau froze over me, then pulled away. "I need another shower."

Then I was left bereft, my eyes opening just in time to see his bare backside disappearing down the hall, leaving me with nothing but a damp spot on my shirt, aching breasts, and an intense throbbing between my legs.

I needed a cold shower myself.

Chapter Ten

*B*eau returned fully clothed. He must have gotten dressed right out of the shower, because his shirt stuck to parts of his wet body, and his hair formed damp curlicues on his forehead.

He'd been gone long enough for me to compose myself. Beau sat on the edge of the coffee table and tried to take my hands, but I slid them out of his.

"Bathsheba, I just wanted to apologize. I shouldn't have been mauling you on the couch."

So he was having second thoughts about the yucky human virgin? "No," I said, my voice stiff with hurt. "You should not have."

He looked further defeated by my tone. "I know you're a virgin. You probably want flowers and candlelight dinners, and I can't give you that. But I can make a vow that I won't throw you down on the couch and ravish you because I can't restrain myself."

I frowned. Where was he going with this?

He looked solemn. "I just want you to know that tomorrow night is going to be special for both of us."

Tomorrow night? The night of his heat? "Are you on drugs or something?"

It was his turn to frown. "What do you mean?"

I gestured at the door. "Your girlfriend—"

"Ex-girlfriend," he insisted. "I'm not dating anyone in the clan. Not her, not Savannah."

"You've never said who Savannah is to you."

"Savannah is my cousin. She's like a kid sister to me. Which is why I want you."

"Correction," I said. "You want anything female and convenient. Remember Rosie? Bachelorette number one?"

"Why, Bathsheba, you sound almost jealous. Would it help if I said that once I heard your voice, I didn't want anyone but you?"

Oh, yes. "No," I said. I picked up his novel and pretended to read, determined to ignore him.

He plucked the book out of my hands and tossed it across the room. "We need to talk about you and me."

I got up to go after the book. "There is no you and me."

He stood, too, blocking my way. "That's what we need to talk about."

I glared at him and tried to move around him. He stepped in front of me again. I sighed and crossed my arms over my chest. "What?" Damn, why did the man have to be so tall? And broad? I felt small next to him.

He brushed my hair off my shoulders, playing with it. For some reason, he loved my hair. I thought of Arabella's short curls and felt rather smug—she might have had a kick-ass body but I had prettier hair. Stupid, I knew, but I'd take whatever victories I could get.

"Bathsheba," he said, his voice grave. "I am extremely attracted to you. I wanted you the first moment that I saw you."

Flattery happened to be my weak spot. Damn the man.

His fingers dipped to my chin, lifting my blushing face to meet his gaze. "But I have a big problem. Tomorrow when the sun goes down, Savannah will go into heat. Normally when a female cougar goes into heat, she leaves the area so as not to affect her clan. But she doesn't have that choice this time, and because she is a female in my territory, it's going to affect me. I can't do anything about that. I'm . . . I'm stuck, really."

His gray eyes searched my face, as if he was hoping to find answers there, or encouragement. "If you and I aren't going to work out . . . I need you to tell me now. Otherwise I'm going to have to chase down that bitch Arabella and ask her to spend the night with me. I don't want to. Hell, the thought of having to do so makes me furious—but if my only other choice is that, I'm going to have to go after her."

He was laying it all out for me, his eyes earnest. I realized then that all his flirting and heavy-handed possessiveness was for my benefit. If I said no right now, he'd let me go shut myself in my room and never touch me, because he wanted to honor my wishes.

And instead he'd just sleep with that bitch Arabella.

I wavered between my loyalty to Sara and my attraction to Beau. My life revolved around Sara's safety, but right now I had an opportunity to take something for myself. Maybe I could have this one small interlude before we went on the run again. And I realized, quite suddenly, that I wanted this, and him, very, very much.

He was obligated to have sex, but he wanted *me*. And I liked that.

I fingered his shirt, smoothing over a damp wrinkle. "You realize that you've put me in a very awkward position, don't you?"

He actually blanched, bless his heart. "I know, sweet Bathsheba." His hand moved from my hair, sliding to my cheek. He caressed my skin with his knuckles, as if he simply had to touch me.

My heart always gave a little flutter when he said my name like that. "This isn't exactly how I planned my first time," I admitted. "I know we're stuck in this cabin together and you *have* to have sex tomorrow, but . . ." It felt a little odd. More than a little odd to think that I'd be de-virginized tomorrow night.

"I'll make it special for you," he vowed. "I'll give you romance."

"Romance?" My brow furrowed. "What do you have planned?"

He smiled. "Leave that up to me."

I trailed my finger down his shirt. His pectorals were so hard that I could practically feel the definition of the muscles through his shirt. "Well, if you truly have no choice, then I suppose we have a date."

He grinned and leaned in to kiss me. "You won't regret it."

I tilted my face up for his kiss, thinking that Sara was going to give me such shit when I saw her again—

"Sara!" I blurted, moving my head just before he could kiss me.

His mouth landed on the edge of my jaw. "What about Sara?" he said, not breaking stride.

I gently pushed him away. "You said everyone in the clan is affected by this heat thing, right?"

I could have sworn his eyes gleamed slightly when I mentioned the word "heat." "Every cougar is, true."

"So what about Sara? She's staying with the guys."

He pulled me against him again. "I told them to hit town tomorrow night. The ones that don't have a mate usually have a local girl on the side."

"And who's going to stay to make sure that Sara is safe?"

"Ramsey. He's not affected by the heat."

"Why not?"

"He's a were-bear. Only cougars will be affected by the heat."

My relief nearly made me sag. "So what is a were-bear doing in the Russell pack?"

"We're not really a pack. We're a clan. More of a corporation." At my arched eyebrow, he explained. "Were-cougars tend to be loners, drifters. Packs are a wolf thing."

"But I thought the Alliance was a pack itself."

"The rest of the Alliance tends to flock to clans, or packs. Vampires have a leader. Werewolves have packs. Fey have their own strange hierarchy. In our world—because we're so different from everyone else—family and friends are everything. My father realized a long time ago that as loners, we were putting ourselves in a weak position. That if we were going to stand a chance against the rest of the affiliations, we needed to have one of our own. My father created the Russell clan, but not everyone is a cougar. The majority are, but some, like Ramsey, are different."

"And only two girls? Just Savannah and Arabella?"

"Shifting seems to be a recessive gene. That's what makes a heat so important and so damn annoying as well. Because cougars have a wide territory, everyone in the entire pack with cougar blood is affected. Savannah and Arabella are the only two cougar women in the Russell territory. There's more females up in the Northwest, but their men are rather possessive. I've never met one."

"Too bad for you," I said wryly.

That heart-stopping grin that made me turn into Jell-O returned. "I'm not complaining. I rather like how things have ended up."

A blood-curdling scream woke me in the middle of the night.

I froze in Beau's bed, afraid to move a muscle.

The scream echoed again; it sounded inhuman. I'd heard Beau's wildcat cougar scream and this wasn't the same. This was nightmarish, twisted.

Not good.

I rolled over and stared at the window, which was covered in frost. I couldn't see out, but I could see the heavy line of salt covering the windowsill. A faint red sheen flickered in the window, as if there was some sort of red light outside.

Wariness made me slide to the floor, and I reached for the sharpened stake I'd made from the woodpile and stashed underneath the bed.

The scream rose through the woods again, closer, and I raced for the bedroom door. It opened before I could touch it. Beau stood there, grim-faced, his hair tousled, his chest bare.

He looked at my stake in surprise, then shoved something into my other hand. "Take this."

I felt relief when I realized the cold, heavy weight was a gun. "Is this loaded? Safety on?"

He grunted. "So you know how to shoot? You always surprise me."

Little did he know. *I've even killed a man.* I tucked the stake under my arm and flipped open the chamber of the gun. Six bullets loaded. "Of course I know how to shoot. I work for a business that deals with undead and werewolves. Are these bullets made of silver?"

"Silver-lead alloy," he said. "Stay in this room,

understand? Get under the bed, and I'm going to coat the doorways with salt. I don't want you moving until I come back."

"Waaaait a moment," I said, grabbing his arm before he could turn away. "Where are you going?"

His mouth was a grim line. "I need to find out what's out there."

"What's the salt for?"

He leaned in and kissed my forehead. "It keeps evil spirits from crossing the threshold."

"Evil spirits?" My voice rose to a near shriek. "Are you kidding me? Is that what this is?" I could deal with horny shapeshifters, or the occasional love-struck vampire who showed up at work, or a little sister who sprouted fur when she got nervous. Evil spirits were far out of the standard territory.

He was already turning down the hallway, pulling on his shirt. "I don't know what this is, Bathsheba. That's why you need to stay in the bedroom and lock the door. That's the safest I can make you."

Stay in this big house by myself, hiding under the bed while he ran off into the woods?

"Fuck that," I said, outraged. "I'm going with you." I chased after him, carrying the gun with careful hands as I crashed down the stairs. "I'm not staying here alone."

"You are not going with me," he said, turning

back to look at me with a furious gaze. "It's too dangerous."

"How do you know I'm safer here? What if it's not an evil spirit, and the salt doesn't do anything but pickle my remains?"

He gave me an exasperated look. "Bathsheba—"

"I'm going with you." I wouldn't feel safe trotting through the woods with scary stuff out there, but at least Beau would be by my side.

He looked torn. "Bathsheba—"

"If you leave me here, I'm just going to follow you," I said. "Classic stupid horror movie move. And you *know* bad things always happen to virgins in those."

He gave me a grim smile. "Wait here and I'll get you a coat and shoes."

This was, quite possibly, the stupidest thing I'd ever done. I trudged through the snow in heavy boots, too big for my feet but tightly bound at the ankle, so they weren't so terrible. Beau's jacket hung off of me like some misfit Eskimo outfit, and he paced ahead of me in the snow in cat form.

It felt weird to be doing this.

Beau had kissed me before shapeshifting, a quick, possessive kiss. "I need to be in cat form for this, sweet thing. If you see anything in animal form other than me—be it deer, skunk, or cougar—you shoot it and think about the consequences later. If anyone else is on my land, they're trespassing—so don't hesitate to shoot."

I nodded at that.

Beau in cougar form was a beautiful sight. His cat body was a long, lean buff beige covered in soft fur and thick cords of muscle. I hadn't watched him shapechange—that seemed a little personal—but when he'd finished shifting, he'd moved back to my side, his feline body enormous and a little frightening until he'd licked my hand with his raspy tongue. After that, I'd lost my fear.

Beau had circled around me once and then headed into the woods. I'd followed as silently as possible. The thick woods were pretty from a distance—like from inside Beau's cozy cabin. Snow had fallen, unusual for Texas, and the darkness was cold and dismal. I decided right then that I hated the woods.

It was eerily silent, as well. Every sound I made, every step that crunched into the snow, was overly loud. I winced every time I stepped on something, knowing that it was messing Beau up, but he simply paced through the woods on silent feet, his cat-nostrils working quietly, his breath whuffing.

We walked through the dark woods for a long

time. My toes were icy, my fingers felt frozen, and the gun was ice-cold in my grip. The odd screams had stopped, replaced by a silence that was even creepier.

We'd seen the reddish orange lick of light from the window, and I assumed that was what we were heading for. Beau seemed to be leading us in a straight line, his steps slow and easy . . . until he suddenly dashed forward.

I raced to follow him, my feet crashing through the underbrush, curses stringing through my mind.

Beau had paused just ahead, and I followed after him like an awkward penguin. We stopped at a thick stand of trees, the moonlight peeking through the leaves overhead. The snow had been a thin blanket of white covering the ground, but here it was churned and dirty. At first I thought leaves were flung liberally through the snow, but the uneven splotches were too thick and too wet to be anything but blood. I swallowed hard.

Beau paced around the campsite, his nose to the ground, sniffing. His tail lashed angrily back and forth, and I kept a bit of a distance, gun in hand. Whatever had made those big bloody spots might come back.

Minutes later, Beau circled in on one spot, digging at the bloodied snow with a giant paw. He lifted his head and looked at me, eyes gleaming greenish yellow in the darkness.

"What? You want me to come over there?"

One slow, deliberate blink. Then another.

Since he couldn't talk to me, I'd assumed that was a yes. I trudged over warily. "What is it?"

He tapped his paw at something in the snow, looking for all the world like a cat batting at a toy. I couldn't make out what it was on the ground, so I reached down with my bare hands. My fingers closed over something cool and slightly damp, cylindrical and kind of firm but spongy. "I'm going to beat you on the head if this is something gross, you realize that, right?"

His tail flicked against my leg and then he moved into the woods again.

I followed after him, mind churning. What had happened here? Some animal making a kill in the woods? Or a shapeshifter leaving a message for us?

We circled around in the woods for a good while longer, until I was no longer frightened and just weary as hell. I dragged behind Beau as he raced through the night snow, pausing to sniff the ground and circle back once again.

Nothing else attacked. Nothing else happened. It was quiet. *Too quiet*, as they liked to say in the movies.

We stumbled into a clearing and I blearily realized that we'd somehow made it back to his house. "Thank God," I said, and started forward.

Beau stopped in front of me, forcing me to pause. The cat looked up at me, flicking his tail in irritation. His head moved from side to side—was he shaking his head no at me?

"You want me to wait here?"

The deliberate double blink again. I sighed. "I'm going to assume that's a yes," I said, leaning against a nearby tree.

He nosed the hand holding the gun, his nose wet and cold. Then he disappeared into the house, tail flicking with agitation.

Right. He was reminding me to be alert. I lifted the gun and scanned my surroundings. If I saw anything, I was going to blow its head off.

Long minutes ticked by, and I glanced at the house, starting to get worried again. What was happening?

A shadow appeared in one of the windows and I sucked in a breath, pointing the gun toward it. But then Beau appeared, changed back to human form—naked again—and headed down the steps back to where I was hidden at the tree line. "Bathsheba, it's safe to come inside now."

I lowered the gun and went inside, studying my surroundings warily. Salt was all over the floor, covering the doorway. The only tracks I saw seemed to be Beau's. I turned to look at him. "What's going on?" My teeth chattered as I spoke; I hadn't realized I was that cold. Or that scared.

He shut the front door, locked and dead-bolted it, then helped me with my coat, oblivious to his own nakedness. "I think whatever has been stalking you followed us out here."

I realized I was still clutching the gun and handed it to him.

"You might want to give me that as well," he said, gesturing at my fist.

I uncurled my hand and nearly threw up. The spongy cylinder was a finger, damp with blood and shredded at one end. "Oh, God," I said, my stomach heaving, and flung it at him.

Beau snatched the object in midair and dropped it on the counter, then steered me toward the sink so I could have a nice, long vomit. And I did.

When I was done, I wiped my mouth and took the glass of water he offered. I pointedly looked away from where the finger lay. "So who does that belong to?"

"It smells like shifter," he said, grim. "Wolf."

I stiffened, finding it suddenly hard to breathe. "W-wolf?"

Wolf was not good. Wolf was not good at all.

Beau sniffed the finger. "Smells like Cash's

pack. Maybe Wade or one of his boys, if he's back in town."

"So what's a werewolf's finger doing on your property without the rest of him?" I said, gulping down water to try to calm my stomach. I knew what the wolf was doing around here.

He was looking for my sister.

But what had attacked the wolf prowling around the property?

"That is the question," Beau said. He moved to wash my sick out of the sink. Once the water ran clear, he began to clean his own hands of dirt and blood.

Seeing him wash his hands made me painfully aware that mine were filthy as well, and I shared the tap and soap with him, scrubbing at my skin. "Did you smell anyone near the house?"

"No," he said. "I only smelled you, me, and Arabella. Whoever was lurking around didn't get close to the house."

"So what do we do now? Call the police?"

"No. We wait for Ramsey to get here in the morning and see if he's heard anything else or had any other strange experiences."

I looked up at Beau, troubled. "You do realize I'm not going to be able to sleep for the rest of the night?"

"I'm sure we can think of something to do," he said.

I raised an eyebrow at him.

He chuckled. "Come on. Even I know that the last thing on your mind is sex." Beau leaned forward and pressed a comforting kiss on my forehead. "I'll play cards with you, if you want."

"All right." I glanced down. "But you might want to put some pants on first."

We played poker until three or four in the morning, both of us tense and edgy. It wasn't fun, but trying to beat the other person took our minds off of things.

After we were done with the cards, I crawled onto the couch and lay down, and Beau let me rest my head on his knee as he played with my hair. I drifted off at some point, the soft sound of his purring in my dreams.

Chapter Eleven

I awoke to the sound of voices in the kitchen. Beau's smooth tones were interspersed with an impossibly deep voice that had to belong to Ramsey. Still wiped out after last night, I dragged myself to my feet and shoved my hair back, hoping I didn't look too ragged from lack of sleep.

As I approached the kitchen, I was disappointed to see that Sara wasn't here. I was even more disappointed when both men stopped talking as soon as I entered. Rather annoying of them. They gave me polite nods. Ramsey was dressed in a flannel shirt and jeans—very lumberjack—and Beau wore his signature dark T-shirt. At least he was fully dressed.

"Sara?" I said by way of greeting. "Is she here?"

"Not here," Ramsey said in a gruff voice. "Safe."

Disappointment crashed through me, but I hid it

and pulled up a chair at the table. "All right," I said, feeling rather awkward at the moment. "Savannah?"

"Still missing," Beau said, his voice short.

Not the most cheerful of mornings, then. I managed a half smile. "Well, it's nice to see you again, Ramsey, even if it's under bad circumstances."

Ramsey just stared at me.

Even Beau looked like something was sticking in his craw. Puzzled, I shoved my hair off my face and tried to finger-comb it a little. It was a puffy snarl around my face, a cloud of blond tangles. "Something wrong?"

Beau's throat worked as he swallowed. Neither one of them said anything for a long moment, then Beau's mouth turned tight-lipped. "Nothing. I was just briefing Ramsey on the situation last night."

"Great," I said, giving up on the finger-combing as my mind set to work. "Don't mind me. I'm just going to hunt for some coffee." It would be the perfect opportunity to listen in on their conversation and find out what they thought about things, all under the guise of being sleepy and careless.

I headed around the small island. There were several large boxes on the counter. I didn't ask how Ramsey had gotten them here, though the mental image of a bear pushing a shopping cart through the forest was a funny one. I opened the first box, but Ramsey moved past me and pulled the box out of my hands, then shoved a different box in my direction.

"Thanks," I said, giving him a faint smile, determined not to let him scare me off. "I think."

Beau stiffened and turned abruptly. "I'll be outside chopping wood." He slammed the door behind him as he left.

What the hell? I blinked. "Did I do something wrong?"

"No," Ramsey said, his voice curt.

I glanced out the window, then back at Ramsey, waiting for further explanation. None came. Well, all right then. "Are you . . . just going to stay here?"

He gave me a short nod.

I looked out the window again, back to Beau. "I'm guessing that he doesn't want you leaving me alone?"

Another short nod, and Ramsey looked more and more uncomfortable, as if he hated having to converse. For some reason, that made me feel like laughing. Poor Sara, stuck with this surly man all week for company. "Well, if you're here and you're bored, you might as well help me unload."

The big man moved across the kitchen and opened the box closest to him, setting to work without a word. It seemed odd that he would take orders from me. But if he considered me Beau's woman, I guess it wasn't that weird after all.

The sound of wood chopping rang outside. It sounded rather . . . frenzied. Obsessive. I frowned and glanced at the window again. "What's bothering him?"

"Heat."

I peeked out the window, watching Beau swing the axe with grim, relentless determination. "I realize you're into the monosyllabic thing, but you're going to have to give me a bit more than that."

He continued to unload the boxes of goods, not looking at me as he responded. "You bother him. Your hair is messy with sleep. Your feet are bare. You wear his clothes. It . . . affects him."

Oh. For some reason I hadn't thought that the heat would do anything more than give him a boner. "Is he going to be like this all day?"

Ramsey gave me a level look. "You tell me."

Oh. I blushed. Maybe I liked Ramsey better when he was silent. "Er, how long does this heat thing last?"

"'Bout twenty-four hours."

Good Lord. I tried to imagine being in the bedroom with Beau for twenty-four hours, but my virgin-mind (despite all the dirty books and Cinemax I'd watched) couldn't quite wrap around it. "Oh."

He gave me a grave look. "Someone will be watching over the cabin while you are occupied."

"I . . . oh. That's nice," I said faintly. So strangers were going to be wandering around outside, knowing that Beau and I were shagging like minks inside? Oh, the embarrassment. "And Sara?"

"She is fine."

"She is," I agreed. "But is someone going to be watching over her? At all times?" The whole situation felt very surreal, unloading groceries while scary things prowled the forests.

Ramsey's eyes narrowed as he looked over at me. "I will keep her safe."

Looking at the massive man, I had no doubts of that. I nodded.

Chop chop chopchopchop—Beau was attacking that wood. I imagined his body covered in sweat, muscles rippling, and felt the sudden urge to fan myself. Instead, I kept unpacking, reaching for the next box and pulling out the contents.

He'd bought enough groceries to feed a small army. In with the staples—rice, beans, canned meat, peanut butter—I found . . . lubricant? I dropped it as if stung and stared down into the box. Accompanying the industrial-sized bottle of lube were three extra-large boxes of condoms and what seemed to be a gallon of massage oil. Good Lord. How much sex did Ramsey think we were going to have?

I shut the box hastily and pushed it aside.

By the time everything else had been unpacked,

I figured our woodpile was the size of a beaver dam.

The coffee had finished brewing and I poured myself a cup, dousing it with enough sugar and cream to make a cake. "You sure Beau is all right?" I looked out the window. "He just seems very . . ." Angry? Jealous? Miserable? "Unhappy," I finished.

Ramsey shoved a baseball cap on his head, as if he was preparing to leave. "Heat," he said again, his expression not concerned in the slightest.

"Ah." Well, if it was normal for him to be this hormonal, I'd stop worrying. "Thank you, Ramsey. I appreciate it."

Ramsey paused at the door, as if warring between the idea of staying and going. After a moment, he sighed, then glanced back at me. "Beau is our leader . . . similar to a wolf alpha. His natural instinct at the moment is to compete and dominate. Right now he is trying very hard not to come in here and attack me for being near you."

I wasn't sure which was more disturbing—the fact that Ramsey had used so many words at once, or what he was actually saying. I forced a tight smile to my face. "Thanks for the advice. And you're positive I'm safe with him?"

Ramsey gave a jerky nod, then sighed again when I continued to stare at him expectantly, as if it was bothersome to humor a human. "You are safer with him than anyone else, Bathsheba. He will not let you come to harm from anyone—certainly not himself."

Swell.

I gave him a wary thumbs-up. Ramsey nodded at me and quickly exited, as if he couldn't wait to get away. Not a chatter, that Ramsey. I heard the chopping stop, heard the two men converse, their voices low. I yearned for supernatural hearing so I could hear what they were saying. But then the chopping began again, and I peeked out the window to see Ramsey strolling away into the cold woods, his hands tucked in his jacket.

I stayed in the kitchen, making eggs, hash browns, and toast. I cooked an enormous amount of food—Beau ate a lot, thanks to his shifter metabolism. He eventually came inside, his body gleaming with sweat, his shirt stuck to his chest, his hair a damp, curling mess on his forehead.

We ate a silent, awkward meal. The heat stood between us. I remained silent, not wanting to antagonize the already touchy Beau, and he seemed content to slap his cutlery around as he ate. He thanked me for cooking, but other than that, we said little. I ate fast so I wouldn't have to linger at the table, and Beau seemed determined to do the same.

So much for romance.

After breakfast, he disappeared back outside and I showered, then dressed in the clothes that Ramsey had brought for me. Jeans and long-sleeved shirts, sweaters, and the like. Cute bras and underwear. I suspected that Sara had had something to do with that, because everything fit.

I picked the laciest, sexiest bra and underwear and put them on under my jeans and sweater. Lingerie was ammunition in the war of the sexes, and I planned on loading my guns.

Chapter Twelve

*B*eau slinked into the living room a short while later, clothing changed. "Get your coat on. We're going out."

I looked up from my book and blinked from my corner of the couch. Then I looked out the window. The unusual snow continued, coming down outside in big, fat flakes. Like any Texan face-to-face with snow, my instinct was to burrow indoors. "We're going out? Why?"

"We're going to do something romantic. To make today special. I told you I'd make this special for you, and I plan on keeping my word." He sounded irritated. Well, gee, this was an auspicious beginning.

"Sure," I said, tucking the book aside and slipping on my new sneakers. "We can go out."

He was there in moments, handing me a brand-new jacket and jamming a knit cap over my head.

I'd fixed my hair in two pigtailed braids to keep it off my neck, and I probably looked thirteen under the cap. But I allowed him to help me dress—in his mood it probably wasn't wise to stop him—and followed him as he headed into the front of the house.

A picnic basket was parked by the door. I glanced out the window again. Still snowing, quite heavily.

I looked back at the picnic basket and frowned. Did Beau really expect to have a picnic outside? But I jerked on my gloves and followed him out as he picked up the basket.

Beau wasn't wearing a jacket—I guess the cold didn't affect him like it did me. He wore a light flannel shirt and raked his hand through his hair, staring at his surroundings.

I paused behind him. "What are you looking for?"

"Nothing," he said tersely and began to plow through the fresh snow, heading to the woods.

This was going to be *so* much fun. I shut the door behind me and followed after him, zipping up my jacket.

We trudged through the snow in silence. If it hadn't been so windy, it might have actually been quite pretty outside. The snow was falling and the woods were blanketed in white, mixed with the ev-

ergreens in the distance. I was also cheered to see
that we were sticking to the clear, open areas.

If my companion hadn't been so tightly wound,
it might have been a bit of an adventure. If you ignored the blood and the finger from last night, of
course. I couldn't help but be a bit nervous today,
even in broad daylight.

"Just ahead," Beau barked at me, and I trotted
after him. My sneakers didn't exactly keep out the
snow, and my socks were getting wet. More fun by
the minute.

I nearly ran into Beau's broad back when he
slammed to a halt, and I placed my hands on his
waist to steady myself.

He jumped away as if burned. "I'll get set up."

I eyed him with frustration, then gave up. We'd
stopped at the banks of a creek that cut through the
trees. Frost and snow lined the muddy banks, and
the icy water trickled delicately over rocks. It was
very pretty.

I turned to look at Beau, who had thrown a red
blanket onto the snow. A red, heart-shaped blanket, and now he was unloading the rest of the picnic basket.

What. The. Heck.

"Come sit down," he said. He must have realized how grumpy that sounded, because a grudging "Please" followed it.

I sat down on one side of the heart, trying to ignore how cold I was. A picnic on a heart-shaped blanket was very sweet. Judging from the jagged edges of the fabric, he'd cut the blanket himself. Though, at the moment, I wished I could wrap it around me.

Beau pulled out chocolate-covered strawberries, champagne, and a pair of flutes. He popped the cork and began to pour the liquid with the grim, methodical look of a man on a mission.

Operation: Romance.

I gave him a bright smile when he handed me a glass, then I took a small sip. It tasted lovely, but it was really cold. My teeth chattered against the lip of the glass, so I opted to just hold the drink instead.

He picked up one of the strawberries with a determined look. "Shall I feed this to you?"

Was he serious? But resolute Beau was far more palatable than sulky Beau, so I ignored my discomfort. "Sure. Why are we doing this again?"

"I'm romancing you," he half-snarled. "Don't you want to be romanced?"

"No, this is fine," I hastily agreed.

He moved to my side and leaned over me. His body was radiating heat, and I immediately wanted to crawl under his shirt. My body was starting to feel like it had stopped giving off heat about ten minutes earlier. Still, he was trying hard to give me the "romance" he thought I wanted, so I smiled gamely and opened my mouth.

The strawberries were a mistake. They were like blocks of ice. Tasty blocks, but I had no desire for more. After one bite I declined the rest. "I must not be that hungry."

He lifted my champagne glass. "More to drink?"

The bitter wind seemed to bite right through my clothing. I could see little flakes of ice forming in the glass, and my jaw began to chatter again. "No thanks."

He put the glasses aside, leaning them in the snow, and moved toward me. His hands slid over my coat and I recognized the hot look in his eyes. "Your mouth is so red," he said, leaning in for a kiss.

Not blue yet? Impressive. I tilted my face toward his and his lips captured mine. Hot, warm, wet—delicious. He tasted like I wanted the champagne to be. Beau made a low noise of satisfaction in his throat, and the kiss became demanding, devouring. I loved the feeling of his mouth on mine, and I sank into the sensation. My gloves wrapped around his shoulders and I leaned into the embrace, not protesting when he pushed me backward.

Until the snow hit my lower back. I jerked and the champagne glasses flipped over, splashing onto the backside of my jeans. "Cold," I shrieked against his mouth.

He jerked away from me in surprise, glancing at the champagne flutes as I scrambled away from the wetness seeping onto my end of the blanket. My entire backside was wet, and so was the blanket—the part that wasn't covered with the drifting snow.

"Are you okay, Bathsheba?" His brow furrowed.

My teeth clattered.

"Your mouth is turning purple. Why didn't you tell me you were cold?"

"Because y-you didn't seem l-like you were open t-to f-feedback—"

He swore. "Bathsheba, don't be stupid. I have a different body temperature than you. You're going to have to tell me when you're cold."

"Fine," I gritted. "I'm cold. It's very sweet, but I think it's the wrong time of year for this."

His mouth tightened. "I'll take you back to the house."

His tone didn't make that sound like something we'd be doing together. "Are you going to stay with me?"

He shook his head. "I think I need some time away. I'm losing control and this just isn't working." He ran a hand down his face roughly. "Don't worry, I'll make sure you're home safe first."

Frustrated and too cold to argue, I stood up and flexed my fingers as he packed up the food. As he stood up with the basket, the blanket lifted off the ground with the wind and slid past me, heading for the creek bank.

I was closer to it. "I'll grab that." I moved toward the bank, my shoes sinking into the mud.

Beau was at my side within moments, trying to move past me. "You're cold and weak. Let me."

I shoved at him, irritated. "I'm human, you jerk not crippled." The blanket was just out of reach, so I took another step forward into the mud, angling my body on the steep bank to keep my balance.

I grabbed at the blanket at the same time as Beau did, and the stubborn ass jerked it out of my hands.

I lost my footing and slid down the steep bank toward the icy creek. Mud slid up my pant leg and sucked at my shoes, and I had a moment to cringe before my legs slid into the icy water.

I yelped.

Beau called my name just before my shoulder smacked against a branch, stopping my fall when I was three-quarters submerged.

Strong hands were on me before my brain could process anything besides coldcoldcoldcold. Beau lifted me out of the water, ripping off my sodden coat. "This is why you need to let *me* do things, Bathsheba," he said in a frustrated voice.

I wanted to punch him, but my entire body was quaking so hard that I couldn't even glare. "Fuck. You," I chattered. My feet were freezing, my socks icy weapons of torture. "If you had let me get it, I wouldn't be a popsicle right now."

He took off his shirt and wrapped me in it. It was warmer, but the rest of my wet clothing still clung to me like an icy skin, and my jaw chattered so hard that I thought it would fall off.

"I'm sorry, sweet thing," he said, scooping me up in his arms and tucking me against his bare chest. I burrowed close, pressing my lips against the warmth of his neck.

I was sooo going to kill him when I warmed up.

The walk back to the house felt unbearably long, with the snow coming down and my legs numbing up and my teeth clacking as if they'd been trying to escape my mouth. Beau was a blazing hot furnace and I curled into his heat as much as possible, pushing my wet chest against his, wrapping my arms around his torso and basically trying to crawl into his skin. I heard a low growl in his throat, but I didn't care. I simply wanted the bitter cold to go away.

Finally, Beau pulled his keys out of his pocket,

unlocked the front door, and then we were enveloped with warmth. I could have cried in relief, but I feared the tears would freeze on my face.

Beau set me down at the doorstep and turned to look me in the eye. His eyes gleamed greenish for a moment. "I'm going to check the house to make sure nothing is amiss, and then I'm going to come back here and build a fire. I want you to strip off your clothing and jump in the shower."

As he raced off, I hesitated, my mind dull with cold. Strip off my clothing? In front of a man—a were-cougar—obsessed with having sex with me? Cold and modesty warred for a brief moment, and then I uncurled my slow, icy fingers and peeled off Beau's borrowed shirt, worn over my wet clothing. It was now as damp as everything else.

He reappeared a few moments later, firewood stacked in his hands, and growled at the sight of me, still mostly dressed. "I'm not going to ravish you while you're dying of hypothermia."

"I know," I said in a wobbly voice, but I still couldn't seem to get moving.

Beau noticed this and picked me up in his arms, where I huddled against him as he moved to the bathroom and turned on the shower. Heat immediately blasted into the small room. "Get in there. Once you've warmed up enough to move, take your clothes off. Understand?"

I nodded, stepping inside the shower and letting the hot water run over my body, gasping at the burning warmth. It felt wonderful, and I closed my eyes and let the hot water cascade over me.

"I'm going to get the fire going," he said. "Then I'll be back to check on you."

I wished I could sink into the hot water and never come out. It felt so good against my icy skin. When I unthawed a little, I began to grow irritated at the feeling of my wet jeans against my skin—I wanted all of me under the hot water. I glanced at the doorway where Beau had disappeared—still cracked open.

Screw modesty. It wasn't like I didn't want him to see me naked at some point, right? My fingers fumbled with the zipper and button of my jeans and I managed to get them undone. I slid them down my legs and stepped out, leaving the sodden lump on the floor on the far side of the shower.

I tried pulling my sweater over my head, but my arms were too drained of strength and the sweater was too soaked. I hauled it to my neck and then got stuck, unable to grasp it properly. "Beau," I whimpered, my head trapped in the wet fabric. "Help here."

A warm body was at my side in the shower in an instant. He pulled the rest of the heavy, water-soaked sweater over my head.

I stood there in the spray of the shower, wearing nothing but lacy panties and a bra that were so wet that they left less to the imagination than my imagination did.

Beau stiffened and suddenly I felt too exposed. His eyes began to gleam in that hungry, predatory way I recognized. "You want to take those off?" he growled.

I bit my lip, deciding. "You won't look?"

"Bathsheba," he said, his voice sounding strangled. "You can't stand in front of me like that and ask me not to look."

Fair enough. I turned slightly, presenting him with my back and letting the water pound against my front. My hands went to the long, wet ropes of my braids and I pulled them forward over my shoulders. "Can you undo my bra?"

His hands slid up my back in a hot, slippery motion, the gliding caress like liquid fire. The clasp on my bra popped and his hands stroked up and down my back. I pulled the bra off and let it fall to the tiled floor. Crossing my arms over my breasts protectively, I looked at him over my shoulder. "Thank you." The words came out low, husky.

I could see that his clothes were soaking wet now. And judging from his expression, that was the last thing on his mind. His hands slid to the low band of my wet panties and then underneath, caressing my bottom. "Take these off," he said, his breath hot against my ear and neck, sending shivers through me.

As I protectively cupped my breasts, shyness overwhelmed me. I didn't want to move my hands, "You do it," I whispered, an utter thrill shivering through my body at the thought of him sliding them off my body.

His hands slid under the wet lace and began to skim that last bit of fabric slowly down my thighs and calves. His body followed, and I could feel his mouth graze the small of my back. Tingles shot through my body.

"You have the prettiest ass," he said, cupping it. "So round and soft."

I shivered at that, and he reached past me and turned the water off. "You're still cold?"

"I, uh . . ."

Within seconds, he wrapped a thick towel around me, completely blanketing my nudity. He shoved me out the bathroom door, ignoring the fact that his clothes were dripping water all over the place, and propelled me toward the fire. It crackled and blazed in the fireplace, and he sat me on the brick hearth. Before I could think, he removed my towel. A thick blanket plopped over my shoulders.

Confused, I pulled it around me, then turned around. Beau faced away from me, one white-knuckled hand clutching the mantel, his shoulders heaving.

The heat was affecting him, badly.

"Wrap up and sit there until you stop shivering," he said in a harsh voice.

Obediently, I snuggled into the blanket. It was warm and very welcome, but my heart fluttered at Beau's obvious distress. Maybe I should have told him that I was shivering due to desire?

The words clamped in my throat as he left the room, stripping off his own wet clothing. I was doing this all wrong. He wanted to seduce me, I *wanted* him to seduce me, but I couldn't seem to get things started.

When Beau reentered the room dressed in athletic pants, I stared at that golden expanse of muscled chest and my mouth went dry. He moved closer to me and I instinctively raised my face toward his. His fingers brushed against my cheek and he frowned down at me. "You're still cold. Wait here and I'll make you some coffee."

He disappeared again, leaving me vaguely disgruntled. I had been enjoying the shower so very much, and he'd turned mother hen on me. I thought of Beau's warm hands and his bare chest pressing against mine and wondered if I had the courage to ask him to get under the blankets with me.

Because oh, I really liked the sudden visual in my mind.

So what was I waiting for? Here was a ridiculously hot man that I was crazy over, who wanted to make love to me. Being shy wasn't going to help me with this.

Beau returned a few minutes later with an enormous coffee mug. Concentration furrowed his brow, but the front of his pants showed that he was still thinking about me despite the polite smile on his lips.

I shook my head when he offered the coffee mug. "My front is cold," I said, shoring up my courage.

"Turn to face the fire—"

"Then my back will be cold," I said, trying not to get peevish at him. Crap. I was really bad at flirting. I stared at his bare, delicious chest and opened the blanket a fraction, showing a hint of my bare breasts. "Would you . . . could you come under the blanket with me?" I thought my cheeks might catch on fire with the blush climbing up my face.

He stilled, those catlike eyes gleaming. "Bathsheba," he said, his voice a near groan. "I don't know if I can keep—"

"I know." I held out one corner of the blanket to him. "Come sit with me."

He put the coffee mug down and sat next to me, avoiding looking in my direction.

I slid closer to him. His eyes closed and I saw his shoulders tense. Encouraged, I let the blanket drop and placed my hands on his shoulders. When his eyes didn't open, I placed my leg on the far side of his and slid forward until I straddled him.

He leaned back against the stone and groaned.

I slid forward a little more, rocking my hips against his erection. "Beau," I said softly. "I've dropped my blanket."

He opened his eyes and looked at my face, so close to his own. Heat was burning in his eyes, dark and full of need. But he leaned over and got the blanket, tucking it around my shoulders as if I'd been a child.

Irritated, I grabbed the corners of the blanket in each hand and wrapped my arms around him. When my breasts pressed against his chest, I forgot everything except the feel of his skin against mine. My nipples ached and my pulse throbbed in my veins. I needed more.

He moved under me, his entire body tense. His hand slipped to the small of my back.

"Hold me against you," I encouraged, tucking my head against his shoulder. "You're so warm and I'm so cold."

A harmless white lie. Right now I wasn't thinking about the cold at all, but how I could get him to put his hands on me.

He sat up so that his chest pressed against mine. His hands grabbed my ass and pulled me tighter against his hips. It caused my legs to stretch a bit wider, leaving me open and bare against the bulge in his sweatpants. The fabric rubbed against my sensitive skin, sending shock waves through me with the slightest touch.

"Sweet Bathsheba," Beau said, his hot eyes devouring my face. "I'm sorry about today."

"It's okay," I said, brushing my breasts against his chest and hooking my arms behind him. He was so warm and delicious. "Though for a few minutes there, I was starting to think you were a polar bear and not a cougar."

His expression was tortured. "I wanted to give you romance."

"Romance is overrated," I said, then licked my lips. "You know what else is overrated?"

His gaze was focused on my mouth. "What's that?"

I leaned in, my tongue tasting the seam of his mouth, flirting with his. "Virginity," I whispered.

Beau's mouth pressed fervently against mine as if I'd just unleashed him. "I wanted this to be special for you and I've been doing this all wrong.

I've never slept with a virgin before. Or a human. I wanted to make this right for you."

I'd be lying if that didn't give me a thrill. I brushed my fingers along his jaw, feeling the stubble rasp against my skin. "Beau, this is going to sound terribly corny, but just being here with you feels special. I've waited twenty-five years, and I think I've waited long enough."

His response was to grab my hips and press the junction of my legs against the hard erection in his pants. The breath sucked out of my lungs and I closed my eyes, letting the sensation wash over me.

"Look at me, Bathsheba," Beau said in a low voice. "Don't close your eyes."

I opened them and gave him a shy look.

Gone was the tense Beau of the past twenty-four hours. "No need to be bashful with me," he said, his mouth curving into a slow, sexy grin. "I want to see you looking at me when I touch you."

I squirmed a little at that thought. It seemed wickedly intimate, but I didn't avert my eyes.

His hands kneaded my hips gently, his eyes skimming over my body in an intimate caress all its own. I wanted to wriggle or cover my breasts, but I forced myself to remain stock-still, my breath caught as I waited for him to make his move. He looked like a ravenous man trying to decide what delicious thing to eat first at a feast.

His hands slid onto my thighs, stroking up and down the smooth muscle. "Do you know how long I've wanted to touch you?"

My mouth quirked. "About five days?"

He chuckled and my nipples hardened in response to the vibrations in his body. "Ever since I laid eyes on you. You had such a serious expression, as if you wanted to discourage me from even thinking about touching you. And I wanted to kiss that frown right off your face." His hands went to my damp braids and began to undo them, his fingers lacing through the wet plaits until the damp hair cascaded down my back. "And right after I saw this glorious mass of hair I wanted to do this." He pulled some of it over my shoulder, letting it cover my breasts in a medieval fashion.

"And I wondered about your pretty nipples," he said, his hands sliding over my waist, skimming my ribs. "Would they be dark and pouty, like your lips? Or pale and delicate, like your skin?"

He was seducing me with words alone, and it was working beautifully. I suddenly needed to touch him, and my hands slid up his arms, feeling the cords of muscles in his triceps.

His thumbs slid forward, grazing over the tips of my nipples, rubbing my long, silky hair between his skin and mine. I gasped at the sensation, my fingers clenching against his arms. "And they're

pale, just like I imagined. Small, soft, and pink."
Rub rub—the slow motion was going to drive me
insane, twin points of madness. "I've been dreaming about these beautiful breasts for days, too."
His thumbs slid away.

I made a sound of protest. It felt so good, and
made my pulse pound hard inside my body. And
I wanted to hear more sweet talk. "What about
them?" I breathed, and fought the urge to push my
breasts back into his hands.

"How they'd feel in my hands," he said, and one
large hand clasped my left breast, teasing the nipple
against his palm in a circular motion. I gasped and
my hips rocked against his, echoing that motion.

But he wasn't finished. "How they'd look
with all this sexy hair falling over them," he said,
and brushed my hair aside, exposing the white
globes of my breasts. "And how they'd taste in my
mouth." He leaned in and brushed his lips against
the sensitive tip of my breast.

I made a strangled sound of pleasure and surprise. I hadn't expected that to feel quite so good.

Encouraged by my response, he nuzzled at my
nipple, teasing the peak with his lips and giving it a
soft, playful bite. I arched against his mouth when
he pulled away, and my hands wrapped around his
shoulders and slid to the back of his neck as I tried
to pull him back toward my breasts.

"Do you want me to touch you, Bathsheba?"

My hips rose in response.

He nipped my neck as if he couldn't stop tasting me. "Tell me what you want."

The words were shy in my throat. "I want you to . . . touch me, Beau."

His hand slid down my belly, stroking my skin. "So you wouldn't object if I touched you here?" His fingers swirled around my navel. I shook my head.

"Here?" His fingers tangled in the pale curls between my legs, and my leg muscles clenched against his again.

His hot eyes held mine, and then he looked down. "What if I touch you . . . here?" I watched as his middle finger slid past the curls and disappeared, sliding into the slick folds of flesh, open and exposed by my straddling him.

And then he touched my clit, and my brain nearly exploded. I gasped and shuddered, my fingernails digging into his shoulders and neck. "There," I gasped, my hips arching. I wanted more from those wonderfully invasive fingers.

His other hand clamped onto my hip, holding me in place, and his fingers circled my clit. I leaned forward against him, breathing hard and fast, my forehead pressed against his. He touched me lightly, fluttering over the most sensitive spot and then moving away, and I wanted to scream in frustration.

He captured my mouth, swallowed my panting into his own breath. "You're so slick and wet for me," he said, and bit at my lower lip. "You've touched yourself before, haven't you? You know just how to touch yourself and give yourself pleasure, don't you?"

I moaned in response.

"Put your hand over mine, sweet Bathsheba. Show me how to touch you to make you come."

I stiffened a little. My virgin libido wasn't quite sure how to take that. I pressed a few more kisses to his mouth, trying to change tactics. But then those fingers fluttered past the sweet spot of my clit once more, not quite hitting the mark, and I groaned, frantically kissing his mouth to show my ardor and need.

"You show me, sweet thing," he said, his fingers stilling. "Put your hand over mine. Use me."

I slid a hand over his. His fingers were damp from my body. I looked at him uncertainly, but his gray eyes were heated and he gave me a soft kiss of encouragement, his fingers wiggling against mine in that most sensitive of places. I wrapped my fingers around his hand, his index finger extended, and guided him.

The pad of his finger rubbed against the nub

of my clit, and I pressed harder with his fingers, rubbing in a quick, fast motion. I was so wet with desire that his fingers slid against me too easily, and I forced him to circle slowly, rocking my hips against his hand, increasing the friction.

"Sweet Bathsheba," he groaned, leaning forward to nip at my breast again. "God, you feel amazing."

When he kissed my breast, my fingers curled in his hair and pressed his mouth harder to my flesh as I rocked against his other hand, letting his fingers tease my clit, hard.

It was only moments before I shattered, a gasped sob choking out of me. Wave after wave of orgasm hit me and I shuddered against him as he continued to rub at my sex, even though my fingers were clenched against his and could no longer guide him.

After long moments passed, my body slowly unclenched and wound down. A hot flush crept over my face. I had just writhed on top of him like a madwoman.

"Sweet Bathsheba," he said, his voice husky. "That has to be the hottest damn thing I have ever seen."

Chapter Thirteen

*B*eau's hands gripped my hips again and he picked me up as if I didn't weigh a thing. Startled, I wrapped my hands around his neck, anchoring my body against his. He tossed my blanket onto the floor and lowered me to it, pinning me between the blanket and his hard flesh. This time, his hips ground against mine in an obvious manner, and the excitement started to build in my body again.

"You're still dressed," I said, reaching for his elastic waistband and giving it a tug. "I want to see what I'm getting out of this deal," I teased.

"You're awfully frisky now." The stubble on his face scratched against my jaw as he pressed kisses against me, and I tilted my head to give him better access to the sensitive skin of my neck. "Not shy any longer?"

"I like this," I admitted. "I like being here with

you." A mind-blowing orgasm already, and Beau's cock was still rock hard in his pants, which spoke of good things to come.

His fervent mouth moved down to my breasts, and I felt him nuzzle against one nipple again. I arched, gasping when his teeth flicked against the tip. His fingers slid to my other breast, teasing the peak there in tandem.

Beau," I gasped. "I want to see you naked." I wanted to see everything.

He sat up and reached for his waistband. "Can I do it?" I asked. He stood, pulling me up with him, then he watched me with hot eyes.

I slid my hand up and down the hard front, feeling the hot length. I wasn't the best judge of these things, but he seemed to be packing quite a wallop. "That seems . . . impressive."

He chuckled low in his throat. "Why don't you take it out and find out?"

I slid his sweatpants down his legs. My cheek brushed against his cock as I did so. I stole a peek at it as I grabbed the waistband of his underwear and gave them the same treatment.

He was magnificent.

Even though I was a virgin, I wasn't completely in the dark. I'd seen penises in art and movies and internet porn. But I didn't recall them being quite so big or firm. I slid my fingers along the darker tip.

"There's quite a lot of you here," I whispered, my fingers skating down the length of him and then back up again.

He was silent.

I glanced up at him and saw his jaw clench, as if he was trying very hard to keep control. "Beau?"

"Yes?"

I pulled a lock of hair forward and tickled the head of his cock with it. I had no idea if he'd find that sexy or not, but I enjoyed it. "What are you waiting for?"

"Waiting?" He was having difficulty speaking. His cock jerked near my fingers—fascinating.

I ran the lock of my hair up the side of his thigh and across his belly button. The man had abs that you could eat dinner off of, they were so flat. "Aren't you going to ravish me?"

He swallowed hard.

I lay back down on the blanket, fanning my wet hair out over my head in what I hoped was a seductive fashion, and the thread of control he'd been hanging onto snapped. His legs spread mine wide, and I felt the stretch of underused thigh muscles as he exposed all of me. His hands went to my folds, sliding his fingers into the most secret part of my body. I gasped at the invasive feeling and squirmed. He silenced me with a deep, longing kiss, and I felt his hips settle against mine, felt the slide of his cock against the slick juncture of my thighs. That felt . . . delicious.

He pulled back for a moment, then I felt the head of his cock nudge against me. I tensed, and the next moment, he thrust into my body in one swift stroke that felt like it broke me.

All the air sucked out of my lungs and I whimpered. It hurt.

Beau groaned low in his throat, thrusting inside me again, stretching me to the limit. I tensed against the pain. Pulling my hips up against him, he thrust into me again. There was less pain with his next thrust, replaced with a curious fullness, a pleasure/pain mix that made me ache and crave more. When he raised my hips a third time, I followed his motion.

"That's it, sweet thing. Come with me."

He thrust into me again, and there was no pain, just the delicious sensation of being filled. I squirmed underneath him, wanting more. He slowed, his fingers reaching to tease one of my nipples. "Are you all right?"

I nodded, suddenly shy at his intense scrutiny as I was impaled under him. He'd gone completely still, and I wasn't sure that I liked that. "Better than all right." I wiggled to show him my approval.

He groaned low again, grabbed one of my legs, and hooked it behind his back. The other he grabbed and pulled over his shoulder, then thrust hard.

And oh *wow*, that was nice. I dug my fingernails into his skin with his next thrust. "That was good, too," I breathed.

He thrust again. "And this?"

I moaned my affirmation.

"And . . . this?" He thrust again, and then again, the thrusts coming harder and faster, as if he was sure now that I wasn't going to break. "Sweet little Bathsheba," he said in a raspy voice, punctuating each word with a thrust. "So sexy . . . all mine."

My hands fell backward and curled into the blanket, trying to anchor into place. Our flesh slapped together hard, fast and wild. The excited pulsing grew in me again and my soft cries filled the air, mixing with his grunts as he pushed me toward the precipice again.

And then he jerked, the cords in his neck standing out, his body tensing as he came. He growled my name under his breath, his hips rotating against mine one last, wonderful time as he filled me with his release. I leaned into it, feeling vaguely out of sorts that I wasn't getting a second orgasm.

It must have been apparent on my face, because he gave me that slow, lazy smile and leaned back, his fingers sliding down to the wet curls that joined our bodies together. His fingers slid right to my clit and rubbed gently, teasing my flesh. "You didn't tell me if this was all right, too."

I writhed against him, his kisses swallowing my responses. Within moments I was crying his name, too.

Once my shudders stopped, he leaned over me and pressed a satisfied kiss to my mouth.

I stilled. "Hell."

His eyes flew open, studying me. "What?"

"Condoms." A whole box full of industrial-sized ones, still in the kitchen.

Beau looked smug. "That's cute."

I sputtered. "What do you mean, 'That's cute'? Are you fucking crazy?" The most boneheaded virgin move ever—I'd totally let myself be seduced without protection.

He brushed a stray lock of hair off my cheek. "Don't worry. It's extremely rare for a shape-shifter to make a human pregnant. Odds are that I can't make you pregnant at all."

My breath exhaled in a whoosh, and I closed my eyes. "For a moment there, I was having visions of spawning a litter in nine months."

He chuckled. "You're safe from that. Our biology's pretty much incompatible unless you carry a shifter gene. Sometimes it's latent, which is why there's a small chance. The odds would be higher if I turned you into a shifter, but even that doesn't always take."

I was silent. I knew that I had a total absence of any shifter gene in my bloodline. I was completely immune. He could bite me a thousand times and it would never take.

I didn't share that with Beau, though. It was just as well—he probably wanted children with some nice were-cat-lady. Just the thought made me clench my fingers into his shoulders possessively.

He nipped at my chin, watching my expression. "Are you mad?"

"No," I decided to distract him. "Then what's with the condoms that Ramsey brought?"

He grinned. "You never know who has diseases. Shifters are immune, remember?"

So I was the diseased one? I shoved my hand in his face and pushed him away. "Oh, very nice. You have the soul of a romantic. You and Ramsey both."

He grinned and licked the tip of my breast.

"So . . . what now?" I asked, shivering.

"Now, we take it slow."

Oh boy.

He got to his feet and reached for my hands. "Let's take a shower."

"And are you going to wash me?"

The dark look returned to his eyes. "Absolutely."

Oh, my. My pulse fluttered as I put my hand in his.

Chapter Fourteen

One of the things I liked best about Beau's rustic cabin was his anything-but-rustic bathroom. There was a glassed-in shower that was larger than every closet in my house and a sunken marble tub in the corner.

I'd given the shower a couple of runs so far, but not the bathtub, and it was more tempting at the moment. So when he took my hand and steered me to the shower, I steered him back to the tub. "Bubbles."

Beau took my cue and began to fill up the tub, adding bubble bath—a light strawberry scent that I suspected he'd bought for me. As the tub began to fill, I smiled. "Pink bubbles? Your masculinity is in grave danger, sir,"

"Can you blame a man for wanting to see you covered in suds?" His hand slid down to cup my ass.

I wiggled out of his grasp. "So what are you going to do while I take a bath?"

"Get in there with you and wash your back." He pressed a kiss to the top of my head and then climbed into the tub, sitting at the far end. It was absurd—the big, masculine were-cougar surrounded by a frothy pink bath, and I bit my lip to keep from letting a wild giggle escape.

He patted his lap and a wave of bubbles splashed the side of the tub. "Come sit here, sweet thing."

I frowned at him. "We're both not going to fit."

"That's mighty flattering of you to say so," he rumbled, his voice mixed with a low purr, "but I assure you that your luscious ass will always fit on my lap. Now get over here."

As I stood at the edge, hesitating, he grabbed me by the waist and dragged me in. I shrieked at the loss of control and the slop of water over the edge of the tub, but he didn't seem to care. He spread his legs until my butt slid between his thighs, and I felt the heat of his cock against the cleft of my ass. He wiggled a little, getting comfortable, and then his legs wrapped around my waist, pinning me against him. "See? Cozy."

I snorted at that, pushing at his knee. "I told you we wouldn't fit."

"You're too focused on what shouldn't be, you know that? Now be quiet and let me wash your hair." And with that, he dumped a handful of water on my head.

I sputtered, wiping the trickles of water out of my eyes as he did the same thing over and over again. "You realize it's going to take you a million years to wet all my hair with your little handfuls?"

The answer? A huge gush of water over my head that left my sodden hair plastered over my face. I twisted around to look at his hand, and he held a plastic pitcher in it. I could hear him chuckling. "Where did that come from?"

"I put it in here last night. All part of the big romantic day I had planned."

I heard the shampoo bottle squirt and then Beau's hands were in my hair, massaging my scalp. The scent of strawberries filled the air. "I take it you like strawberries?" I said, closing my eyes and relaxing.

I could feel the rumble of his laugh. "Not until recently. You make me think of a strawberry. Soft, sweet, and luscious."

"Flattery will get you everywhere," I teased. "Keep this up and I might let you get to third base."

"I already had my hand on third base," he said, and a bolt of desire shot through me. I grew very aware of the hard line of his cock against my bottom. The heat was still strong within him, and it gave me a little shiver of excitement.

"It's so strange," I said. "I've known you for just a week and here we are in a tub together."

"What's wrong with that?"

"I feel like we should know each other a little better," I said, wiggling my toes in the water.

Beau pressed a kiss to my neck. "That's easily fixed. So tell me about you."

I hated talking about me. Talking about me led to Sara, and there were too many secrets to keep. I scooped up a handful of bubbles and pretended to blow them off of my palm. "What's there to tell?"

"Why were you a virgin at twenty-five?"

I splashed him. "You do *not* ask a girl that."

"Fair enough," he said, chuckling. His soapy hands slid from my hair to my shoulders, rubbing the tension out of them. "It occurred to me that I don't know anything about you other than you like math and you work for Giselle. Do you have a big family?"

"Sara's the only one I claim." I kept my answer short and breezy. "What about you? Family?"

"Yes." His fingers ran up and down my back in a relaxing motion. "But we're talking about you right now. Your parents are dead?"

I sighed. "One is."

Those magical hands resumed their kneading, and I wanted to lean in and let him do that for hours. I sighed in bliss.

"Out of contact with them?" he asked in a low, easy voice.

"You could say that," I admitted. "I haven't seen my dad in ten years." When his fingers didn't pause, I decided to tell him just enough to get him off my case. "My birth mother died not long after I was born, and my dad married Sara's mom when I was three. She didn't like me much—Sara was still a baby and my dad left almost as soon as the honeymoon was over. He drove a truck for a living, so he was gone a lot, and after a while he just stopped coming home. I took care of Sara when we were kids. When my stepmom wasn't at one of her jobs, she was piss-drunk. So I learned how to keep house and take care of things early. I did the laundry, I went grocery shopping, I went to Sara's teacher-parent meetings. I did everything for Sara."

His hands had stilled on my back.

Sara's drunk of a mother wasn't able to understand what happened to Sara. When she saw her daughter turn into a wolf, she went after her with a frying pan. And when I saved Sara from that, her mom tried to turn Sara over to the police for being a monster. Luckily they were familiar with drunk Mrs. Ward and her stories, so they dismissed her

tales of her werewolf daughter. The betrayal devastated Sara. I was perfectly happy never to see
that awful woman again.

I picked up another handful of suds, staring at
it blindly. "Sara's always been everything to me."

He began to pour water over my hair. "Is that
why you put her ahead of your own needs?" He
didn't sound like he was judging.

"Mmm."

"And is that why you don't date?"

I shifted in the tub, uncomfortable. "Can we
talk about something else?"

"I'm curious. You're lovely, smart, and delicious. Why weren't you snatched up by some
human long ago?"

I gave him a scowl over my shoulder. "Can you
drop it? Maybe I just don't like to be touched."
I always worried about Sara's scent every time
someone touched me.

His hands stilled on my back. "Do you want me
to stop touching you?"

I sensed the tension in his body, and I knew
that if I said a word otherwise, he'd never touch me
again unless I asked for it.

"Actually," I said, sliding a hand down the
thigh pressed against my side, "I like it when *you*
touch me. I don't want you to stop."

His hands skimmed down my spine, making

me shiver. "That's very good, because I have no desire to stop."

"So what about you? How was your home life?"

"Remember, I told you that my dad was the leader of the Russell clan—he actually started it. Between that and the multiple jobs he held down, he was rarely at home. Since I was the oldest, it was up to me to take care of the family. My father was always picking up stray members of the Alliance without homes and setting them up someplace they could be safe. It was a loose clan, even if we didn't have an official designation. Were-badgers and were-eagles and all kinds of creatures. It was a rough time for a supe on their own: they had to pay protection to the vampires or the wolves. So if you weren't lucky enough to be born into a clan, you had a hard, poor life. My father wanted to stop that, and he came pretty close."

Only close? The Russell clan seemed well established, so that surprised me. "He didn't succeed?"

Silence. Beau poured more water through my hair, rinsing it off. "When I was in high school, my father stepped into a fight between my best friend and Savannah. My friend had hurt her, and he thought it was his right as a male to claim a female. My dad disagreed. JT ripped out Dad's throat." A pause filled the air, and I wondered if I should speak. But Beau continued. "So Dad didn't get a chance to finish achieving his dream."

I hurt with sympathy for Beau. "What did you do?"

He clipped my wet hair atop my head and squirted body wash across my shoulders. "The only thing I could do. I challenged JT for the right to lead our mismatched clan, and I won. And then I exiled him. And spent the next twelve years getting everyone's shit together. Went to college, got my business started, and got this place out here for quiet time. I set up the Russell clan as a corporation, and others came to us for protection. As an Alliance, we have enough power to withstand the bullying from the vampires and werewolf packs. Now loners don't have to worry about seeking protection—they have the Alliance looking out for them. We've grown stronger every year, and now we've got a major toehold in the supernatural world. It's come a long way."

He sounded genuinely proud, not resentful of the fact that he'd had to pick up the pieces his dad had left behind. I knew what it was like to put your own dreams on hold to care for others. I'd wanted to leave home and go to a college as far away as I could. But when Sara's boyfriend had bitten her, it had changed our lives. I'd given up a full university scholarship because Sara hadn't been able to come with me. Six years later, our lives still revolved around keeping her safe.

"Your path was decided for you by family. Did you ever want something different?" I asked.

He rubbed the wash across my shoulders, then down my arms. "Never. The clan is mine. I built it up." His slick hands slid around my front, palming my breasts, and I gasped at the twin flickers of sensation as he stroked his thumbs across my nipples.

I leaned back against his chest, arching under his hands with a soft moan of pleasure.

One of his hands strayed down my stomach, leaving a sudsy trail. His breath tickled my ear. "How do you like your bath?" His fingers circled my belly button.

Warmth flooded through me. As his other hand circled and teased my nipple, I pressed back against him, gasping. "I like it," I admitted, blushing.

"We'd better finish washing you," he said in my ear, his voice husky, "before the water gets cold." His hand slid down to the curls at the juncture of my thighs. One thick finger slid against my sex, and I bit my lip as he searched for just the right spot.

A delicate brush, and then a rocketing sensation as he found it, his finger swirling around the sensitive spot. "Nice and slick," he murmured, kissing my neck. My hand slid down to cover his, unsure if I wanted him to stop the tormenting pleasure or to press him to do it harder.

"I need to make love to you again, sweet Bathsheba," he said, licking the sensitive skin of my neck between words. "I'll be careful if you're too sore." His teasing fingers slid through my folds, delving lower, and one finger slid inside me.

I inhaled sharply, rearing back against him. It stung a little, but the initial discomfort was soon replaced by startling pleasure. "Not too sore. Should we get out of the tub?"

Beau's legs untangled from around me, and he grasped me by the waist and moved me onto his lap. Then he ran one hand down my thigh and lifted my leg over the side of the tub. He did the same with the other leg, lifting it over the other side, and I sucked in a breath, a little startled—and turned on—at how open I was.

His hand slid between my legs again, teasing my parted flesh, and my hips bucked as he circled my clit. "Tell me if anything hurts you, Bathsheba. You're still sensitive." His hands slid under me, lifting me slightly, and I held on to the edge of the tub as he tilted me forward. Then I felt his hard cock nudge between my legs and I sank down on his body.

I felt tight, stretched. Delicious. "Feels so good," I panted, encouraging him.

He thrust with the barest hint of movement, but I felt it down to my toes. I moaned in pleasure at the sensations that rocketed through me, trying to imitate his motions. His hand slid down my front again, plucking at my nipples as he thrust again, slow, precise.

"Not going to last for long," he said, his breathing harsh. "So sweet and tight . . . so damn hot."

His hand slid between my legs and he rubbed my clit hard with his next thrust, and I shattered. A high, keening cry came out of me as the orgasm swept over me, his fingers dancing over that hot spot as he thrust again, and then again and again, the movements smaller but sharper and more frequent. He bit at my shoulder again, thrusting hard, and I heard a feline snarl. He growled my name, and came inside me again, pressing down hard against my hips and grinding my flesh into his. My shoulder hurt where he'd bitten me, but it was so overwhelming that I didn't care. I simply clung to him, my fingers wrapped in his hair, as his body subsided against mine.

Both of us were panting when his tongue rasped against the sensitive spot of my shoulder where he'd bitten me. It was rough like a cat's, and

I froze at the odd sensation. He continued licking my shoulder, and I winced.

"I'm sorry, sweet thing. I bit you. Fuck." He sounded angry with himself. "I lost control."

Sure enough, he'd bitten me hard enough to break the skin. A set of bite marks circled the white flesh of my shoulder; I'd probably be bruised in the morning.

And I found I didn't care. I smiled. "That's all right. It's not like you can turn me into a were-cat if you don't break the skin."

He stilled. "How do you know?"

Oops. I couldn't tell him that it was personal experience, that I was immune to turning. "I think Giselle mentioned it once," I said casually.

"Bathsheba," he said in a low, serious voice. "When we're together, you have to tell me if I'm hurting you. With the heat . . . I . . . I can't control myself very well." The hard, raspy note was back in his voice, and I felt him stirring against me again.

Already?

It excited me, even through my exhaustion. I wiggled against him again, delighted that I could cause him to lose his mind like that. "I like what you do to me, Beau."

He pressed his forehead against my shoulder. "Let's give this a few minutes." He seemed to be trying to compose himself.

But I liked the wild, untamed Beau. I was disappointed when he lifted me out of the tub and set me on my feet, our bodies sliding apart and leaving me with a sudden jab of loneliness. As I moved to the long counter where our towels lay, a glance in the mirror showed that Beau was still in the tub, his eyes closed. I frowned.

I toyed with my long hair and let it fall down my back in a damp cascade, the wet ends teasing the small of my back. "Would you dry my hair for me, Beau?" My voice sounded breathy and excited. His eyes opened and I ran my hand through the long, tangled strands, then deliberately leaned over the counter, my ass in the air, and glanced at him over my bitten shoulder.

I heard that same leonine snarl, and fast as lightning, Beau was across the room. He pressed me against the counter, my stomach sliding along the cool marble, and his hot, thick cock rammed into me from behind, hard and delicious. I cried out in surprised pleasure and Beau plunged deep, hard, and fast, and his hand clamped down on my shoulder, holding me against the counter as he pumped over and over again.

As I spiraled toward the newest orgasm, I wondered if I'd last until morning. And when my body stiffened with pleasure and I cried out his name, I decided that I didn't care.

Chapter Fifteen

Several hours, seventeen climaxes, and a brief nap later, I pulled Beau's discarded shirt over my head and went down to the kitchen for a drink. Beau was sleeping upstairs, his movements restless. I suspected that he'd wake soon and we'd go for another exhausting, wonderful round of sex. He'd woken me up twice during the night, his body demanding more in a wordless call that I was happy to answer.

My entire body was deliciously sore and my hair had long ago formed a mass of snarls that framed my face. I shoved it out of the way as I filled a glass with tap water, then squinted at the bright sunlight pouring through the window as I drank. I was wrecked. Happy, but wrecked.

There was a small red box on the counter, about the size of a book. A jaunty white bow covered the top and there was a tag on the cover. *For Bathsheba. You can do my books anytime, sweet thing.*

I lifted the lid and laughed at the calculator inside. A small ten-key, complete with rolls of tape in pastel colors. My name ran along the side of the calculator in alphabet stickers.

It brought tears to my eyes and I dabbed at them, feeling like an idiot and yet unable to stop smiling.

No one had ever bought me presents. My stepmother had rarely remembered, and when we'd had money, everything had gone to Sara. I'd been lucky to get hand-me-down clothing from neighbors. Never a present just to put a smile on my face.

I lifted it out of the box and held it to my breast, feeling absurd. I was about to bawl over a calculator. *This is the part where you separate sex from love, idiot*, I told myself, and put the calculator down. I couldn't afford to get attached. I couldn't.

Beau's cell phone lay on the counter, and on a whim, I picked it up and called the office.

"Midnight Liaisons, this is Ryder. How can I make your Afterlife?"

"Very cute," I teased her, my mood light and sunny. "New company slogan?"

"Just trying out some new ideas," she agreed. "Wow, you sound happy. Things going well with the dates?"

"Just one date," I said. "And yes, going really well. How are things in the office?"

"Good, good," she said in a bored voice. "Got a few new vampires this week, a faerie prince looking for hot changeling action, and a random assortment of shifters. Business as usual."

"And Sara?" I said in a casual voice. "Has she been in?"

"She came to pick up her check when Giselle wasn't in, but other than that, she's been out of the office," Ryder said, and I could hear the loud banging of her fingers on the keyboard as she typed. She always typed as if she were attacking the computer. "She came in with the new boyfriend, too. I had no idea she liked 'em so scary."

She must mean Ramsey. "The big guy? Blond hair? Kind of scowly?"

"That's him," Ryder agreed. "I swear I can't picture the two of them together, because she's so tiny and he's gargantuan, but he was hovering over her like she was some delicate flower that needed to be shielded from the world. Which was kind of sweet to see."

That made me uncomfortable. Did Ramsey have a thing for Sara? Or was he simply being diligent because he knew she was the wolf everyone was looking for and didn't want her to get away?

I changed the topic back to office work. Ryder and Marie were happy to pick up the extra shifts and the additional money, but Ryder confessed she would be happy to have me back because she couldn't seem to make the ledgers balance.

"I guess I could ask Giselle," Ryder said uncertainly. "She's been in the office all day."

"Oh?" I said. That seemed unlike Giselle. Weekends weren't really her thing. "What's she up to?"

"I'm not sure," she said. "Some project with the werewolf packs? She's pulled every single file that we have on the wolves and has been holed up with them."

My entire body went cold.

Giselle wasn't playing around—if I wasn't going to date all the weirdos she had lined up for me, she was going to sell Sara out to the nearest pack. Any traces of happy contentment in me disappeared.

All I wanted was to crawl back into bed with Beau and kiss him until he pulled me close again, but I couldn't. My only choices were getting out of town or holding up my end of Giselle's deal.

I sighed heavily. "Ryder, I need a favor. Did Beau Russell leave a home address on any of his files?" I waited as she banged on the keyboard.

"Nope, nothing. There's an emergency contact number," she said. "Want it?"

"No, that's okay."

As soon as I hung up, I flipped through Beau's

apps on his phone. Sure enough, there was GPS—
which meant I now had a ticket out of Beau's
cabin.

In no time I was hiking through the woods, using
the GPS to guide me. After a while I came out to
the road and a small locked garage and mailbox. I
pulled out a magazine and noted the address, then
called Ryder back, asking her to pick me up.

It took another hour or two before she arrived,
the time ticking by endlessly, with me positive that
Beau would show up and drag me back to his cabin
for more lovemaking. When Ryder's red pickup
pulled up, I was actually a little disappointed that
it hadn't happened.

We drove back to the office in silence. If she
thought I looked like a mess wearing Beau's shirt
and workout pants, my hair in a snarled ponytail,
she was too tactful to say anything. As soon as we
got in the office, I went straight to Giselle's office
and shut the door behind me.

The siren gave me a tight smile, her sharp blue
eyes scanning me with barely veiled anger. "Well,
well, well. Look what the were-cat dragged in."

"Hello, Giselle," I said, calm on the outside.

She gave me a disdainful look. "It's obvious
that it's too late for any sort of discussions." She

crossed her arms over her generous chest. "Do you know how much shit you're in?"

"No," I said, sitting down across from her. "But I'm sure you'll tell me."

She stared at me as if I'd grown another head. "This lip of yours. I don't like it."

I'd always been submissive and quiet before, and my mouth twisted in a wry smile. For some reason, her superior attitude now irritated me instead of frightening me. Maybe being with Beau had bolstered my courage, or maybe there was so much other crap happening that I didn't have time to worry over her. At any rate, it was a refreshing feeling.

"I'm here to tell you that I didn't forget about our deal," I said. "You're not going to touch my sister."

"Our deal?" She sneered the words. "Does your pathetic little human brain recall that the deal was for a human *virgin*? Then as soon as I turn around, you go into hiding and bang the first shifter who sticks his hand in your panties!"

I decided that I'd try to be the adult one about this. "It's not what you think, Giselle."

"No?" She leaned forward, eyes glittering with animosity. "Tell me what it is, then, because it seems to me that we had a bargain and you broke your end, which means I don't have to pay attention to my end of the deal."

"Someone broke into my house and tried to kill me."

Giselle snorted.

"It's true." I detailed what had happened—the terrible stench of the creature, the attack, its strange appearance. As I spoke, Giselle's mouth compressed into an even thinner line of disapproval.

"So how is it that you decided to go stay with Mr. Russell? I assume that is where you went." She slid her fingers along her desk, absently flicking away a speck of dust.

He kidnapped me, I wanted to say. It was the truth and it'd get me off the hook, but at Beau's expense. I didn't want to do that to him, not after he'd been so good to me. So I fudged it a little. "He asked me to go—to spend his heat with him. I agreed."

"I see," she said in a surprisingly calm voice. "So you decided to have sex with him despite our agreement that would keep Sara safe?"

I swallowed. "That's right." When it didn't sound convincing enough, I added, "I was blinded by passion."

She gave me an odd look. "Well, you're of no use to me now. You're not a virgin. His bites are all over your neck."

I clasped my hands over my neck to hide the incriminating marks. "No one has to know but us."

She quirked an eyebrow at me.

"I can fake it. I don't plan on sleeping with any-one else, so I'll just smile and blush and we can keep telling them that I'm a virgin. Nothing has changed."

She made a small noise in her throat and shrugged, clearly mollified but trying to hide it. "You'd do that? What about Mr. Russell?"

My heart was aching as I said, "If he wants to see me, he'll have to go through the service."

Giselle's smile bloomed, a thing of beauty. "Good. I'll line you up some dates, and we'll jump right back into business."

I gave her a wan smile and stood up to leave. "Sounds good."

"Oh, and Bathsheba," she said as I turned to go. "If you break another date with one of my clients, I'm selling your sister to the Anderson wolves. I hear they're looking for another female for their pack. Eight wolves and only one female to relieve their urges. I told them I'd help out any way I could. . . . Understand?"

I swallowed hard. "I understand."

I thought longingly of Beau all day. It made mat-ters worse when I pulled into my driveway and saw a tall, leonine man with brown hair waiting in a sports car in the driveway. To my intense disappointment, it was another Russell were-cougar. Jeremiah had an easy smile and relaxed manner as he explained that Ramsey had insisted he keep watch over the house. I let him have the guest bedroom.

The evening passed agonizingly slowly and I stared at Beau's phone. I could give it to Jeremiah and tell Beau I never wanted to see him again. But for some reason, I couldn't bring myself to hand over the phone. I went to sleep with it on my bedside nightstand.

It was no surprise that Beau invaded my dreams. They were wicked dreams, too. I dreamed that I lay in bed and he pulled the covers off my body, his hands warm as they skimmed the thin cloth of the nightgown. The long fabric had bunched up around my legs and he knelt between them, kissing my stomach through the fabric and murmuring soft words that I didn't understand. In my dream, his eyes gleamed like a cat's just before he ducked his head and I felt his mouth on the apex of my thighs, seeking that one perfect spot and scoring. My breath caught in a shudder and my thighs clenched as I stirred. Warm hands grasped my hips, holding me steady, and a hot tongue drew circles around the sensitive flesh.

I wasn't dreaming.

My outrage changed to a moan of desire as he hit just the right spot and an orgasm began to rocket through me, my legs clenching and my body shattering as his tongue worked its magic.

"Sweet Bathsheba," Beau said, and I felt his breath whisper against my flesh. "You taste wonderful. I thought about doing this to you all day."

I sat up, my hips banging against his nose, and he groaned in pain. I pried his hands off my thighs and scurried to the far side of the bed. "Beau! What are you doing here?"

My traitorous heart gave wild thumps of joy, and my legs still quivered with pleasure.

He sat back on his haunches, rubbing his nose. "I should ask you the same question. Bathsheba, why did you leave? It's not safe."

I couldn't explain it to him. I shook my head, tugging my nightgown down. I wanted to be mad at him, but more than that, I wanted to fling myself into his arms again and kiss him, press his hot skin against my own. "How . . . how did you get in here?"

Beau glanced toward the window. "I climbed the trellis to the window. You should make sure that you lock the windows from now on."

How dare he sound mad at me? "One of your brothers is in the guest bedroom," I said, my face coloring. Oh God, had I been moaning in my sleep? What had Jeremiah heard?

"So that's how you got back to the city," Beau said, spotting his phone and moving to the side of my bed. He grinned at me. "Clever thing."

As he approached, I slid my legs over the side of the bed and went in the other direction. I needed to keep space between us. My legs still felt like Jell-O after his wake-up call, and my body ached for a repeat performance. "Beau, stay away from me."

He stilled on the bed. "Bathsheba, tell me what's wrong. Did I hurt you last night? Frighten you?"

"Nothing like that," I said. "Last night was . . . fine." Terrific. Mind blowing. Amazing. I couldn't tell him that, though, or he'd never leave.

His frustration was evident in the tense set of his shoulders. "Then what is it? Something's obviously bothering you; I just want to know what's happened." His eyes gleamed in the darkness, just like in my dream, and it started an involuntary pulsing in my blood. "It's Giselle, isn't it? Is she blackmailing you somehow?"

I kept silent. I couldn't expose Sara's secret.

"Giselle is a bad person, Bathsheba. She uses people." He moved toward me and knelt beside the bed. "Let me help you."

"You can't help me, Beau," I said, my voice quiet with pain. "Please go. I don't want to have this conversation anymore."

"Bathsheba—"

"Please, Beau, just go. If I could be with any-one, it'd be you. But I can't be with anyone, so please . . . just leave me alone."

He reached out to touch my cheek, but when I turned away, he pulled back as if burned. His voice softened. "I'm going to find out what Giselle has over you, and I'm going to change it. I've claimed you. And when a member of the Alliance marks a woman as his, nothing had better stand in his way."

He stalked to the far side of the room and slid out the open window. I heard his feet thud as he hit the pavement below, and then nothing.

The next day Giselle had me back at work, dressed in an outfit that she'd picked out: a pink turtleneck and long skirt. "Got to cover up the bite marks," she said. "You don't want anyone seeing that Beau has claimed you." Her mouth thinned. "Repeatedly."

Her words brought a hot blush to my face, and I recalled waking up with his face planted between my thighs last night.

I poured myself another cup of coffee and sat down at my desk. It was covered in papers, cases that needed to be matched, client profiles to up-date.

Marie from the night shift sat at Sara's desk. She had headphones on and softly sang off-key to a Bon Jovi song as she worked at her computer. I would have smiled if I'd had anything to smile about.

Instead, I just felt like crying.

My email inbox was full as well. I picked through the messages, clicking past client emails. Beau had emailed me at 3:00 a.m., and I deleted it without reading it. Cold turkey was the best method for dumping an ex . . . and healing a broken heart.

I also had four emails from Jason Cartland. They were simple, conversational, charming. One read, *Had a great time on our date. Looking forward to the next.* The next said, *Heard that you were sick—let me know if you need me to drop by. I make a mean chicken noodle.*

I smiled faintly at that.

Another email popped into my box as I was reading. Jason again? I tamped down the twinge of annoyance. *Lunch?* It read. *You look beautiful in that turtleneck. Not a bit under the weather.*

In shock, I looked up from my computer screen and saw him in the office waiting area, BlackBerry in hand. He grinned and waved it at me, and I was struck anew at how handsome he was—and how completely different he was from Beau. Beau's face was rugged, sexy with hard lines that made his playful smiles all the more thrilling. The angular planes of a Roman soldier who knew what he wanted and took it with force.

Jason was his opposite. His features were refined, perfect—his nose hadn't been broken in bar fights, and he probably used product on his hair. His gray suit was impeccable, and he wore a light pink tie that added a playful note to his suit . . . and just happened to perfectly match my turtleneck.

I glowered at Giselle's door, then gestured for Jason to come in.

"I didn't see you out there," I said, wincing when it came across as surly. The scent of his thick Old Spice put me in an immediate bad mood.

He gave me a dazzling smile. "I heard you were sick. I hope you're feeling better?"

I nodded and gestured at one of the nearby seats. "I'll live." In reality, I wanted to crawl into bed and never come out again. But Jason wouldn't want to hear that, so I feigned a smile and pretended nothing was wrong, like I always did.

"I'm glad." He leaned over my desk, took my hand, and kissed the palm, his eyes on me.

Resisting the urge to rip my hand out of his, I gave him a tepid smile.

He released me and took a chair directly across from my desk. "I heard you were back and thought

I'd see if you were interested in picking up where we left off. I promise not to bite, unless asked."

A date? Right now? The thought made me want to cry.

"Can we take a rain check on that?" I said, trying to smile and failing miserably. "I'm still not a hundred percent." I sat down at my desk and opened his file, paging through the documents. "I'm sure we can find you someone else if you're lonely. I know a great harpy—"

He reached across the desk and took my hand again, and the heavy scent of his cologne met my nostrils. "I don't want anyone else," Jason said, all sultriness, his eyes intense. "I want you to spend time with me so we can get to know each other better, and so I can wipe that sad look off your face."

I pulled my hand out of his uncomfortably. I hated the touching. But he was such a nice guy that I felt like a bitch. "Jason, I don't know . . ."

Giselle strolled into the office, a tall Starbucks in her hand. Her lovely face lit up at the sight of him. "Jason, dearest. How are you?" She moved to his side and he stood to greet her. They exchanged a quick kiss on each cheek in the European way. "What brings you here today?"

"I can't get Bathsheba out of my head." His white smile flashed across his face. "I thought I'd see if she wanted to go out on a date tonight."

Giselle gave me her most delighted expression. "A date? How lovely of you. Poor Bathsheba has been in such a slump lately." She gave me a pointed look. "Isn't it thoughtful of him to come by?"

I was beginning to suspect she had engineered this little "surprise" visit. "Very thoughtful," I said, forcing an equally fake smile. "A date will be fine."

Chapter Sixteen

I made a quick stop home on my lunch hour.

Sometime during the day, a cleaning crew had stopped by and the house smelled of furniture polish and lemon-scented cleaner. It was just like Beau to send in a crew to take care of things. A small part of me was disappointed that the Russell clan was no longer staked out here, but maybe I didn't matter anymore.

I didn't have time to dwell on my hurt, though. I grabbed a change of "date" clothes and returned to work, dreading my date with Jason that evening. Giselle had scheduled it at a fancy French bistro.

The afternoon dragged by. The only thing to break it up was a quick meeting with Giselle; apparently Garth the naga wanted to see me again, despite the fact that I'd ditched him.

Giselle was thrilled and scheduled it for the

next night. "Leave all your nights free," she crowed. "Business is going to be better than ever."

I managed to keep a polite smile on my face.

My dark mood blackened further when I went into the bathroom to change clothes and noticed the scent of strawberries mixed with roses, which immediately made me think of Beau. On a hunch, I opened the wastebasket and peered inside. Sure enough, a bouquet of beautiful red roses and a pretty container of chocolate-covered strawberries had been thrown in the trash. I picked the card out of the garbage and saw my name on it.

Damn Giselle. I'd have liked to have seen my present before she'd thrown it away.

I changed into a light gray sweater dress with opaque tights for my date with Jason. I'd found one of Beau's love bites on my calf, and the sight of it had made me blush (and get hot at the same time), but my skirt hadn't been quite long enough to hide it, so I'd had to change clothes before my date. The new ensemble itched, but it covered me from ear to toe, and that was important.

Giselle had seen the love bite, as well. She'd not been amused.

Jason was all boyish charm that evening, and I

could tell he was out to impress me. He bought expensive wine, he told funny anecdotes about banking, and he encouraged me to talk. He was one of those touchy-feely types, too. He'd reach across the table and touch my hand, and I imagine any other woman would have been dazzled at the display of affection.

It annoyed the hell out of me. I pulled my hand away every time he reached out to touch it. For once the blushing virgin act did me a favor.

"Shall we go dancing?" he suggested as he handed the waiter his credit card and I toyed with my cherries jubilee. "There's a great salsa club downtown that I can get us into."

Salsa dancing? Shoot me now. "I have two left feet," I admitted.

His white smile flashed again. "So modest. I thought all women liked dancing," he teased.

The thought of dancing with Jason made my stomach lurch. Maybe it was because I'd be so close to him that his cologne would smother me. "Perhaps we'd better end the evening. I'm not feeling so well." It wasn't a lie; His heavy, musky cologne had become choking after ten minutes.

He looked crestfallen. "Is it me, Bathsheba? Have I done something to offend you?"

Great, now I felt like a monster. "It's not you," I said, forcing myself to reach across the table and grasp his hand to reassure him, because I knew he'd appreciate the gesture. "I'm just . . . not in a great place tonight."

Or tomorrow. Or ever again.

He gave me an understanding look, and his hand squeezed mine. "I totally understand." He accepted the bill from the waiter and signed his name without looking at the tab, then added several large bills—more than I'd spent at the grocery store in the past month—as a tip. "I recognize when my date's too distracted to concentrate on dinner."

Maybe it was the three glasses of wine or the soft, understanding tone of his voice, but I smiled at him. "You can see right through me."

Frankly, I was just relieved our date was coming to an end. I couldn't wait to get away from him. I let him tuck me into his nice, bland, champagne-colored Lexus and him drive me back to the office.

At least, I thought we were going back to the office. When we pulled up to a huge electronic gate with the initials JTC wrought into the ironwork, I gave him a suspicious look. "Why are we going to your place?"

"It's entirely innocent, I assure you," he said. "I thought you might like a coffee and maybe watch a movie. The evening is still early."

He had a point, and I forced myself to calm the unease that skittered through me. If he dropped me off too quickly, Giselle's radar would be on alert. "All right. Though I'm not really in the mood for coffee."

Jason grinned. "Wine, then. Giselle told me you're a fan of reds."

I forced a tight smile. "Great." I really hated Giselle sometimes.

Jason smoothly steered up the long, winding driveway and I tried not to let my jaw drop as we parked. Jason owned a veritable palace. Versailles, American style. Built as an old-fashioned planta- tion house, it had twenty-four windows along the front, and that was just the porch area. His house probably had well over a dozen rooms, each one grander than the last. The outside was rather spectacular, as well. Pretty columns supported the arching roof, and ivy wrapped around the col- umns.

Holy crap. Jason had *money* money. "When you said you were in banking, I thought you meant loans," I said.

He nodded at the servant who opened my car door, letting me out. "I do loans," he said agree- ably.

"No," I corrected. "I thought you were the paper-pusher. The monkey who writes down the

info. You're the freaking monkey with the money!"
I gestured at the house. "Holy crap."

He gave a boisterous laugh and came around
to my side of the car, tucking my hand in his arm
in an old-fashioned manner. "You're still wrong,
though."

I let him lead me in. Holy crap, was that a crys-
tal chandelier? "I'm wrong about what?"

"Not a monkey," he said affably. "A cougar."
His eyes gleamed green at me, sizing me up in blatant fashion.

A shapeshifter joke, maybe, but it still freaked
me out. "Figure of speech," I said faintly. "I was
kidding."

He grinned. "I like it when you tease me."

Oh, boy. I gave him an awkward smile.

Jason led me into the den, his hand moving
to the small of my back. A massive plasma TV
covered one wall of the study, and lines of DVDs
trimmed the walls instead of books. Speakers were
mounted in every corner of the arched ceiling. The
man liked his toys.

Suddenly he turned me around and pulled
my body up against his. "'Sheba," he breathed.
His fingernails dug into me, pricking through my
clothing and breaking the skin. "I've been thinking about how sexy you look all night."

I could feel a drop of blood slide down my wrist

and I twisted my hands, trying to shove him away. "Jason, let go! Your claws—"

He released me immediately. "I'm sorry," he said, breathing hard as he stared at me. "I don't know what came over me." He reached into a pocket and offered me a handkerchief.

Well, don't let it come over you again. I dabbed at my wrist. The blood was just a trickle, and it dried up within moments. I thanked him for the handkerchief, then hesitated. Should I throw it away?

Jason extended a hand and gave me a rueful smile. "Here, let me take care of that for you."

I handed it to him.

He turned his back and his shoulders hunched, and he didn't move for a moment. I leaned to the side, trying to see what he was doing. Was he . . . sniffing the bloody handkerchief?

My weirdo radar went off.

Jason moved across the room and tossed the handkerchief in the trash, and I wondered if I'd imagined the whole thing. He reapproached me, stalking me like I was his prey. I took a step backward, my body pressing against the wall. My breath disappeared in a gasp as he pulled me against him. His arms anchored my body against his and he bent to my neck, pushing my collar down and feverishly laving kisses on my skin.

"Jason!" My hands pushed his shoulders—

the man was impossible to budge. "What are you doing?"

His hands slid down to my ass. "Let me wipe him from your mind, Sheba," he breathed against my neck, his tongue sliding over my skin. "You're so beautiful, and sexy—"

I squirmed, trying to get away, and managed to slide out of his grasp. "Jason, what the hell?"

He stiffened, staring at me in shock. His eyes flicked to the weird cat gleam, then back again. "Your neck . . ." His nostrils flared.

Shit. I'd forgotten all about Beau's rampaging marks all over my skin. Not that I'd expected to be mauled by my current date. I straightened my high collar and gave him an insulted look. "There's nothing wrong with my neck."

"I thought you were a virgin." There was a dangerous note in his voice.

My face turned bright red. "I'm a virgin, not a nun." I was counting on his not trying to check the virginity thing for himself.

Jason stared at me with hot eyes for a moment longer, then shook himself. "Forgive me. I was . . . overcome."

"I should leave."

"No," he said, and the look in his eyes became soft and pleading. "Please. We'll just talk. I promise. I'm sorry."

I wavered, flustered. "I . . . I suppose."

Smiling with relief, Jason showed me to a plush leather chair in the entertainment room. As I sank into the seat, he said, "I need to make a couple of calls. Can you give me a moment?"

He was *leaving* me here? When I didn't want to be here anyway? I tried to hide my annoyance and exhaustion. "Look, Jason, we can do this some other time—"

He put his hands on my shoulders, and my eyes watered at the heavy smell of his cologne. "No, please, 'Sheba."

Why did I find his stupid nickname for me so irritating?

"I promise I won't be long," he continued. "And then we can get to know each other better." His eyes were pleading, and his thumb brushed against my shoulder as if he could convince me the more he touched me. "I want you to stay."

He seemed to want it rather desperately.

How long it would take for him to tattle to Giselle if I left? "Sure," I said after a moment's hesitation. "But I can't stay too late. I have work early . . ."

He winked at me in a way that screamed total cheese. "I won't keep you out too late, I promise. Let me have one of the servants bring you some wine while I make my calls."

Servants? How very posh of him.

Jason disappeared, leaving me alone and sucking in clean, fresh air. What was it about him that seemed so overpowering and choking? His cologne was heavy, but I'd smelled stronger. Maybe he just wasn't Beau, and so I rejected him. Beau always smelled clean and musky and delicious, never overpowering.

I shook away those thoughts and moved to examine the DVD collection. Lots of war movies, black and white movies, and foreign with subtitles.

Sheesh. Give me *Revenge of the Nerds* over *Casablanca* any day.

I picked through his movies for several long minutes, bored and checking my watch. He'd been gone for a while now.

"Miss?" There was a small knock at the door. A maid appeared with a tray holding a wine bottle and two expensive-looking glasses. She seemed nervous, and was small and thin, with limp brown hair and an oversized gray uniform. "The master sent me in to see to your needs."

The "master"? Jason clearly had issues.

I pulled out my cell phone. "What's the address here?" When she recited it, I typed it in, texting Ryder: *COME GET ME NOW*.

The maid looked at the tray uncertainly when

I was done. "The master instructed me to bring this."

I gestured to a nearby end table. "Just put it there. Thank you."

She set the tray down, but the weight was balanced wrong, and as soon as she released it the whole thing toppled over, wine spilling into the pale silk Persian carpet.

We both sucked in a breath at the same time. I quickly reached for the bottle, placing it on the table. The damage was done—a deep red stain the size of a basketball had already soaked into the carpet. "Do you have any towels nearby? We can catch the worst of this before it sets in."

No response. I turned and looked at the maid.

Her eyes were wide with fear, her pupils dilated. She wrung her hands, silent tears dripped down her cheeks, and shudders wracked her form.

Oh, Lord. "It's just a little wine," I said with a reassuring smile. "Towels?"

She fell to her knees and began to sob as if she'd been given a death sentence.

Either she was a total drama queen, or she was frightened out of her mind. Frowning, I went out into the hallway, looking for other servants. "Hello? Is anybody there? Jason?"

Another woman in gray appeared from another doorway. She looked at me with hunched shoulders, as if she expected to be backhanded instead of greeted.

What was wrong with these people?

"Can I help you, miss?" she said in a soft voice.

I nodded and pointed at the door. "Can you come in here for a second?"

She followed me like a timid little mouse. When she saw the other woman, prostrate and sobbing with fear, and the wine stain on the rug, she turned on her heel and ran.

"Are you running to get towels?" I called, unease niggling inside me. "Hello?"

I could hear her feet slamming up the stairs and a door shutting behind her.

All right, that was it. I didn't care that Ryder wasn't here yet—I'd wait outside. I took a pen and a grocery receipt out of my purse and wrote a note to Jason.

> Can't stay tonight. Sorry about the wine I spilled. I'll pay for the cleaning service. Can we catch up some other time?

I signed it and handed the note to the maid. "Look, I'm going to take full responsibility for the wine, all right? I was reaching for the bottle and knocked it over—that's the story we're going to use." I gave her a friendly smile.

Her tears dried a little, and her breathing calmed from those awful, gasping sobs. "Yes, ma'am."

Something really weird was going on, and I wasn't going to stick around to find out what. I gave her an encouraging smile and grabbed my things, then headed out of the house. Jason was creeping me out big time.

The mansion's driveway was long and cobbled, and it snaked through the woodsy area surrounding his estate. Given that it was rather dark outside and my nerves were shot, it wasn't the most relaxing walk. I kept hearing noises in the woods, and I walked even faster.

I punched the release for the gate and slipped out before it had even finished opening, then trotted down the street a ways so I could watch the oncoming cars.

Of all fortuitous, lucky things, a large truck slowed next to me. Ryder. Thank God.

I peeked inside to double-check that it was her, but the door opened and Beau slid out of the passenger seat. A squeak of protest erupted from my throat, and I stared inside the cab. Ramsey was driving.

"Where's Ryder?"

"We were at the office and I told her I'd take care of this. Hop in."

"How do I know this isn't all some hilarious

plan to kidnap me again and take me back to the Love Lodge?"

Beau's grin was feral. "You don't."

I scowled and glanced back at Jason's mansion on the hill. Creepy overbearing cougar in the mansion? Or too-sexy-for-my-own-good cougar I was trying to break up with? There was really no question, but I pulled my phone out to text Ryder and noticed that she'd sent a message a few minutes ago.

Don't be mad. Beau is very determined to see you.

No shit, Sherlock.

"Why were you at Midnight Liaisons?" I asked.

"Marie had promised to pull some records on the Anderson wolves for me, to see if we could match up all their addresses."

I softened, seeing the worry on his brow. "Still can't find Savannah?"

He shook his head, then gestured at the truck. "You going to get in?"

I slid inside the cab. Beau got in beside me, shut the door, then pulled me into his lap.

While this was slightly better than being squeezed against Ramsey's glowering hulk, it was still awkward. "Beau," I said, trying to slide off, "I can't sit in your lap."

He gave me a teasing look but refused to let me go. "Remember that last conversation we had, where you said you didn't want me in your life?"

"I remember," I said, trying not to look him straight in the eye so I could hold onto my resolve.

He shrugged, and my eyes were drawn back to those wide shoulders like some starving nympho. I couldn't have him in my life. I *couldn't*.

"I don't accept that," he said.

I shook my head to clear it. "Accept what?"

"Your rejection of me," he said, taking my hand. His hand was so warm and comforting. "I've decided not to take no for an answer."

I shivered at the thrill his words gave me. I forced sarcasm to my voice. "Do you think I can just give you a nice little kiss and pretend that I haven't dumped you twice?"

"That sounds real good to me." Then his mouth was on mine, his hand moving around behind my neck to hold me against him.

Me and my big mouth.

Him and his delicious, *sinful* mouth. His lips were soft, warm, delicious. He knew what he was after, and like a single-minded general, he came, he saw, and he conquered. After the first stroke of his tongue into my mouth, I was lost. His tongue swept through my mouth, possessing and playful, and I met it with my own. No one tasted as good as Beau.

I was *so* not over him; I wanted him despite

everything. My hand curled into his shirt, and I slid my thigh over his.

Ramsey cleared his throat, and I crash-landed back down to earth. Beau's mouth stretched into a faint smile.

I punched him in the shoulder. "Stop doing that to me."

He put his hands up as if surrendering, and his eyes locked on me. "Who were you with?"

I tucked a lock of hair behind my ear. "None of your damn business."

His eyes flashed in the darkness, the werecougar version of having a temper tantrum. "You reek of cologne."

Yeah, well, so did my date. "Beau, stop it."

"Did he kiss you?" Was that a note of strain in Beau's voice?

I shot him an angry look to cover my lie. "Some guys are polite enough to not maul a girl on a date."

Not Jason, but I'm sure there were some guys out there like that.

Silence. Then a smug "Good."

It irritated and thrilled me at the same time. Thrilled that he was being possessive when it came to me . . . irritated that he was being such an ass about it. Damn it. My heart broke a little. I couldn't have this. I couldn't have him. "I can't do this, Beau."

"Don't," he said softly.

"I can't be with you. I'm sorry." My eyes burned with tears.

A few minutes passed in awkward silence, then Beau spoke again. "I need your help, Bathsheba. You've met a lot of Alliance members at your job, right?"

It seemed an odd question. "I guess so."

"And all applications are done in person, correct?"

"Giselle uses in-person interviews, yes. Some of the customers are several hundred years old and slow to catch on to new technology." Vampires were notoriously bad with computers and couldn't type worth beans. "Why?"

"Because I need help identifying a few bodies."

Chapter Seventeen

I must not have heard him correctly. "What?"

"I know it's a lot to ask of you, but I need your help."

My *virginity* was a lot to ask of me. This was just weird.

We rode in silence until the car pulled up at the medical examiner's office. The parking lot was nearly deserted at this time of night. We went to the door, then rang the bell. After a few moments, the door buzzed and the three of us went in.

The technician who met us at the door looked rather familiar. He had Beau sign in. "Think she can do it?"

"Worth a shot," Beau said calmly.

The lab tech led us down a long corridor to a door that said Morgue. "Give me just a moment to get clearance."

The door shut and through it I heard " . . .
Bjorn . . . to see the dead girl . . ."

". . . relation to the deceased?" another voice
asked.

That made me nervous.

The door opened and the tech smiled, and I
remembered where I'd seen him before—he was
one of Beau's men who had come to secure my
house.

"Follow me," he said, and Beau and I stepped
inside. Ramsey stayed in the hallway.

The room was large and sterile-looking, with
small white ceramic tiles covering the floor and a
row of metal drawers lining the back wall. Our escort pulled out one drawer in a puff of refrigerated
air. On the slab was a sheet-covered object just
about the right size for a body.

Oh God. Even though I'd expected this, my
knees felt a little weak.

"Steady," Beau said, and his arm went around
my waist.

The lab tech pulled back the sheet and exposed
the face of the victim.

It could have been a wax Barbie doll; whatever was human about her had long fled. Her face
was cold and gray, her features refined and pretty.
Beautiful, even, but that wasn't a surprise if she
was in the Alliance. Her ears weren't pointed, so

that eliminated the chance of any sort of fey creature. Her blond hair was brushed back from her head, almost as pale and colorless as her skin.

Could I identify her? She looked vaguely familiar. I leaned in to Beau and whispered, "What is she?"

He whispered back, "Shifter. Don't know what kind. She's not from around here."

That definitely narrowed down the field. Female shifters of any kind were rare, so most were snapped up right away. Which made Giselle's business very difficult at times. "Any markings?"

The tech pulled the sheet down a little, revealing a tiny paw tattooed over the right breast. At the sight of that paw, I remembered. It was too tiny to be a wolf, the five small toes tipped with dainty claws.

"Mink," I said. "Regina St. James was one of the few were-minks in the database. She showed me her tattoo once." I stared down at the body. Lord, it didn't look like Regina. She'd been so pretty, with a zesty, bubbly personality. This cold stranger wasn't her. "She liked to date a lot. Giselle loved her."

Our tech nodded and made some notes. "We'll check with her family and see if she's been reported missing."

"Do you want to see the other body?" the other tech asked from the other side of the room.

Our small party headed over as she pulled out the slab. When she uncovered the face of this woman, I couldn't tell who it was again. The face was rounder, sweeter than the last. Younger. The hair was a bright yellow-blond that made the pallor of her skin seem unnatural. Her figure was slightly fuller than the were-mink's.

She had no identifying tattoos and she'd been found in the river, her scent long gone. They didn't know what sort of shifter she was, or if she was one at all.

"I'm sorry," I told them after a few minutes. "I don't recognize her. I can check the records at work tomorrow, if that'll help." I glanced over at Beau, who was eyeing the corpse with a grim expression.

He glanced at me, then back down at the corpse. He looked murderous, intense, his eyes changing from normal to feline. "Both women are blondes. How long is the hair?" he asked the shifter tech.

The man checked a chart. "Mid-back on both."

"How tall?" he rasped.

Again, the guy checked his chart. "One was five foot eight. The other was five nine."

Beau's mouth thinned into a line. "Both tall with long blond hair." His gaze focused on me. "They look like you."

I frowned. And as I stared at the second corpse, I felt pricklings of alarm.

"How did they die?" I asked.

The tech shook his head. "We don't need to get into that at the moment—"

I'd suspected something like that. I grabbed the sheet so I could see the rest of the body, not just the face, which looked a little too similar to mine with every moment.

Beau put a hand over mine, halting me. "Bathsheba," he said in a low voice. "You don't want to see. She's . . . parts of her have been eaten."

Beau refused to let me go home that night. I protested all the way to the Worthington Hotel, but Beau got his way.

"Leave Giselle a message," he said calmly. "It's not safe there for you right now. Not with someone hunting tall blondes."

I was a little scared, too. After all, whoever had been in my house a few days ago was hunting me, too, as well as that scary creature.

And I felt safe with Beau.

My *panties* weren't safe, but the rest of me was, at least.

"You should take me to where Sara is. This isn't safer than that," I complained as we went through the massive lobby.

I vividly remembered the last time I'd stayed

here. He'd wrapped his body around mine, and I'd snuggled into the musky scent of him. My nipples grew hard with longing just thinking about it, and Beau gave me a hot look as we reached the room door.

"Why do you keep doing that?" I whispered, jamming the key-card into the electronic lock. It gave a silent click and the light flicked to green. I shoved the door open.

"Doing what?" His voice had a tense edge to it.

"Look at me that way . . . sometimes." I couldn't explain that it happened when I thought dirty things about him. "It's almost like you can read my mind."

"I can't read your mind," he said, his tone mild.

The door clicked shut behind us and he pulled me against the wall, his hard body pressing against mine.

"But I can smell you," he said softly, and his lips brushed mine. My body thrilled at the contact, and my breath left me. His finger slid down my cheek, caressing me. "Ever since we made love in the cabin, I can smell the softest things about you—what kind of perfume you wear, the shampoo you use, the detergent you use to clean your underthings." His nostrils flared and I realized he was smelling me right now. "I can smell when you get turned on. I'm attuned to your scent. I could pick you out across a room."

A hot blush covered my face. Oh my God. "You can smell *that*?" Was that what he was sensing every time he gave me that odd look?

He pressed against me, demonstrating the thick erection in his pants. "I'm half-wild with wanting you." His mouth captured mine. "I catch whiffs of your arousal and it drives me crazy with desire. I hunger to taste it on the air again, to know that you're thinking of me." His hands dropped from me suddenly. Then, slow, and almost unsure, "*Are* you thinking of me? Or someone else?"

"I'm thinking of you," I said softly.

He crushed me against his chest and our mouths melded once more. We fell into bed together, all hands and hot, needing lips. I was all over him, and he reciprocated with hot bites of pleasure. His hand pulled my ponytail free, and my hair poured over both of us. He groaned hard, and I rubbed his erection through his slacks.

He ran his fingernails down the leg of my tights, and they split open.

"Claws." He grinned and stroked my now-bare leg.

"I can smell you," he growled against my neck, ripping the last of my tights off. His hand slid between them and he pressed over me, his weight exciting and heavy.

I unzipped his pants and pulled them down, my breath mingling with his in a hot melody. His hand slid under my knee, spreading my leg wide, then his weight settled between my legs, the head of his cock sliding along the wet heat of my apex.

I inhaled sharply, my nails digging into his buttocks.

He froze. "Bathsheba?"

I squirmed underneath him, bucking my hips against his erection. "If you stop now, I swear I'll never speak to you again."

He chuckled as the head of his cock teased my entrance. "Can't have that happen," he whispered, and his cock slid home.

That delicious stretching feeling of him inside me filled my whole body. I gasped as he stroked into me again, and my hands pressed against the sides of his face, drawing him down for another kiss.

I raised my hips to meet his, and his chest brushed against mine, my nipples skimming his flesh as he pumped again, over and over. Faster and faster we collided, his body stroking against mine at just the right spot until I cried his name, and he exploded just after I did.

We collapsed together, my legs. still wrapped around his waist, quivering with aftershocks.

"Hell," I muttered. So much for turning him away.

A smile curved his mouth. "Is this a breakup? Because if so, I think we've already kissed and made up."

I punched his arm and tried to get up, but I was trapped under him. "Let me go."

"Do you promise to stay here with me tonight?"

Grudgingly, I nodded, and he released me. I scooted over a few feet on the bed. "Where else would I go tonight?" The obvious answer was *back to work*, but I didn't want to hear the third degree on my date with Jason. And if Giselle knew I'd seen Beau again, she'd flip out on me.

"Where else?" He shrugged. "I don't know. You keep a lot of secrets."

I ignored him and stared at the blank TV. In the reflection I could see my pale legs sprawled on the bed, and it reminded me of the corpses at the morgue. I shuddered, feeling chills skitter across my skin. "Who would want to eat those girls?"

Who would want to eat me?

"I think it's a Wendigo. Or a pack of Wendigo."

"A what?" I slid forward, and the sheets brushed against my sensitive spots. I blushed hard, a quiver rocketing through me again.

Beau turned to stare at me with hot, gold-green eyes and I blushed even harder, knowing what was going through his head. "Sorry, I slid wrong. You were saying? . . ."

"Wendigo," he sat up on the edge of the bed and rested his elbows on his knees, as if he was exhausted from the day.

I watched him with concern. In my mind, Beau was strong and tireless. Seeing the weariness settle around his eyes and mouth made me feel horrible for giving him so much trouble. I knelt behind him, placing my hands at the base of his neck and kneading the tight knot of muscles there.

Beau groaned with pleasure, tilting his head back and leaning into my hands.

It was a pleasure to stroke his neck and feel the fine hairs there, the soft skin behind his ears, the hard muscles below his collar. His shirt was in my way, so I leaned forward and unbuttoned it. "So tell me about the Wendigo."

He sighed heavily. "They're . . . cannibals."

My hands paused, then pushed his shirt down his arms.

"Have you heard the Native American legends of the Wendigo?"

I kneaded his shoulders, soothing him. "No. What are they?"

"Some of the tribes believed that a man who ate the flesh of another man could steal his power. But if you did so, you became a Wendigo—a terrible creature that needs another creature's flesh to survive. They smell foul, like the grave. They're stronger than any other living creature, and thirst for blood." He paused. "Those legends were mostly wrong. Only a shifter can turn Wendigo."

"Oh." I removed my hands so I could wring them in silence. "And of course, everyone we know is a shifter."

He said nothing.

"Both of those girls at the morgue looked like me. So does this mean that someone's going to try and eat . . . me?"

"They shouldn't. You're not a shifter."

"So why are they going after me?"

"I don't know," he said darkly. "But I intend to find out."

Chapter Eighteen

The next morning, my cell phone woke me out of a sound sleep. My head was cushioned against Beau's broad, warm chest, my legs tangled with his. On his nightstand, my cell phone buzzed, and Sara's ringtone played.

I jerked up at the sound and winced when I realized my long hair was caught under his head.

He opened his eyes and smiled at me. "Good morning. Sleep well?"

I untangled my legs from his. "I don't remember going to sleep at all," I teased.

I wanted to slide underneath him and feel his heavy, wonderful weight over me. I wanted to burrow against his chest and let the world fall away.

As the phone continued to blare my sister's ringtone, I sighed "I need to get that."

He reached over and handed the phone to me.

I flipped open my cell phone. "Hey."

"Hey, Bath!" she said, entirely too chirpy. "You took forever to answer. What's up?"

"Nothing," I said, hoping she wouldn't hear the blush in my voice. Beau pulled me back down against him and I squirmed away. "How are you? Is everything all right?"

"Everything's good. Very quiet. We've mostly been playing on the computer. Ramsey's terrible at it, but I think he keeps trying for my sake." I could hear her munching on something—probably toast. "How about you? Are you keeping busy?"

I choked. "Uh . . . yeah, I'm—I'm fine." A nervous laugh escaped my throat. "Just staying busy with work and all."

"Mmmhmm." She paused. "Beau's right there, isn't he?"

Oh, God, shoot me now. "No, he's not. Whatever makes you think that?"

"You have this high-pitched squeak in your voice." Munch munch. "And Ramsey told me that Beau was crazy about you. You like him, too, don't you?"

Beau snorted and rubbed his foot against my calf. "I never used the word 'crazy.'"

Of course Beau could hear everything Sara said. What could be more humiliating than that? "Nothing's going on," I said, even as Beau's hand slid to my very naked behind and pinched it, making me squeak.

"Of course something's going on. You're dating him. You're *sleeping* together."

"We'll talk about this later," I said, stifling the moan that threatened when Beau's fingers lightly danced along the inside of my thigh. "What's going on?"

"So, uh, I don't know how to break this to you," Sara said slowly, and my heart dropped.

"What is it?" My mind automatically went to panic mode. If we left town tonight, we could still get away. Pack up under the cover of darkness . . .

"Ramsey knows," she said.

"He knows what?" My heart pounded in my chest. Maybe we were talking about two different things.

"About the wolf thing?" Beau said lazily. "He's always known."

I stopped breathing. I couldn't think. "I'll call you back," I said breathlessly to Sara, then hung up the phone. "What do you *mean*, you know? What wolf thing?"

"Your sister is the wolf the Anderson pack has been looking for," he said, following me up the bed, a cat stalking its prey, as I shrank backward.

I was stunned. "How . . . how did you know?"

He shrugged. "Any shifter with a nose can tell

as soon as she walks in the door. I kept smelling wolf on you and thought it was some sort of carry-over from work, and when I met Sara it all clicked. That's why Ramsey's shadowing her—he's going to keep her safe until we get Savannah back."

Tears blurred in my eyes. I felt . . . I didn't know how I felt. I was a volcano, ready to explode with rage. I was a balloon that had just been deflated. I repeated Beau's words, still not comprehending. "He's going to keep her safe?"

His hands slid to my waist and he pulled me down the bed and under him, then began pressing kisses to my belly button. "That's what I said."

"But . . . but the wolves . . ."

"We would never give your sister up to them in return for our sister," he said, and nipped at my stomach. "You realize that, don't you?"

Sara was totally safe? No one would trade her to the wolves, taking her away from me forever? The relief was so overwhelming me that I felt like sobbing. For six long years it had been us against the world, always hiding, always frightened. Knowing that we had people to share our burden stunned me into silence.

"Do you want to talk about it?" Beau asked.

No!

But that wasn't fair. I knew I had to say the words somehow. I breathed deep, trying to bolster my courage. "When I was in my first semester of college, Sara met a man. She was only seventeen and he was really controlling. When I found out she'd moved in with him, I went home to talk some sense into her. She got so upset that . . . she changed into a wolf right before my eyes. That was when I learned about werewolves. And that she'd been bitten. We tried to hide from him, but he came back for Sara and . . . I killed him. Shot him."

Would he hate that I had killed a man? I had blood on my hands, and I wasn't regretful in the slightest.

Beau rested his chin on my stomach, looking up at me. "It was necessary," he said simply. "You needed to keep her safe."

"I shot him after he bit me, too," I said softly. "He was going to kill Sara, and I shot him dead, and buried him in the backyard."

Beau's eyes gleamed, and I knew that he didn't disapprove of me. He understood doing whatever it took to keep loved ones safe.

He pressed another kiss on my stomach, then glanced up at me. "But you didn't turn?"

I shook my head. "It didn't affect me at all. I don't know why Sara was more susceptible than me, but she just was. She became a wolf and I became . . ." Her keeper, I wanted to say, but it sounded so unfair. Sara hadn't chosen it. When I'd found her she'd been broken and frightened and so close to being wild, and I'd nursed her back from the edge. I regretted nothing.

He didn't look surprised by my words. "It happens. Some people are born immune. The theory is that most people have an ancestor that could shift, or so they carry the gene and are susceptible. It's rare to find someone who's totally immune."

"Sara and I have different mothers," I reminded him. "But you know what this means?"

"What?"

I swallowed hard. "You can't turn me. I'll never be a shifter. I'll never be able to have a shifter's children."

I waited for him to grasp that I couldn't ever be the right mate for him, to stiffen and move away. Instead, he nipped my hip hard enough to make me squeal in surprise. "Hey! I'm trying to tell you something here!"

"You're telling me that you can't have my litter, so I can bite you as much as I want," he said, his voice a low, contented rumble. "Or did I miss something?"

"You don't care?"

His fingers flexed against my hips, the same way a cat might knead, and he gave me a serious look. "If it matters to you, we could always adopt.

I know of a gentle were-bear that could use a home—"

I snorted. "Absolutely not."

He grinned. "You're distracting me from your story. So you and Sara killed the rogue wolf and ran from the wolf pack?"

I nodded. "We moved to another state, looking for someplace with fewer wolves. Giselle offered me an office job but wouldn't say what it was, and I nearly passed out with fright when I realized exactly what her business was. I thought she'd set me up."

He chuckled. "I bet."

"But we needed money so badly we had to stay. No choice." I ran my fingers through his hair. "A few weeks passed, and Giselle said nothing about Sara. Then she suggested that I hire my sister to help out in the office. Sara was tired of running, so she went in that first day expecting Giselle to bust her, but . . . nothing. Giselle had no idea what Sara was—or at least, I thought she didn't. It seemed like the perfect way to keep tabs on the wolf packs and hide right under their noses, if we were careful." I sighed. Telling the story was taking an immense weight off my shoulders. "We've been careful for six years now. Sara can control it a little better, but she still has bad moments—a lot of them."

"And you never dated? Anyone?"

I shook my head. "It would have put Sara at risk."

"You've had a tough life, but it's made you strong." He rested his chin on my stomach, as if thinking, then said, "Is that why you said you don't want to be with me?"

"That was the original reason. But now Giselle knows Sara's secret. And she's going to sell her to the wolves unless I keep dating other men that she sets me up with."

A low, possessive snarl started in his throat. "You're not going to date anyone else. You're going to be with me, and together we're going to protect Sara. Understand?"

I wasn't sure if I could turn over Sara's well-being to someone else that easily. I was too used to taking care of it all, of always remaining vigilant.

"Or is it that you really don't want to date me, either?" Beau's gray eyes searched my face. "Is that why?"

It dawned on me that I'd hurt his feelings. "You know better than that, Beau."

"Actually, I don't." His voice sounded grim.

I stared at him, vulnerability warring with shyness. I opened my mouth, and a squeak came out. Mortified, I cleared my throat and tried again. "I . . ."

"You . . . ?" He lifted an eyebrow, waiting.

I slapped his naked chest. "I *like* you, all right? At first I only dated you because of the Rosie thing, but I slept with you because I like you. I'm in this bed with you because I like you—not because of anything I owe Giselle. I like you a little *too* much, maybe."

He grinned, all self-confident cat once more, and brushed a strand of hair off my cheek. "I know."

"If you knew, why did you make me say it out loud?" My face burned hot. I hated leaving myself open like that.

Beau tilted his head, regarding me. "I wanted to make sure you knew it, too."

"Oh, thank you, zen master," I said sarcastically and pushed at him. He didn't budge. With a sigh, I ran my hands down his back. "I suppose I should call the office and tell them I can't come in for a few more days. Lay low until we figure all this out and both Sara and Savannah are safe."

"You should," he agreed. His muscles flexed under my hands, clearly enjoying my petting.

I continued to glide my hands over his back, fascinated with the play of muscles under his smooth skin. His spine had the most amazing indentations, and I trailed my fingers down to the swell of his buttocks.

If all shapeshifters were made as wonderfully as him, why did they need a dating service at all? My fingers slid to his buttocks and I grasped them, fighting the sudden urge to bite the rounded muscles.

Beau's eyes gleamed that catlike green-gold. "You're doing it again," he said in a husky voice.

"Doing what?" I looked up at him with glazed eyes.

"Thinking about sex," he murmured, then his mouth descended on my neck.

"It's a shame that thinking is all that's happening," I teased.

His hand slid under my leg, hiking it up around his waist, and the rest went just as I'd hoped.

No one was answering the phone at the office. That disturbed me, and when I suggested that we check things out, Beau didn't protest. It would allow me to explain to Giselle face-to-face why I needed to be absent, and would also let me find out what was going on.

I pushed open the door.

The front office was silent. Were Marie and Ryder taking a few hours off? If so, who was manning the office? Giselle? That would explain why the phones weren't being answered—she thought she was too good for that. A quick glance at her office showed the light was on, the door shut.

I told Beau, "I'll talk with Giselle and get some time off of work. You stay here."

"I don't smell anyone," he said and moved past

me. "No one recent, anyhow." His nose wrinkled as if he smelled something. "Old Spice?"

Jason's cologne was so strong that it had probably lingered, and Beau's sensitive nose had picked it up. "A client who came in yesterday," I said.

He headed for Giselle's office, and I planted my hands on his back and steered him toward the file room. "Let me talk to her first, Beau." When he balked, I continued, "Five minutes. That's all I ask."

"And you'll stay with me until we figure this out, so I can protect you?"

"Yes, but I have to let Giselle down easy. She won't like it if you come in and start throwing your weight around, demanding things. Let me handle her."

"All right. Five minutes. But no more."

I nodded, headed for Giselle's office, and knocked on her door.

No answer.

I cracked the door open and peeked in.

No one was there. That was odd. If Giselle wasn't in, then who was running the office?

That did make bailing out of work a little easier, though. Flickers of guilt bothered me as I realized that no one would be in, but I couldn't stick around and hope someone showed up. I went to the other side of Giselle's desk and grabbed a piece of her stationery to leave her a note.

Giselle, family emergency has come up. Call me on my cell and I'll explain.

I wrote down my cell number and signed the note, hoping that she'd understand. I studied the note for a moment, biting my lip. Oh, who was I kidding? She wouldn't buy it. I drummed my fingers on the desk in frustration and accidentally hit her mouse.

The computer monitor blinked to life, and Giselle's screen lit up.

I froze. Giselle would kill me if she knew I'd seen her screen—her desktop wallpaper was a rather incriminating picture of her and three sailors. Oh, my. How she could look at that every day and still get work done, I didn't know.

Windows were flashing on her screen, and I clicked on one. A chat messenger—BigWilly69 (lovely man, I'm sure) was sending frantic messages. *R U STILL THERE? R U ALIVE? HELLO LOL.* All dated at 10:49 last night. Odd. I clicked on a few of the other messages and found the same thing, although one had sent a picture of his dick. Nice. I quickly clicked away.

Maybe she'd just forgotten to turn off her computer when she'd left the office?

A new message popped up. *Giselle, are you there?*

The screen name was Jason_ontheprowl.

Jason?

I hesitated a moment, then typed. *Hi, Jason, it's Bathsheba. I'm borrowing Giselle's computer.*

A long moment passed. Then Jason's response lit up on the screen.

Bathsheba—a smiley face followed my name. *Are you okay? You left so fast last night. I was hoping we could talk. Tonight, maybe? Drinks at my place?*

Ugh. He'd gone straight to Giselle to try and set up more dates? *Something has come up,* I typed. *Can we catch up next week?*

Or never. Never would be a really good time to catch up.

Sure, he typed, another smiley tagged on. *I'll call you.*

I good-bye'd, then logged out of chat. The calendar was underneath the chat box, and I took a look at it.

She'd booked three more dates for me today. Garth again, Jason in the evening, and some new guy named Ricardo in the afternoon. She'd thoughtfully tagged each appointment with the client's profile ID, the sum he'd paid to date me, and an email address.

I fired off quick emails to the men explaining that I would be out of town, then deleted the incriminating evidence from Giselle's Sent folder.

"Bathsheba?" Marie's inquiring voice called out.

"In here," I called back.

She stepped into Giselle's office a moment later, thumbed a gesture behind her, and gave me a curious look. "I found a stray. Can we keep him?"

Behind her, Beau came out of the shadows and grinned at me. "It's been ten minutes." He lifted his head and sniffed the air once, then rubbed his nose. The scent of Old Spice must really bother him.

"I was just shutting down Giselle's computer. Then I'm done."

Marie was looking at Beau with a rather adoring look on her face. "Take your time. I can make some coffee if you're going to be sticking around," she said, and I realized she wasn't talking to me. Irritation flashed.

Beau grinned, but his eyes were resting on me. "Thank you, but we need to get going."

I nodded and moved around Giselle's desk. My shoe slid across the tile, and I nearly face-planted on the floor, but Beau lunged past Marie and grabbed me. "Sorry," I breathed, distracted by his proximity. "I slipped on something."

I glanced down and saw dark smears on the tile, sticky and red.

Blood.

Beau's face paled. "I didn't smell it," he murmured in surprise, even as he ushered me out of Giselle's office and hurried through the main office.

"Where are you going?" Marie cried behind us. "What's going on?"

"Bathsheba is in danger." Beau didn't break stride, urging me toward the door. "I'm sending someone over here to look after the office. I want you to come outside with us, understand?"

She gave him a frightened nod and glanced back at Giselle's office, then followed us out.

I wasn't moving fast enough for Beau. He swung me into his arms as if I weighed nothing and carried me out to the car. Ramsey had gotten us a rental car at some point last night, and Beau shoved me into its backseat. "Lie down and cover up with that coat until I tell you otherwise."

I heard Marie slide into the front seat and lie down, her terrified breathing loud and raspy. For God's sake. It wasn't like snipers were going to be shooting from the rooftops or something. "Beau, are you sure—"

"Lie down," he snarled, and I did. He shut the door after me, and I lay there, scarcely daring to breathe. Outside he paced back and forth, jingling the keys, ready to move.

It seemed like an eternally long time before I heard other voices, and I sat up to sneak a peek. The other Russell clan members had arrived. At the sight of them, Marie was let out of the car—I was given a firm glare and stayed put—and Beau and his men investigated the building. One of them stood outside, protecting me as I lay in the back of the car, and then Beau reemerged. The men talked in low voices, but the body language was a bit more relaxed. Safe for now.

Beau opened my door and I slid out of the car. "Marie will be okay?"

"Yes. Two of the boys will stay with her."

"How come you didn't smell the blood?" I asked.

"There were too many other smells—the dust, the cologne, flowers. You." He glanced over at me. "The Old Spice was bothering my nose, so I focused on the smell of you and nothing else." He looked angry. "It was stupid of me."

I sat in flattered silence as Beau got in, then pulled out onto the street. I had a million questions, but all I could think about was that pool of half-dried blood under Giselle's chair.

We drove back to the hotel in silence. I was lost in thought, and Beau didn't seem inclined to talk, either. The hotel was bustling this morning—people getting coffee before heading off to conferences or meetings, people with suitcases checking out. I shivered every time someone looked at me, then realized it was because I was wearing a dirty sweaterdress and no tights in winter.

My hand clenched tight in his, Beau led me back

through the maze of hotel rooms, his face bleak, his eyes slitted and cold. Determined. Angry. He paused in front of our door, sniffing the air, then pulled out the key-card.

"Beau," I said, "I don't have any clothes." With the angry protective state he was in, I might not emerge for days.

He gave me a hard look. "You're not going back home."

"So what am I supposed to do?"

He glanced at my dress. "Wash it in the sink."

Typical male response. "Are you on drugs?" An elderly couple passed us in the hallway, staring. Maybe I'd been a little too loud. Oops. I leaned in, dropping my voice to a whisper. "I don't have any panties."

A slight smile lightened his expression. "Are you flirting with me?"

"No! I'm telling you I need some panties," I whispered furiously. "We need to go to the store—"

"Too risky," he interrupted.

The store? Risky? Was he mad? "Then you need to call Ramsey and tell *him* to bring me panties."

He stared at me for a moment. "No."

I blinked in surprise. "What do you mean, no? I need clothing."

He pushed the door open and gestured for me

to go in. "Your life is in danger. You can go shopping later."

I pinched the bridge of my nose. The vein throbbing there was going to burst soon if I didn't get to punch something. "You're not listening to me," I began.

"You're not listening to me," he said, putting his hand on the small of my back and basically shoving me forward.

I planted my feet, furious. "Beauregard Russell. If I have to stand in this hall all day arguing over panties to get some, then by God, that's what I'm going to do." I braced my feet against the door frame, glaring at him.

He tickled my sides and I collapsed in a fit of giggles. He grabbed me by the waist and carried me inside, dumped me on the bed, then crawled on top of me. A hint of a smile had returned to his stern face.

"Panties?" he asked.

"Panties," I affirmed. "Jeans and a T-shirt would be appreciated, too."

He leaned over and kissed me. "Your wish is my command. I'll see what Ramsey can scrounge up."

I had mental images of a bear scrounging for frilly underpants, and snorted. "Maybe Sara should help him."

Chapter Nineteen

*R*amsey knocked at our hotel door an hour later, bags in hand. Beau stepped outside to have a private conversation with his lieutenant, and I spent the next few minutes picking through the clothing and changing into jeans, a T-shirt with Beau's business logo on it, and fresh panties. There was even a pair of Keds slides. Nice.

I tucked my cell phone into my back pocket and it immediately began to vibrate. Surprised, I pulled it out and stared at the screen.

It read *Gis-cell*. I flipped it open and answered warily. "Giselle, where are you—"

"Hello, Bathsheba." The voice was overly sugary, smug. I didn't recognize it, and it sure wasn't Giselle. There was something about the tone that niggled at my memory. "Be very quiet and listen to what I say, or your sister Sara is going to die."

I went cold, blackness crawling before my eyes.

The breath whooshed out of my lungs. How had they gotten Sara? Ramsey was keeping her safe . . . I glanced toward the hallway, where I'd just seen him, then swallowed. "Who is this?"

"This is Arabella. Remember me?"

"I remember you." I looked at the door, but the men were still murmuring out there. I moved to the bathroom and shut the door behind me. "You have Sara?"

"I do," she crowed. "And your boss, too, who happens to be in terrible pain at the moment. Want to talk to her?"

God, no. But that wasn't a good answer. "Yes."

There was a bit of static, and then I heard a groan of pain, followed by a sob. Giselle?

The phone jerked away and I heard Arabella's soft laugh. "Oops. Sounds like she can't come to the phone right now. Too bad."

"Let me talk to Sara."

"She's currently unconscious."

My heart froze. "If you've hurt her—"

"I haven't yet," she interrupted. "At least not too much. I'm going to leave that for the wolf pack, since they're so hot and bothered about finding her. Unless you and I want to work something out?"

Every ounce of my body wanted to fling the phone away. "Yes," I gritted. "What do you want?"

"Good." She sounded pleased. "If you want your sister to live, I need you to do a few things."

I hesitated. Giselle gave a shout of pain in the background, and that decided me, even though I had an awful feeling in my stomach that this wasn't going to turn out well. "I'm listening."

"I want you to meet me," she said calmly, as if she'd been discussing a dinner date. "Alone. I'm going to text you the address, and I want you to be there in a half hour. If I get one sniff of someone helping you or accompanying you, I'll cut Sara's throat. Understand?"

I swallowed. "I'll come alone." I didn't know how I'd get away from Beau, but I wouldn't let Sara down.

"Good." She chuckled. "Be here in a half hour or I start cutting off fingers. And claws. Your little sister can't afford to lose much more."

She hung up.

I clenched my fists, trying to think. I couldn't break down. I had to do something. Fast. If I told Beau, he'd stop me from going and Sara would die.

I needed a plan.

The room door shut and Beau called out, "Bathsheba?"

I smoothed my hands down my jeans, wiping away the clamminess. "Be out in just a minute." I took that time to compose myself and then left the bathroom, my face carefully blank. One wrong facial expression, and Beau would figure me out.

"If I get one sniff of someone helping you or accompanying you, I'll cut Sara's throat."

So I had to get rid of Beau. I ignored the smile he was aiming in my direction and sat on the edge of the bed. "So what's the plan?"

He came and sat next to me, his warm arm rubbing against mine. His arm slid around my waist and he pulled me closer. "What do you mean?"

I pried away from him and leapt off the bed. Time to play innocent, to get him off the trail. "I mean, what's your plan to find out where Giselle is? What if the same people that are after me have her?"

He looked exasperated. "Giselle can take care of herself, and I don't give a damn where she's at. All I care about is keeping you safe."

I nearly crumbled at that, but I decided to use it against him instead. "So you're just going to leave her there, helpless? What if the wolves have her and are torturing her to find out where Sara is?"

He shook his head. "They wouldn't torture one female to get another. And Giselle is anything but helpless."

No, she wasn't. If there was anyone that could turn a kidnapping into roses, it would be Giselle. But then I remembered the blood under her desk. "We can't just leave her with whoever has her, Beau. She's my boss." My voice rose an octave.

"Leave it alone, Bathsheba."

"No. We need to help find her."

He glared at me as I paced. "You're not going to let this go, are you?"

"No." *I can't.*

"Why are you so loyal to her? She's used you over and over again."

"She's given me a job. A good-paying job," I shot back. "She's stood up for me. The least I can do is not leave her to the wolves."

"Not wolves," he said dismissively. "Whatever is behind this attacked the wolves."

"It was a figure of speech," I snapped, starting to get worried at how close he was to the truth. "We have to rescue Giselle. I won't be able to live with myself if we don't. Remember that finger on your property? Whoever is behind this is eating people. And they have her."

"I realize that," he said patiently. "But your safety is first and foremost in my mind. Someone is out there hunting blondes. That's in addition to the wolf pack, which is looking for your sister and has my cousin. We have enough problems without trying to play white knight to a woman who was trying to pimp you out to the highest bidder!

Bath," he said, moving to my side and rubbing my arms to soothe me. "With everything that's going on, why don't you just lay low for the next few days and let me take care of things."

The offer was sweet, and thoughtful . . . and meant me sitting on my ass waiting for him to make magic happen.

That wasn't how I worked.

Beau's phone vibrated and he glanced down at the screen, then back at me. "Ramsey's got an update on Savannah. Can you wait in here?"

I nodded. "Sure."

As soon as he was out the door, I plucked the keys from the nightstand and climbed out the window—luckily, we were on the bottom floor—and then I shut it again. Then I dashed across the parking lot to the rental car. Even if I was running into a trap, I'd do it. Sara needed me.

As I pulled out of the parking lot, my cell phone buzzed. The message that popped up was a text with an address.

I memorized it without really comprehending the words and pulled onto the highway.

Beau would be panicking, wondering where I'd gone. He'd asked me to trust him, and I hadn't. As soon as he'd turned his back, I'd run. Again. If I ever saw him again, I hoped he would understand.

Chapter Twenty

*T*wenty minutes later, I pulled off the highway and onto the service road, following the
GPS to the address I'd been given.

I had no plan. My mind was racing at a million
different angles, and the best I could come up with
was *Free Giselle and Sara; escape by any means necessary.* In other words, I was doomed.

I pulled up to a familiar driveway, my eyes
widening at the sight of the iron gates with JTC
emblazoned across it. No fucking way. What was
Arabella doing at Jason's house? I remembered the
maid's fright and the way he'd sniffed the bloody
handkerchief, and I swallowed hard.

I pulled up to the speaker box, pressing my finger on the call button.

"Who is it?" Arabella's sweet voice came
through the speaker.

Who the hell did she think it would be? "It's me. I'm here, and I'm alone."

A buzz sounded and the gate began to swing open. "If you're *not* alone, I'm going to disembowel Sara," she warned.

My finger stabbed at the button, my mouth watering as if I was going to throw up. "Don't hurt her," I yelled in. "I'm *alone*. I swear."

No response. I drove up the long, winding driveway.

No one came to the door to greet me. I hesitated before ringing the doorbell, and headed to the side of the massive house, trying to look into the windows and see what I was up against.

Most of the windows were closed, the heavy curtains drawn over the panes. There was a window at the back of the house, though, and it revealed an empty, white-tiled kitchen bigger than my first apartment. A sunny, cheerful yellow split door nearby led into the kitchen. I placed my hand on the doorknob. What if there was an alarm? Well, Arabella was expecting me anyway. I turned the knob.

No alarm. Good.

My heart hammering, I tiptoed into the house. Around me was a blanket of silence, uncomfortable and oppressing. My shoes sounded heavily on the floor. I crossed the kitchen quickly, spotted a knife in a butcher block, and grabbed it. No sense charging in without a weapon. Clutching it tight in my hand, I turned down the hall.

Somewhere in this maze of a house, Arabella was waiting for me. To kick my ass or eat me, I had no idea which. I slid forward along the wall, and I suddenly understood why they did that in movies. If you had your back to something, you felt less vulnerable. If I could have pressed both my front and my back to the wall, I would have done it.

The stairwell loomed up ahead, and I walked toward it. Quietly.

A whiff of Arabella's heavy perfume, powdery with a rancid undertone, caught my nose. At the smell a few things clicked in my brain. Whenever we'd been at a scene where the Wendigo had been present, the smell of rot and decay had been present. Inside my house, the putrid stench had been chokingly strong.

That was why Arabella had been able to hide her true nature for so long—she'd nearly choked us with her perfume, disguising the awful smell of death that accompanied her stolen powers. Jason wore an equal amount of cologne. And now I realized why Arabella was hiding at Jason's house.

They were working together.

My eyes watered and I crouched low, eyeing

my surroundings. No sign of her. Maybe the smell was everywhere inside.

The house felt eerily deserted. I glanced at a nearby clock—I still had a few minutes before my deadline. With a final glance around me, I proceeded silently up the stairs. If I had been a vicious Wendigo looking to get revenge on my ex-boyfriend, I'd have hidden my prisoners on the highest floor, in the most inaccessible room.

The second floor was more open than the first, which made me nervous. I stuck close to one side of the hallway, pausing only to quickly pass a red and white bathroom.

Then I paused again. And turned back.

The bathroom wasn't decorated in red.

Blood covered the floor, splattered across the ceramic bowl of the toilet, across the edge of the columned sink. The edge of the fabric shower curtain was soaked in it.

A hand dangled out of the bathtub, long red nails perfectly manicured.

I knew whose hand that was.

Giselle's.

Where was Sara? Was she still alive?

Jason's voice rang out from down the hall. "'Sheba, I see you've arrived."

Gripping the knife tighter, I followed the sound of his voice.

I found him two rooms down, reclining on a pool table. His hair was a mess and his neat, expensive clothes were ripped at the shoulders and seams. He grinned at the sight of me. "You're here. Welcome!"

I froze, fear pounding through my blood. "Where's Sara?"

"I haven't seen her," he said, his grin widening. I could smell his thick cologne from where I stood several feet away.

A very, very bad feeling crept over me and I turned back to the door.

Arabella stood there, reeking of floral, powdery perfume and rot. A bit of red tinged her mouth, and as I watched, she delicately wiped at the corners. "Oh, is Sara not here?" she said in a dulcet voice. "Shit. I guess we lied. That makes me a bad, bad girl, doesn't it?' "

I took a step backward, reaching for the wall. *Back against the wall. Back against the wall.* My palms began to sweat, and I adjusted my grip on the knife, "Sara's not here?"

Arabella grinned at Jason. "What a moron."

Sara wasn't here? Relief flooded through me. My sister was safe, then.

Arabella went over to the table and caressed Jason's jaw. "JT's plan was brilliant."

My gaze grew horrified as a few more things

clicked into place. Beau's story about his childhood friend, then enemy. The absolute terror of his servants. The big honking JTC on the main gate.

I *was* a moron. "Jason . . . you're JT?"

His smile seemed entirely too toothy. "I was wondering how long it would take for you to catch on. I really had you going."

"You sure did," I agreed, moving along the wall until I bumped into the corner, and huddled there. The smell of both of them was overpowering, and coupled with my frantic mind, I thought it might make me faint.

With a possessive look on her face, Arabella watched JT slide off the table.

"So," JT said as he sidled toward me.

Cornered, I brandished the knife and glared at him. "I suppose this is the part where I'm supposed to ask you what you plan to do with me."

He took another step forward and I swung, but he was unnaturally strong and fast. He knocked the knife out of my arm so hard that I thought my wrist would snap from the impact, then he shoved me against the wall. The plaster gave a little behind me, and the wind was knocked out of me from the force of his blow.

I struggled for breath, trying to gasp it in. When it finally returned, I sucked in huge, noxious lungfuls of Jason's scent and gagged.

He planted his mouth on mine, forcing his tongue into my mouth. I gagged at the taste of carrion and tried to shove him away, but it was like shoving against brick itself. I pounded on his shoulders, waiting for him to be done with me.

Arabella cleared her throat, sounding annoyed. "Jason."

He pulled away from me and chucked me on the chin, looking amused. "You, my dear, even taste immune."

"Immune?" I stared up at him.

He grinned. "Yes. My Arabella isn't fond of the physical changes of being a Wendigo. Legend says that to transform back, you have to drink the blood of an immune. And I wondered where would we ever find such a creature?"

I swallowed hard.

"Then . . . I started stalking a little female who'd gone out with my enemy. She was sweet and pretty, but human. And because Beau wanted her, she was going to have to die," he said, gazing at me in a possessive fashion. "At least eventually, after I'd had my fun. Humans are so easy. Easy to stalk. Easy to frighten. Easy to follow and scare."

All the times I'd been sure that something had been wrong in my house. I couldn't put my finger on it. The dead blondes who looked like me. The occasions when Jason had shown up out of nowhere to woo me. How long had he been playing with me like a cat with its prey?

"Then I found out from Giselle that my little human had a werewolf for a sister. And I thought that was odd, because her older sister didn't smell like a wolf at all. Isn't that fascinating?"

I looked over at Arabella, whose eyes were glittering as she focused on me.

"Arabella said your blood smelled pure to her, so I checked for myself. And sure enough," he said, digging one claw under my chin until blood welled. His nostrils flared and a leer flitted over his face. "You smell nice and clean."

I jerked my knee up, trying to catch him in the groin.

His hand grabbed my knee before I could make contact, his movements whipcord-fast. "Nice try."

"So you brought me here because you want to eat me? Is that it?" I said bravely.

"Actually," Jason said, "we brought you here because you're Beau's mate. First we're going to lure him here and kill him. That's for me. *Then* my darling Arabella gets to eat you. Something for both of us."

Chapter Twenty-one

True to their plan, they didn't eat me right away.

They tied me to a chair. At first they'd tied me spread-eagle on the pool table, but when Jason had eyed me with a little too much interest as he'd fixed my bonds, Arabella had insisted on a chair instead.

And so we sat, and waited.

It seemed that Arabella was a different sort of Wendigo from Jason—less powerful and more drawn to the blood, though his reek was as strong as hers. Every so often, Arabella would shudder and convulse, and disappear for another round of eating Giselle. I guessed that she needed the flesh more often.

No wonder she wanted to change back.

During one of these interludes, I decided to work on Jason. I twisted my hands behind the chair, trying to loosen my bonds. They weren't that tight, and I didn't suppose it really mattered—they'd be on me within seconds and I'd be unable to escape. Still, it made me feel better to work them.

"Why are you doing all this?" I asked.

Jason looked up from his BlackBerry in surprise. "That's a rather asinine question."

"I'm an asinine human," I shot back. "Humor me. I thought Wendigos were supposed to be strong and invincible."

He pocketed his phone and moved across the room toward me. "There is no greater power in the world than that of a Wendigo. I have the strength of those that I have devoured."

"So why eat me and change back?"

"My mate is not happy with her transformation. This is for her."

I squirmed a little. "Okay, I get that. But why drag Beau into this? What has he done to you?"

He squatted near my chair. "Why am I after Beau?" Jason seemed to be amused by my concern. "Are you truly that worried about him?"

I shrugged. "Just curious. He was only using me for his heat."

"I'm not so sure about that." Jason reached forward and began to pull my T-shirt out of the waistband of my jeans. "At any rate, I'm sure we'll find out shortly."

I jerked as he tugged at my clothing. "What are you doing?"

He sliced my T-shirt open with his claws, jerking it apart and dragging it across my shoulders so it exposed my pale torso and my bra. "Making sure our kitty cat takes the bait, my sweet." He picked up a roll of masking tape from a table and pulled off a piece. Then he crammed a sock into my mouth and slapped the tape over it, muffling me and making me gag. My heart hammered in my throat, my eyes went wide. What was he planning on doing?

Jason slid around the chair and wrapped his arm around the back of it, curling it around to rest on my breast. I yelled against the sock, shoving my tongue against it to try and loosen the gag.

He held up his phone and snuggled up to me, grinning at its camera. "Smile for your boyfriend," he said and pinched my nipple.

I snarled as I heard the click of the camera.

To my relief, he got up and wandered across the room. His thumbs flew across the keypad as he typed in a text message, whistling to himself. Jason clicked one final button, then glanced over at me, the toothy smile revealing itself again. "All done. We'll see if that brings your boyfriend out to play."

I gave him a mutinous glare.

Jason just smiled, moving back toward me again, and chuckled when I shied away. He pulled my hair free of the ponytail and arranged it over my shoulders, looking at me thoughtfully. "It's a shame you're human," he said, trailing a finger over my bra again. "But if Beau can look past it . . ."

My breathing stopped in fear.

But he simply smiled at me, stood up, and left the room.

Hot tears of fright threatened, and I gave in for a few seconds before nearly choking on the gag. I forced myself to recompose, and thought hard, my mind frantic.

How could Beau possibly take down two superfast, superstrong shifters?

How could I?

"Well, well," a voice cooed near my ear. "It looks like the cavalry has arrived."

I looked up, half-conscious, from where I was slumped in my bonds. Arabella loomed over me, and I blinked at her.

She slapped me across the face so hard that lights danced in front of my eyes. "Wakey wakey."

Bitch. I groaned, "Fuck you" around the sock.

She put her hands on her knees and stuck her face in mine, eyeing me with entirely too much interest. Her fetid breath fanned my face. "You are just full of surprises, aren't you?" She reached out and poked the end of my nose.

Alarmed by her too-chummy attitude, I looked around for Jason. But it was just me and the crazy girlfriend. Lucky day.

Arabella sliced my bonds from the chair and grabbed me by the arms. Her grip was so tight that I thought she was going to break my arms, and tears of pain streamed from my eyes. My nostrils flaring as I sucked in a frightened breath, I struggled against her grip, but it was useless. Despite my terrified jerking, she dragged me over to the window.

Was she going to throw me out of it?

She flung open the curtain and shoved my face against the glass. "Take a look, sweet-cheeks. Take a good look."

It was a little hard to look with my face plastered to the window, but I quickly scanned the wintry lawn, looking for anything out of the ordinary. Bare trees. Large patches of muddy lawn, and . . .

I gasped and nearly gagged on the sock. It took me a moment to recover before I could look again and make sure I wasn't mad.

Beau stood down there in cat form, his large body visible near the tree line. He was beautiful— long, swishing tail and buff feline form. There was nothing to distinguish him from any other cougar, but I knew it was Beau. He'd come for me.

Oh God, he was going to get killed.

More shadows melted out of the trees, and with them, more animals. A giant brown bear appeared at Beau's side. Ramsey.

More shadows—more cougars, who stood a few feet behind Beau, unequivocally stating that he was their leader.

Beau began to walk forward and then it was like Noah's ark threw up on the lawn. Animals of every shape and size, predators of every imagining, began to appear on Jason's front lawn. A giant Siberian tiger prowled next to Beau, at his other side, a lion. An eagle circled in the sky, swooping low around them. I counted dozens, then I gave up when they continued pouring out of the trees. I could even pick out Sara's small wolf form.

They were showing their allegiance to him. Supporting him in his bid to get me back.

It was beautiful.

It was very, very bad.

Arabella grabbed the back of my head, her hand snarling in my messy, loose hair. "You must have a magic snatch for him to bring out the cavalry like this." She grabbed between my legs in a painful clench: I snapped my thighs shut, trying to shove her away. She laughed, but there was a desperate edge to it.

I shoved at her and bolted, but she grabbed me

by my hair and threw me to the floor, knocking the wind from me. "Dumb bitch."

I flexed my hands, gasping for breath to return. The pool table was enticingly near and I crawled under it, then worked on pulling the tape off my mouth.

A pair of new shoes appeared on the other side of the pool table. "Arabella," Jason said warningly. "Have you seen the front lawn?"

"I have," she said, sounding a little defensive. Was she scared of Jason, too?

"Didn't I tell you quite specifically that he was to come here alone if he wanted to see her alive again?"

"That's what I told him," she said, her voice rising. "Since he's not listening to you, he must want her dead." A hard, raspy edge entered her voice. "Let's just eat her, already."

I stilled, not daring to breathe.

"Not yet. He wants her. I know he does," Jason said, furious. I watched as his feet thunked across the floor and over to the window. "He filed for a mate visa yesterday. He's trying to get her permanent status in the Alliance."

A mate visa? Beau wanted to marry me?

"He what?" Arabella sounded furious. "He can't possibly mean to mate a human; he'll be laughed out of the Alliance."

"Then why is my lawn filled with a display of force?" His voice was becoming rougher with anger. It was frightening to hear. "He needs to come up here, alone."

Alone? No—they'd kill him.

Jason looked under the pool table and grinned at the sight of me. I stared at him, muffling my defiance and hoping he didn't notice that I was missing the tape across my mouth. I'd spit out the sock and clutched it in my hand.

He grabbed me by my ankle and dragged me across the carpet like he would a rag doll. He stroked my hair and admired me like one might a fragile possession. "Arabella's not hurting you, is she?"

I looked over at Arabella, who was glaring at me with hate.

"Good," he said, taking my silence for obedience. His hand continued to stroke my hair in that odd, possessive way. "If he intends to have a siege, we'll give him one." Jason smiled coldly. "But I have to wonder how long it will last when he hears your screams when I'm fucking you." He gazed down at me, almost tenderly. "Do you think that would bother him?"

Yes, I thought and tried to shove him away.

He batted my hands away as if they'd been nothing, grinning.

"It would bother me," Arabella snarled and

shoved between us. Her force knocked me against the nearby wall, and my head cracked against a painting. "You said I could eat her! Not that you would fuck her."

Jason gave her an amused look. "My dear, I have no interest in a human." He took her hand and began to kiss her wrist, then delicately up her arm. She watched him with intense, crazily possessive eyes. "But think of how much it will bother him. First I steal *you* away from him, then he finds that I'm fucking his little pet human."

"But I don't want you touching her," she whined.

Jason stared at Arabella, his mouth thinning as if he was finding her needy side very annoying. After a moment, he sighed. "All right, my pet. I won't touch her. She's all yours—"

Arabella's smile was brilliant.

I swallowed hard.

"—as soon as we've killed Beau," Jason finished.

"But—" Arabella began.

"I have to go to the bathroom," I blurted.

Both of them turned to stare at me in annoyance.

"Sorry," I said in a small voice, trying to sound pathetic. "I can't hold it much longer."

It was the oldest ploy in the world. *Please let them fall for it.*

To my vast surprise, Jason acquiesced. "Take

her to the bathroom, and we'll finish where we left off."

Oh, boy.

Arabella gave me an impatient look and grabbed my arm. "Come on."

She dragged me toward the bathroom. Giselle's bathroom. Bile rose in my throat and I clutched a hand to my mouth. "Not that one," I said between pressed fingers. *"Please."*

She looked at me in disgust and wavered for a moment. I knew what she was thinking. Give in to my stupid demand, or push me into the bloody butcher shop and risk Jason's wrath if I freaked out?

"Come on," she said gruffly and dragged me across the hall and down the stairs, back to the first floor.

Thank God for that small miracle. I allowed her to drag me through the house with no protest, and when she threw me into the bathroom, I didn't utter a squeak as I slapped against the wall. "Five minutes, or I break your leg," she snarled at me. "I can still eat you with a busted leg."

I nodded at her as she closed the door of the bathroom. When it shut, I heard her pacing the hall.

I had five minutes to think of something, fast.

I ruled out the window right away. Instead of regular glass, there were small blocks of thick, bubbled glass too small to squeeze through.

Think, Bathsheba, think.

I had two massively powerful shapeshifters in this house with me. Beau and his small army waited on the lawn. Neither was going to make a move until the other did. Beau wouldn't come inside unless he knew it wouldn't cost us our lives. Arabella and Jason wouldn't vacate because right now they held the advantage.

I had to get Arabella and Jason out of the house, somehow.

A small, decorative set of candles on the back wall caught my eye. A fire! Candles needed matches.

I quietly pulled open the drawer under the sink and rummaged through it. No matches.

There was nail polish, hairspray, hair doodads, a curling iron, and a blow-dryer. Arabella's stuff. My hand passed over the nail polish again, and then the curling iron, and then stopped.

The curling iron might get hot enough to start a fire.

Excited, I glanced around and looked for an outlet. There—on the far end of the wall. Good. I plugged the curling iron in, turned it on high, and looked for someplace to hide it.

A half-full wastebasket sat on the far side of the toilet. Even better. I shoved the curling iron in the bottom, and filled the rest of the wastebasket with loose toilet paper, then dripped the nail polish over it. Last, I set the aerosol can next to the curling iron. That would explode, right? I hoped so. If I was lucky, it'd catch fire.

"Hurry up," Arabella yelled, and I hastily flushed the toilet. I took a quick look at the cloth shower curtain, then shoved the wastebasket over as far as the curling iron's cord would stretch and tucked some of the shower curtain in it. Perfect. Unless you were looking closely, the beige cord of the curling iron was invisible against the wall, and the shower curtain ruffles hid the basket.

The faint stink of hot metal was already starting to fill the room, mixing with the scent of nail polish, and I panicked. I needed to conceal the smell. I grabbed the nearby perfume bottle and smashed it on the floor.

Arabella flung the door open. "What are you doing, you stupid bitch?"

As soon as she opened the door I bolted past her, barreling for the kitchen.

She grabbed my elbow and snapped me backward so hard that my arm throbbed and burned, and I collapsed at her feet. Arabella wrapped her hands in my shredded clothing and dragged me back down the hall. "You're done."

Exhausted and hurting, I cradled my arm and let her drag me back to the pool room, praying for a miracle.

Chapter Twenty-two

*T*he day passed unbearably slowly. My nerves were so tight that I thought my entire body would snap. Nothing was happening. It was a standoff of strange, bizarre proportions. The host of Alliance shifters was still on the lawn, circling the house in animal form, prowling.

The only bits of news I got were from the few short, terse words exchanged by Arabella and Jason. They'd bound me again, and alternated between glancing at me and then uneasily back at the lawn.

Beau's backup had thrown a major wrench into their plans.

"We need a way to draw him in," Jason said after a time. "He's too confident out there, surrounded by the others. In here we can destroy him, steal his power. Once he's downed, the others would fall like cards."

I shuddered. *Come on, fire. Any time now.*

Arabella gave a small shrug. "Why not hurt her? Take her out on the balcony and remove a few fingers to get him moving." Her eyes gleamed.

As if considering this rather horrible plan, Jason studied me. "Take your clothes off."

What? "No." I glanced at Arabella, whose mouth had thinned into a line of disapproval.

"Take your clothes off," Jason repeated, staring at me with intensity. "We need to make him think the worst."

No, no, no. I scooted my chair back.

Jason strode over to me, a crazy light in his eyes. His hand extended toward me, and as I watched, it twisted and bubbled, transforming into something hideous. The distorted flesh formed a paw, and then kept going. Muscles bulged and ripped, and the claws grew even larger.

I scooted back another inch. Arabella's eyes began to gleam and transform, as if she was excited by the thought of the violence.

Oh, God.

The repulsive paw touched my shoulder, and a shudder rocked through me. I tried to wriggle away. "No! Don't touch me!"

His lips curled back as if amused. Claws sliced through my already shredded T-shirt and snarled on my bra, leaving painful red welts. Then he sliced through my bra. Jason methodically tore my clothing until it hung off me in shreds, exposing my trembling body and leaving long red scratches across my pale skin.

After my clothing was demolished, Jason took a step back, flexing his distorted paw. "Why don't you mess her up a little, my dear?"

Arabella pushed forward and decked me across the face.

Red and black edged my vision, and I tasted blood. Hot blood ran out of my nose, and my head rang with pain.

"Just enough to make her look roughed up," Jason cautioned. "We want her mobile enough for him to know she's alive. Make her scream."

He knew Beau's ultra-sensitive shifter hearing would pick up my cries. Well, I wouldn't give them the satisfaction. I bit my lip and closed my eyes, bracing myself. Arabella's next fist got me in the gut. She punched me a few more times, but I remained silent, choking back sobs of pain.

Jason pushed Arabella aside. With one quick swipe, he ripped his claws across my shoulder and breast, tearing my skin. Blood ran from the shallow wounds and my chest felt like it was on fire.

I gave a long cry of pain, unable to swallow it.

"That's better," he said, and rubbed his crotch as if my pain excited him. Then Jason grabbed me by the wrist, dragging me up against his body. His claws cut through my bonds and my wrists fell free.

I immediately started to thrash, trying to break free of his grasp.

"I like it when you fight," he said, his eyes gleaming with madness, a feral grin on his face. "Let's go see your boyfriend, shall we?"

One of the large bay windows led out to a balcony. Jason pulled me in front of him as a shield, setting off waves of pain, and glanced at Arabella. "Stay out of sight."

She snarled, a more Wendigo-like sound than I would have liked to hear. "Why?"

"Because they think I'm here with her alone. The element of surprise will work in our favor." He gave her a cold glance. "And because I said so."

With that tone, he wasn't messing around. Arabella shut up and kept away from the door.

Jason pulled it open and went out, my back pressed against his stomach. I struggled weakly, then sagged. Still reeling from Arabella's beating, I found it hard to concentrate. The side of my face was sticky with blood, but even worse, I couldn't seem to focus. The pain was too distracting.

"Beauregard," Jason bellowed. "Show yourself."

The lead cougar strode forward and began to shift. I winced, anticipating a disgusting change like Jason's. To my surprise, Beau's transformation was fluid, almost seamless. His skin rippled slightly and changed, his bones elongating grace-fully. Within moments he was in his human form, completely naked. The look on his face was lethal and his eyes scanned me with possessiveness.

"I am here," he said, proud, strong.

Jason's hand clasped around my throat and he lifted me off the ground, demonstrating how he could manhandle me.

My hands went to Jason's, trying to pry his fingers off my throat before he cut off all my oxygen. I heard Arabella chuckle inside the dark room, and a plan formed in my mind.

I let my hands fall back down to my sides and clenched my fists, leaving two fingers out as a sig-nal that there were two of them . . . if someone would only look at my hands.

"I've been having fun playing with your human," Jason said, then grabbed me between the legs in a startling, painful grip. I twisted and gave a gasping sob of pain, writhing. "It's a shame that they break so easily."

Beau's jaw clamped into a hard line, and I could practically see the muscle ticking in his jaw.

"She's not fond of my games, though," Jason continued in a mocking voice. "I don't think she'll last much longer if this siege continues."

"What do you want?" Beau's voice was deadly with anger.

"You meet me inside this house. Alone."

I wiggled my two fingers and looked desperately at the sea of animal faces. Had they seen my gesture?

"We meet, just you and me, and we settle our rivalry once and for all." Jason's lie rang across the twilight courtyard.

Beau would never take such a stupid deal.

"And you won't hurt her?" There was no hesitation in his voice.

I heard a pleased chuckle from inside the room.

The two of them would kill him!

Jason's hand slid across my chest and squeezed my breast, and Beau's face darkened as if he wanted to kill him.

"There's two of them," I yelled. "Two of th—"

Jason's fist clipped me across the face, and I nearly bit off my own tongue. Darkness swam over my vision and I barely heard Beau's roar of anger and Jason's curses as he dragged me back inside. The door to the balcony slammed shut, and Jason flung me to the floor.

I skidded across the tile with the force of his hit and slammed into the wall.

"The stupid bitch is trying to ruin this for us," Jason seethed, and Arabella stroked his arm in a soothing gesture. Both of them glared hatefully at me from across the room.

"Let's kill her," Arabella agreed, her eyes shimmering green-gold. "She doesn't matter now. Let me drink from her throat." Her hands began to bubble and molt.

"You can't kill her until the others are gone," he snarled. "You need your powers to beat them."

"But what if I don't have another chance?" Arabella whined.

A window broke downstairs, and they looked at each other with triumph. "He's coming," Arabella said.

Then something detonated downstairs. The floor shook beneath my feet, and the loud boom was deafening. The pictures on the walls crashed to the floor as the fire alarms went off madly, filling the house with an earsplitting chorus of warning beeps.

"What the fuck are they doing?" Jason bolted out into the hall. "Stay with the bitch," he called after him.

Arabella waited only a moment, then followed him.

I picked myself up off the floor, my first instinct to hide. I fought against the thought—if the house was on fire, it would be supremely stupid to stay here.

So I needed a weapon. I frantically looked around and saw the rack of pool cues. I could use one of those.

I yanked one from the rack. It wasn't very heavy, but it was better than nothing.

A feral voice snarled, and Jason pounded up the hallway. "I'm going to kill that bitch for setting my house on fire!"

I smiled grimly. Like they weren't going to kill me anyhow? I clutched the cue stick tightly in my hands and hefted it, standing in plain sight on the far side of the pool table. Jason skidded down the hallway and caught sight of me, and his mouth curled in a ruthless smile.

"Bathsheba!"

The two Wendigo froze in the hall at the sound of Beau's faint call. Smoke drifted upstairs and I could hear the crackle of the fire now; it must have covered the entire bottom floor.

Jason turned his black eyes back to me and I saw that the front of his pants had popped a tent. I took an involuntary step backward. Fire and violence seemed to turn him on. Bad news for me.

"We have to get out of here," Arabella said, coughing on the smoke. She tugged on his arm, turning him away from me.

Jason flung her away and she crashed into the wall, knocking down and breaking the rack of pool cues. "You stupid bitch. They'll slaughter us if we try to make it out." His eyes turned back to me, gleaming. "You trapped us, didn't you." He moved toward me, stalking his prey, and slid his hand down the front of his pants. "You trapped us with the fire."

My fingers tightened on the cue stick and I took another step backward. "I'd do it again, too." I sounded way braver than I felt. If Jason got any closer, he was going to hear my knees knocking together.

He snarled. In a completely inhuman move, he leapt onto the pool table and flew at me.

I barely had time to swing the pool cue at his head before he was on me. The stick splintered as if it had been a toothpick and he shoved me against the wall, pinning me against him and forcing his erection against my stomach. A horrible grin stretched his mouth and he grabbed a handful of my hair and sniffed it.

I squirmed, trying to get away, my hand shoving at his face. He only laughed.

"Forget her!" Arabella launched herself at Jason, tugging on his arm as she gave me a hateful look. "We need to leave *now*. We'll find another immune later." When he didn't budge, her voice turned coaxing. "Those pathetic creatures are no match for us. We'll crush them like bugs beneath our feet and gain more power from their deaths."

"Power," Jason echoed, his black eyes intent on

my face. He leaned in so close that his nose pressed against my skin, he thrust his hips at me. I gagged. "I need more power," he murmured.

"Yes," Arabella cried, tugging on his arm again.

To my surprise, he turned to face her. The ghoulish smile was still on his face. "Power," he said, and ran his fingers along her jawline. She preened at the momentary pleasure, arching her throat and gazing at him with devoted, fanatical eyes.

He leaned in to her—and tore her throat out. Blood gushed everywhere.

I screamed as her hands went around him, clutching him as if she would embrace his body for all eternity. Her head went limp, and the horrible sounds continued as Jason hunched over her. There was the snarl and crackle of bones, and the sound of flesh tearing. He was *eating* her. Stealing her power.

I gagged and pushed myself off the wall. *Run away!* I staggered toward the door.

"Bathsheba!" Beau's voice cried my name again, though it was getting harder to hear over the roar of the fire and the shrill beeping of the fire alarms.

Jason's leg contorted and he lashed out, kicking me in the ribs. I went down, collapsing to the floor. My lungs felt like they were on fire from the smoke, and I couldn't breathe. Gasping for breath through the searing pain, I clutched my side and pulled myself toward the door on one hand and my knees.

I just wanted to be out of here. I just wanted to be with Beau. In his arms. Just us in the cabin again. Happy. I slid toward the door, feeling overwhelmed by the distance to it and by the pain in my body. Even if I made it to the stairs before Jason got me, how would I get out? My shoulders collapsed, and I huddled on the floor.

I just needed a quick breath, then I'd keep going.

I heard a ferocious yell, then someone new burst into the room, looming over me. Sluggish from the pain and the smoke, I stared up at my savior.

Beau.

"Oh, God," he said, kneeling down and pulling me to him. His hand skimmed my body. "Oh, God, don't be dead. Please don't be dead."

Did I look dead? I tried to put my fingers on his lips to shut him up, but everything was slow to respond. I struggled to point to the corner of the room where Jason still feasted on Arabella, his body contorting as if he couldn't control the power rushing through him.

Beau pressed a kiss to my forehead; his eyes were streaming from the heat and the smoke. "You clever, sweet thing," he said, lifting me up against him.

I suspected that he'd guessed my fire plan.

We needed to get out of the house, and I was relieved when he stood with me in his arms. "Beau," I managed. "Jason—"

A tearing force ripped me out of his arms, and I went crashing into the back wall. Stars circled in front of my eyes.

Jason had finished with Arabella.

Beau snarled, a feline cry of rage, and my eyes fluttered open to see the two of them circling, forms morphing. Beau was all sleek golden curves as he changed into his cougar form.

"Run, Bathsheba! Run!" he yelled.

Jason was a monster—bulging, rippling unnaturally under the fur. He was hideous to look upon, all claws and fangs. And he was twice the size of Beau.

The ceiling began to blacken, with orange fire at the edges, yet they launched themselves at each other, claws flying in a fight to the death.

We didn't have *time* for this! The burning roof was going to collapse and kill us.

The cats tangled in a mess of flying fur, rolling and scratching, teeth flashing. Jason's gray form dwarfed Beau's sleek golden one; Beau didn't stand a chance.

I frantically looked around the destroyed pool room for anything to use to distract them.

A bundle of broken pool cues lay on the floor and I grabbed one to use it as a club. It was only a foot and a half long, and the wickedly pointed, jagged edge gave me a new idea. I wobbled to my feet, clutching it against me.

I knew that one bad swipe from one of them could kill me and distract Beau at a critical moment. But I couldn't do nothing. I'd forced us into this awful scenario because I hadn't trusted him, but I trusted him now. And I was going to save him.

All snarls and flashing claws, the cats flew across the room with catlike screams of pain and rage. Beau's mouth clamped on Jason's shoulder and tore a huge gouge. When they rolled toward me again, all I saw was Jason's back and I heard Beau's cry of outrage as he was pinned.

I charged toward them, holding the broken end of the pool cue with both hands, then lunged toward Jason's back.

It sank in like he was made of butter.

Jason arched backward, his clawed paw trying to reach his back, but he couldn't as a cat. He began to shift, desperate to reach the I'd stake in his lower back, under the rib cage. He turned toward me with murder in his eyes, then Beau tackled him and ripped his throat out.

My stomach heaved, and I collapsed onto the floor. The pain and smoke finally took me down, and everything went black.

"Bathsheba." Beau tapped me gently on the cheek, and I woke up in his arms. Blood covered his face—his human face—but he was still whole. "Bathsheba, tell me where Giselle is."

We were still in the burning house. I had only been out for a few moments.

"She's dead. Beau, we have to get out of here." My raspy voice didn't even sound like me.

He moved to the balcony door. "Two steps ahead of you," he said, and kicked it open.

He went to the railing and looked over.

Animals waited down below. Too far down below. I clung to his neck, suddenly afraid.

He kissed my forehead. "Ramsey will catch you. Do you trust me?"

I hadn't trusted him earlier today and nearly gotten both of us killed. With a small sob, I pressed my mouth to his in one last kiss. "I trust you."

"Good." He dropped me off the balcony.

I vaguely remembered being caught in the heavy paws of a grizzly bear before blacking out again, this time staying down.

Chapter Twenty-three

*M*y eyelids fluttered open sometime later. A cool sheet covered me, and something hot clung to my hand.

I was in a hospital room—clean, pristine, and white. A tray of uneaten lunch stood at the foot of the bed, and Beau sat beside me, his hands clasping mine tightly as if he'd lose me if he let go. His flannel shirt was a few sizes too big for him (Ramsey's, I guessed).

He looked exhausted. I felt steamrolled.

I groaned and Beau instantly jerked alert. His eyes flicked over my face and body, then his intense look gave way to relief. "You're awake."

"I am," I said and tried to sit up. "Where are we?"

He pushed me back down. "The doctor wants to keep you for a few days to ensure that you don't have any bad effects from smoke inhalation."

"You seem to be totally healthy." The sight of him whole and smiling made relief flood through me.

"There's a few perks to being a shifter." I felt his heavy weight settle on the edge of the bed and he leaned over me, brushing a lock of hair off my face. "Bathsheba?"

My heart fluttered at the tender way that he said my name. "Yes?"

"Don't *ever* pull a stunt like that again."

I grimaced. "Which one? The one where I climbed out the window and stole the car, or the one where I shouted a warning and nearly had the Wendigo eat me, or the one where I nearly blew up the mansion?"

"All of them. When you're dealing with shapeshifters and Wendigo and other supes, you can't possibly compete." His hand clenched mine.

Irked that he thought I was so fragile, I pointed out, "They were both twice your size. I had to do something or they would have killed you."

"Not if that something involves sacrificing yourself," he said, brushing my hair away from my face in sharp motions. He was rather upset, I realized. "Not if it means that I'm going to lose you." Stroke, stroke, stroke. At the rate he was going, he was going to stroke all the hair straight off my head. "He . . . he *hurt* you." There was a world of anguish in that tone.

I brushed my knuckles along the stubble on his jaw. "Just a few scratches. He didn't really hurt me."

"Two busted ribs, a concussion, and lacerations on more than sixty percent of your body," he shot back.

"He didn't rape me."

The tightness left his face.

"And I'd do it again if it saved you," I said softly.

He jerked up and walked away, and I was swamped with burning disappointment. What was I thinking, falling in love with a shifter? I'd gotten too sappy, and he was probably trying to break it off with the human liability that he'd saddled himself with—

"I can't do this, Bathsheba." Beau was back at my bedside, looking tortured.

My breath caught in my throat. "Do what?"

He looked at me with haunted eyes. "I've led the Russell clan for twelve years. I've led the Alliance for eight. Everyone listens to me. If I snap my fingers, things get done." His hands tightened on mine, and he stared at my small hand as if it fascinated him. "Yet ever since I've met you, you haven't listened to a thing I've said.

"I don't know what to do with you. You're independent to the point of stubbornness, and even when you're confronted with an opponent who's stronger and meaner, you don't give up. You go out of your way to protect Sara, who should be just as capable as you. *More* capable, because she's a shifter."

I opened my mouth to protest, but he continued on, his voice dropping low. "You even risked your life to save mine, when it could have killed you."

Sudden tears pricked at my eyes. If this meant that I'd lost him forever, I'd . . .

I'd do it again. Over and over again.

I loved Beau with all my heart, I realized. I wanted to always be at his side, and protect him when I could. "I'm sorry," I whispered.

He wasn't listening. "You're the one person in the world that I can't bend to do my will," he said slowly. "And that's why I can't let you go. I refuse to accept that you want to break up with me."

I stared at him in surprise.

He continued, "The Alliance is a dangerous place for a human—everyone plays rougher, and there's a code you can't even begin to comprehend. It's too dangerous for you. The past few weeks have shown me that." An anguished look crossed his face. "And I can't change you even if you asked me."

I nodded. "I'm immune," I said softly.

His fingers continually stroked my hand. "Everyone warns me that I shouldn't bring you further into my world, further into the Russell clan. But all I can think of is that I need to marry you to keep you safe—"

My heart leapt in my chest, and the heart monitor at the side of the bed beeped loudly. "You want to marry me—just to protect me?"

His grim face lightened a little. "Actually, I want to drag you back to my cabin, lock you away, and never let you out into the world again. I want to keep you at my side so I can watch over you always, and kiss you every time you walk past me." His expression relaxed, changing to something more sensual, and his voice dropped into a husky whisper. "I want to smell every time that you think of me, and I want you to think of me several times a day."

My mouth went a little dry. "Can we have tub sex again?"

He laughed and pressed a kiss to my knuckles. "We can definitely have tub sex."

"It wouldn't be so bad, then," I mused, and I was rewarded with a brilliant smile. "But that's the wrong reason to marry me. I don't want you to marry me just because you want to protect me, Beau. And I can't stay with you in the woods."

His smile dropped away, and he looked devastated. He reluctantly let go of my hand. "I understand."

"*Wait*," I said when he pulled away. I grasped the front of his shirt. "You *don't* understand. I *want* to marry you, you dense, overgrown cat. I love you."

Beau hugged me tight. "I love *you*, Bathsheba. Will you marry me? Join the Russell clan and be my mate?"

It was hard to talk around the emotional knot in my throat. "I can't live in the woods and hide away from the world," I warned. At his puzzled look, I said, "I need to run Giselle's business."

The lines were back around his mouth, but he was listening. "Go on."

I continued, my courage bolstered. "I feel responsible for Giselle's death. If not for me and you and Jason, she'd still be alive."

He raised a skeptical eyebrow.

"And think of the database," I said, warming to my subject. "Every paranormal for six states around is logged into that database. Not just Alliance—werewolf, vampire, and even some fey. Midnight Liaisons can be a common connection for all the paranormals in the area. We can connect couples, or families. And what about bodyguards? Or business transactions? There's so much we could do. A social network for the Alliance would be a terrific way to keep people connected, and the office can help people set up profiles and regulate traffic," I said, getting excited. It was a brilliant concept.

"We're getting married before you go back to that office," he insisted. "You're mine and no one else is touching you. Ever again."

"All right," I said, thrilling at the thought. The heart monitor beeped again.

"We're marrying tomorrow," he commanded.

I shook my head. "Let's wait a week. I'd like to be able to stand upright for my wedding without medical assistance."

"A week," he declared. His face broke into a smug grin, as if he'd just been handed a crown and a scepter.

I asked the last thing that was bothering me. "And my being human won't be a problem with your position in the Alliance? You won't get kicked out of your leader spot?"

He shook his head. "If anything, we're starting a trend. All of my brothers are out prowling the streets looking for naked blondes to jump out of windows and flatten grizzly bears."

I swatted his arm and winced at the pain. "You're an ass. I couldn't possibly have flattened him."

Beau's lips twitched. "Just a little. Sara's calling you Bathsheba Bear-Slayer."

I laughed, even though it hurt. My hand clasped his and I looked into at his smiling gray eyes. "I'd rather be Bathsheba Russell."

"Good. Because you're probably going to want to kill me when you hear what I propose next," he said somberly. "It involves Sara."

As soon as I was released from the hospital, a meeting was set up between the Russell clan and the Anderson wolves. The location was a neutral patch of land not owned by either party. The cause for the get-together? An exchange of women: Sara for Savannah.

I rode with the Russell clan in their convoy of trucks and SUVs. Sara sat with me, remarkably calm. Since I'd last seen her, she'd dyed her short, shaggy hair bright blue, and she wore a ragged old concert T-shirt that I didn't recognize. It made her look younger, but it also made her look a bit tougher. Or maybe it was the events of this last week that had finally hardened her. I wanted to hug her close, but I knew she didn't want that. This was her battle, and I couldn't fight it for her.

This was the only way to resolve the impasse without destroying both groups of shifters. It was the exchange or war.

I held my sister's hand as we lined up at the

meeting site. Beau stood at the front of the clan. Ramsey stood next to him, his immense form nearly dwarfing the rest of us in shadow. Sara and I hung back, the only women among nearly a dozen men.

The wolf pack loped out of the woods in wolf form. After they circled the group once, they broke apart and transformed to their human forms. Naked.

To a one, they were all handsome. I hadn't seen any ugly shifters (except for Garth) but they looked hard. And they eyed Sara with far too much attention.

One stepped forward, his face bearded and lined with years of hard living. "You brought the wolf girl?"

Sara tensed beside me.

"We brought *Sara* with us, yes," Beau said. "Where's Savannah?"

The lead werewolf glanced at Sara and me, shielded by a wall of Russell clan members, then raised a hand in the air. After a moment another man emerged from the woods, his arm around a young, dark-haired woman's shoulders.

"That's Savannah," one of the Russell brothers murmured for my benefit.

Her clothes were muddy and she squinted at the sunlight as if she hadn't seen it for a few days, but she looked whole and healthy. And she didn't seem upset, which was good.

When Savannah got closer, she broke free from the man at her side and staggered, as if recovering. Then she gave him an enquiring look, as if seeking permission.

How odd.

Then she ran for the Russell clan, and was enveloped by the warm hugs of her cousins.

"She's all yours again," the werewolf leader drawled. "Give us Sara."

My sister looked at me and squeezed my hand, letting me know it would be all right, and I squeezed hers back. I was so frightened that something would go wrong. That this would be the last time I would ever see her.

Then Sara stepped forward, a dainty, blue-haired figure among a horde of towering men. I pushed forward, determined to keep my eyes on her.

The werewolf leader sized her up, and his nostrils flared as he checked her scent. Then he smiled wide. "Hello, baby doll. We're gonna treat you real nice."

"I'm going with you of my own free will," Sara pointed out. "A trade is a trade."

The werewolf nodded.

"All right, then," Sara said, and I heard the

slight wobble in her voice. "I'm now part of the wolf pack."

Silence fell.

Then Ramsey stepped forward and dropped one huge hand over her shoulder, nearly covering it.

"In accordance with the law of the Bjorn and the were-bear clans, I claim this woman as my mate."

Turn the page for a special look
at the next sizzling novel
from Jessica Sims

Coming soon from Pocket Books

*M*y sister cast me worried looks on the entire drive to the meeting grounds, her hands clutching mine. I kept my expression serene, knowing Bathsheba was looking for any sign of fear, and then she'd insist on me not doing this.

And then Savannah would probably die and I'd be responsible, and the wolves would keep hunting me for the rest of my life. I'd have to keep hiding the monster I'd become. Keep bathing in perfume to disguise my scent with other shifters. After six years of hiding, I was so very, very tired of living in fear—of waiting to turn the corner and have the world come crashing down, of making the wrong move and ruining everything once again. I knew I'd messed up Bathsheba's life as well as my own. There was nothing I could do about that now.

But I *could* do something about Savannah's life. So I smiled and watched the scenery with interest, hoping Bath didn't notice how sweaty my palms were.

We pulled up at an abandoned tract of land. Tall weeds overgrew the property and the barbed wire fence was falling down in several places. When I got out of the car, I smelled the faint scent of wolves. The back of my neck prickled and my mouth began to water with fear, two signs that I was close to changing into wolf form. I clamped the thought down and bit the inside of my cheek hard, struggling to maintain control. Now was not the time.

My sister scanned the woods, her brow wrinkling, and I knew she didn't realize they were here. Every shifter in the area did, though. The posture of her fiancé, Beau Russell, changed from easy to alert. A few of the other Russells closed ranks around me, and a massive shadow loomed over my shoulder. I didn't have to glance backward to see that it was Ramsey.

They surrounded me like Fort Sara. As if it would do any good.

Then Beau stepped forward and my shadow was gone, the two men standing side by side, waiting for the wolves to emerge. I bit my cheek harder.

After a few minutes, they appeared. The weedy grass led to taller bushes in the distance, which led to a thick stand of trees. I had guessed that was where they were hiding, and I was correct. I hadn't anticipated them appearing in wolf form, though. The smell of them filled my nostrils, overpowering all other scents and bringing with them a wealth of bad memories.

I crouched low in the kitchen, raising my arms over my head. "No, please, Roy . . . I'll be good."

"It's because I love you that I have to teach you a lesson," Roy said, snapping the belt over my head and lashing my arms and shoulders.

I whimpered in pain, knowing he would hit me harder if I screamed and alerted the neighbors. Roy wanted me to be strong. The beatings, he told me, were to condition me to pain.

I huddled smaller and waited for him to be done with his lesson. But then the belt caught me across the mouth and my mouth filled with blood. I spat it on the floor, then looked up to see that Roy was changing, his nose becoming to a wolf's snout, his arms covered with hair . . .

I shivered and pushed the horrible memories aside, my entire body tense. Wolves pushed out of the woods, two . . . three . . . six . . . seven. Beau had told me that the Anderson wolf pack had eight male wolves and one female, so two were missing. I craned my neck, looking for them until I heard Bathsheba's gasp. Her gaze was on the pack, and I looked back to them. They had stopped and now were crouched, changing back to human form. As I watched, one naked man rose and stretched as if he had not a care in the world. He looked over at me and winked, unconcerned that he was naked.

My sister averted her eyes.

I stared back at the man. How the hell had he shifted so very fast? My own shift was always painful and drawn out, leaving me aching and heaving. This man acted like he'd woken up from a pleasant nap.

As the others quickly changed, they lined up behind the other man. He stepped forward and looked at Beau. "You brought the wolf girl?"

I tensed. Roy had always called me "girl" too . . . just before he beat me. Was I going to be just a nameless, faceless creature to abuse? Again? The skin on the back of my neck rippled and I bit down on my cheek again, willing my body under control.

"We brought Sara, yes," Beau said. "Where's Savannah?"

The lead werewolf glanced back at me. I remained where I was. I wasn't moving forward until I had a nod from Beau or Ramsey. My stomach churned hard, and I forced myself to relax my sweaty hand so I wouldn't accidentally squeeze the hell out of Bathsheba's fingers.

The lead wolf raised a hand in the air and motioned someone forward. I heard the rustle in the woods, then a man about my age and a young, dark-haired woman emerged. She smelled like the wolves and her clothes looked borrowed, but underneath I could smell the faint scent of cougar.

"That's Savannah," someone murmured to my sister. As the only human at the parlay, she missed the subtle signals that put the shifters a page ahead of her.

Savannah slowly moved forward. One of the Russells breathed out hard, and I wondered at the angry sound. Savannah gave the wolf shifter at her side a long look, then rushed toward us.

The Russells enveloped her in warm hugs, patting her on the back and clapping her shoulder, but their expressions remained grim. A short distance away, Beau looked furious. Savannah's smile was wide and she wiped relieved tears from her eyes. Her scent was heavy with wolf—one wolf in particular. And noticing her calm demeanor I realized why the Russells were mad.

Savannah was no longer in heat. That meant . . .

"She's all yours again," the Anderson wolf leader drawled. "Give us Sara."

I fought the sick feeling in my gut and gave my sister's hand a squeeze, and then released it. I stepped forward, past the Russells, past Beau and Ramsey, and approached the naked pack of wolves.

All of them were tall and muscled. The leader had a beard and a rather stern face. The others were younger, but I was still the youngest—and smallest—one. The leader's gaze was assessing as I approached, studying my figure, my face, testing my scent on the air. I knew what he was looking for.

He was judging me as a potential mate.

The skin on my back bunched and rippled, and I inhaled sharply. The scent of wolf was almost overwhelming, and my legs were cramping up. Shit! I bit my cheek so hard that I drew blood. I would *never* take another wolf as my mate. I'd die first.

"Hello, baby doll. We're gonna treat you real nice," he said in a mild drawl, clearly sensing my nervousness. His gaze was oddly hypnotic, and I avoided making eye contact. An alpha could control the wolves in his pack, couldn't he? I felt that strange thread of compulsion and I wasn't even officially in his pack. It frightened me.

I didn't dare look back at the Russell clan. Instead, I took another step toward my new "family." I tried not to shudder. "I'm going with you of my own free will," I announced, using the phrases we'd decided on to bring the plan into action. "A trade is a trade."

The werewolf alpha nodded at me.

I turned back to Beau. "A trade is a trade, right?"

He nodded at me, his body tense. Beau didn't take his eyes off me. "Agreed."

"All right then," I said, hating how small my voice was. "I'm now part of the wolf pack."

The alpha smiled, a possessive, smug look. My entire body tensed as I waited for the plan to kick in to motion. Waited for rescue.

Behind me, heavy feet stepped forward. A large hand clasped my shoulder and yanked me backward against a massive, firm body. Ramsey said, "In accordance with the law of the Bjorn clan and the were-bear clans, I claim this one as my mate."

The wolf leader's face flickered with confusion, then contorted with rage. "What the fuck is this?"

I quivered, flinching at the alpha's rage. Normal anger scared me, but the alpha's rage made my entire being shiver. It affected the other wolves, as well—they shifted anxiously on their feet.

Ramsey's arm looped over my chest, protecting me.

The wolves frowned and muttered, exchanging glances. The bearded alpha gritted his teeth and glared at me and Ramsey. A low growl formed in his throat. "This is a trick."

Ramsey's arm tightened, and I squeaked when I realized his protective hand had accidentally cupped one of my small breasts. I didn't think he'd realized it either, and his hand shifted lower.

"Not a trick," he growled back, the rumbling in his throat much deeper than the alpha's wolf-like growl.

My mouth filled with saliva again. God. Not now. I couldn't go wolf now.

The alpha's eyes flashed with anger, anger that he focused on me. "She don't look excited to be your mate, Bjorn. She looks scared."

Uh oh. I put on my chirpy smile and gave Ramsey's hand a little pat. "I'm just surprised that my Huggy Bear decided to declare our love openly. He's kinda private."

Someone snickered. I felt Ramsey's arm tighten on me, and he leaned down and kissed my temple. The oddly tender gesture threw me for a loop.

The wolf leader didn't look convinced. "You two aren't a couple," he declared. "This is bullshit."

"We are too," I blurted, desperate. I turned in Ramsey's arms and looked up at him. He stood at least a foot and a half taller than me, and weighed twice as much. I grabbed the collar of his shirt and tugged him downward, then planted my mouth on his.

I felt a tremor of surprise rip through him but ignored it, kissing his hard, unyielding mouth. I had to make this look as real as possible so I slid my tongue against his lips, coaxing them apart, and then sucking on his lower lip. Ramsey hesitated a moment, and then I felt his big hands cup my ass, pulling me closer against him, and his tongue flicked against mine. I made the kiss deeper, wrapping my legs around his big torso like I wanted to ride him, making small noises of pleasure in the back of my throat for the audience's benefit. Ramsey's sharp inhalation took me by surprise a moment before his tongue stroked deep against mine. Startled, I broke off the kiss and stared up at him. His brown gaze met mine and he gave me another light kiss, as if reluctant to let the contact end. It sent a shiver all the way through me, the way he was looking at my mouth.

Perhaps I was not the only great actor here.

I turned in Ramsey's arms, unwilling to unwrap my legs from around his torso, and glanced at the wolf pack.

I shouldn't have looked. All the naked men were staring very pointedly at me. And several of them had erections.

Oh jeez. Had I just made things worse? What if they didn't believe us and I had to go with them? What if I left with them and they all held me down and raped me? Would they even have to hold me down? Or would the alpha bark a command and I'd just drop to all fours?

Fear quickened my breath, and I felt the tight,

uncomfortable band of a headache surge through my scalp. Oh no. That was another sign of an imminent shift.

The wolf leader put his hands on his hips and stared at Ramsey, then at me, then at the Russells. His body looked tense, his posture wary. "If she's your mate," he growled, "then why's she so fucking scared?"

Ramsey's hand on my ass tightened. "You," he snarled.

The leader looked surprised. "Me?"

"She doesn't like wolves." Ramsey's bass voice rumbled through his body.

"She must have liked wolves enough at some point," the Anderson leader said crudely. "She let one between her legs."

Ramsey's response was a low growl.

A chorus of growls rose from the throats of the wolf pack. Fuck. This was getting worse, not better.

I unhooked my legs from Ramsey's body and slid down him. "Let's be reasonable about this," I said in my cheeriest voice. "There's no reason to—"

The wolf alpha leveled his gaze at me. "Get over here, girl."

Caught by that compelling stare, I shrank my shoulders and moved away from Ramsey, dropping to my knees. I couldn't stand tall in front of the alpha; had to show my submission—

Ramsey roared—a feral sound—and I heard the Russells surge forward, though I wasn't sure if they were going to stop Ramsey or stop the wolves. The Andersons rushed forward as well and I was suddenly surrounded by a pack of naked men as their leader tried to pull me away from the furious Ramsey.

"A wolf belongs with her alpha," the Anderson leader snarled.

"No," I gasped, but I was unable to rise from the ground. My legs tightened. One of the Andersons reached for me, taking my arm in his hand. To my horror, my skin rippled in his grasp. The Anderson wolf gave me a look of surprise and let go of my arm just in time for a convulsive wave to crash over me.

Not here. Not now. My back arched and my body undulated with pain. I cried out and dropped to my haunches, my panicked body beginning the painful transformation to wolf.

*I*n humiliation, I endured the endless rounds of agony. My jaw cracked and shifted, my nose elongating, every muscle stretching like a rubber-band pulled taut. My skin shivered the entire time as the wolf worked her way through me. I tried not to cry out, but this change was so hard and sudden that I nearly blacked out with the pain of it, and I'm pretty sure I made a few whimpering noises.

The clearing was deathly silent except for the sound of my labored breathing and the roaring of blood in my ears as I became the hated half of me. I struggled to go back, turn the tide and remain human, and that made things harder. It was like torture as my hands turned to paws, and I felt each excruciating twist of tendon and bone acutely. Long minutes passed and then my shredded clothes fell to the ground. I gave a long, humiliated body shiver, then rose shakily to my feet. My wolf feet.

Both sides stared at me—the Russells in something like chagrin, the Andersons in surprise. Ramsey's expression was one of disappointment. For some reason that made me feel worse, and my stomach lurched and gagged. I threw up blood in the grass, unable to keep it down. On some of the more painful changes, I vomited blood. Today, it seemed, was one of those days.

The Anderson leader pointed at me and the stink of wolf rolled off him, my nose attuned to the scent. "That," he said, his voice an echoing boom in my sensitive wolf ears, "was a fucking disgusting show."

A small whine crept out of my throat.

"You're letting her kill herself!" he continued. "She keeps transforming like that and she's going to slaughter herself. And you assholes ain't helping her?" The Anderson leader spat at Ramsey's feet. "I thought you said you wanted to be her mate."

I heard the creak of Ramsey's knuckles as he clenched his fists and I looked up at him. He didn't look at me.

The Anderson leader moved toward me. I shied back, but he held a hand out, fingers extended, and the wolf in me felt compelled to sniff them. I did so, and he touched my ears, then ran a hand down the ruff of my neck. I endured it, feeling the wolf's need to please the alpha.

"Ain't supposed to be slow and painful like that," the Anderson leader said, his voice softer. "Ain't supposed to make her puke blood. If that's what she's doing, she's gonna be dead before a year is out."

My sister's breath caught in her throat, the start of a soft sob. "No."

My body was still radiating pain, though it was ebbing slowly. Humiliation tore through my thoughts, along with fear. Was this a trick? Or was he right and I was going to die? What could I do? I didn't want to go with the wolves. I whined. I wanted to go back with my sister. I wanted to run away. My tail flicked.

As if sensing my thoughts, the Anderson leader tried to put a hand on my ruff again but I flinched away, skittering back a few feet, human fear over-riding wolf instinct.

"We can help her learn how to change," he said in a calm, low voice meant to soothe. "Send her with us and we can save her. Even wolf babies know how to shift better than she does. Not only is she putting herself at risk, she's putting others at risk. What if she changes in public?"

Ramsey looked down at me, into my wolf eyes, and must have seen the fear there. He looked back at the Anderson leader and took two steps forward, getting in the man's face. To his credit, the wolf leader did not back down.

"She is my mate," Ramsey said in a low, dangerous voice. "She stays with me. The laws make it so."

The Anderson leader looked at me, then back at Ramsey. "If you aren't gonna let her come with us, then one of us is going to go with you. I'm not gonna let you kill her. She's one of us."

Ramsey growled.

Beau stepped forward. "Hang on. This is an arrangement I am interested in. I want to hear what you have to say."

A half hour later my flesh began to ache and crawl again, and I hurried off to the woods, my sister trailing behind me with my clothes. Several long, agonizing minutes later, I lay in the grass, naked and panting and human, waiting for the nausea to pass.

My sister crouched next to me and handed me my clothes. "Oh, Sara," she said softly. "Why didn't you tell me?"

I sat up and took the T-shirt from her. "Tell you what?"

"About the changes. How it hurts."

I shrugged, slipping the shirt over my head and

then dragging on my jeans. My bra and panties had been destroyed in the change, and the shirt was in tatters. "I didn't know it *wasn't* supposed to hurt. How could I have known?"

"When Beau changes, he's not in pain. I watched him once. It wasn't like yours."

I squeezed my eyes shut. Jeez. I wanted to die of embarrassment. I'd had an ugly, messy transformation in front of everyone. Shifting was private. You didn't talk about it, any more than you'd describe the last time you'd taken a leak. "Let's just go, Bath. I want to hear what they're saying."

But when we returned to the rendezvous, all the deciding had already been done. Beau was smiling and the Anderson leader looked mollified. Only Ramsey continued to scowl. I approached slowly, holding my tattered shirt together.

"It's been decided," Beau said and beckoned me forward. Reluctantly, I went.

"Levi wants to help you," Beau said. "They can teach you how to shift properly. And they want to make sure your mating to Ramsey is of your own choosing. So Connor Anderson is going to stay with you for the next month and teach you how to be a wolf."

Levi—the alpha—nodded, and gestured for one of his wolves to move forward. Connor turned out to be the young, handsome wolf who had brought out Savannah. I wondered what the story was there.

"And what does Levi get out of this?" my sister asked. "My sister doesn't want to live with them. She wants to live with her mate."

"Don't want nothing but the well-being of my wolves," Levi said. His arms crossed over his chest. "I'm the alpha and it's my job to make sure my wolves are safe. All of 'em."

"And in the meantime," Beau added, "we're going to discuss the possibility of the Anderson wolves joining the Alliance. A few have expressed interest in the Midnight Liaisons service, as their pack is looking for a few mates to add to their family."

"Oh," my sister said with pleased surprise. "That would be very good."

Midnight Liaisons was the dating agency my sister and I owned, and it catered exclusively to paranormal clientele.

Seemed like everyone was getting something out of this deal but me. I looked over at Ramsey, whose mouth was still pressed into a tight line of disapproval.

"All right," I said meekly.

Levi clapped me on the shoulder, nearly startling me out of my skin. "Looks like you get to have your Huggy Bear after all, girl. Why don't you go give him a big kiss and wipe that scowl off his face?"

Oh, jeez. It looked like the last thing Ramsey wanted right now was to kiss me. But I was terrified of losing the fragile peace, so I moved forward to Ramsey.

This time I didn't have the courage to do more than give him a light kiss on the mouth. His lips didn't part under mine.

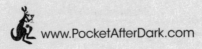

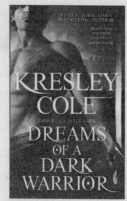